Recent Titles by Linda Sole from Severn House

THE TIES THAT BIND
THE BONDS THAT BREAK
THE HEARTS THAT HOLD

FLAME CHILD

THE ROSE ARCH
A CORNISH ROSE

A ROSE IN WINTER

Linda Sole

This first world edition published in Great Britain 2002 by
SEVERN HOUSE PUBLISHERS LTD of
9–15 High Street, Sutton, Surrey SM1 1DF.
This first world edition published in the USA 2002 by
SEVERN HOUSE PUBLISHERS INC of
595 Madison Avenue, New York, N.Y. 10022.

British Library Cataloguing in Publication Data

Sole, Linda
    A rose in winter
    1. Love stories
    I.   Title
    823.9'14 [F]

    ISBN 0-7278-5653-7

Typeset by Palimpsest Book Production Ltd.,
Polmont, Stirlingshire, Scotland.
Printed and bound in Great Britain by
MPG Books Ltd., Bodmin, Cornwall.

One

I was seventeen the day before I saw him for the first time. My birthday had been celebrated in the usual way, despite the fact that Papa was in London talking to people about the terrible war, which had been raging for the past three years.

'Shouldn't we wait for Papa to come home?' I had asked my mother. 'It isn't fair to have a party without him.'

'Your father sent you a present, darling,' Mama replied. 'He wants you to have a lovely time, Julia. He will come home as soon as he can.'

My mother was a very beautiful woman, her hair almost as dark a red as it had been when she was young, untouched by the silver that threaded Papa's. But then, she was ageless, a charming, gracious woman, as lovely inside as she was out. I knew Papa thought so. He adored her, but he also loved me. He was always giving us both presents, spoiling his precious girls. My brothers spoiled us, too. Mama and I were very fortunate to be so loved.

I had heard my mother telling Papa how glad she was that my brothers and not been forced to join the army.

'Much as I love France, I do not want my sons to be killed there,' she had said, and Papa agreed, though he added that we must all do our duty for our country.

My brothers were both younger than me. Philip was just a year younger, but Lawrence was only fourteen. In some families the sons are made more fuss of than the daughters, but not in ours. I had always been led to believe that I was the special one in my family. I loved them all desperately – especially Papa! I was also thankful that Phil and Lawrence were still at school and too young to fight in France.

I had visited my grandfather Laurent de Arnay and his

1

second wife, Kate, in Paris more than once during the years of my childhood, and I, too, loved France, but I also adored my home. It was a gracious old house and the grounds were extensive. I particularly liked Mama's special garden.

She grew many beautiful flowers and shrubs there, but those I loved most were the exquisite, scented white roses. Even in November there was a sheltered corner where the roses still bloomed. I was carrying a bud I had plucked as I came from the garden that morning – the day after my seventeenth birthday.

I noticed at once the man limping up the drive to the house. He was wearing a soldier's greatcoat, and walked very slowly – as if in some considerable pain. I believed that he must have been wounded during the war and my heart was moved with pity for him. I ran to catch up with him.

'Hello!' I said as I drew near. 'Are you looking for Mr Allington? Papa is in London, but Mama is at home.'

He turned to look at me for a moment and something in his face made my heart lurch. He was an attractive man with soft grey eyes and a generous mouth, but he looked so ill! I thought he was going to collapse at any moment.

'Oh,' I cried. 'Do you feel faint? May I help you? Pray lean on me, sir.'

A faint smile flickered over his mouth. 'You should not be so trusting of strangers, Miss Allington. A young and lovely woman such as yourself should be wary. There are those who would take advantage of your innocence.'

'You know my name?' I stared in surprise.

'You told me,' he said. 'You are Philip Allington's daughter.'

'My father is your friend?' I smiled at him. 'Then you are not a stranger, nor are you likely to take advantage of me. Papa would not have told you about me if he had not trusted you.'

A flicker of appreciation was in his eyes as he bowed his head in acknowledgement. 'Not only beautiful but also wise, just as your father said. My name is Captain Charles Hamilton.' His gaze darkened, grew distant, almost brooding. 'At least, they tell me so. I fear I have no knowledge of my family or myself – beyond what I have been told.'

'How awful for you!' I cried, feeling immediate sympathy

for his plight. He had suffered terrible wounds, of course. I could see a livid scar at his left temple, though he had pulled his cap forward in an attempt to hide it. 'That must be most unpleasant for you, Captain Hamilton.'

'It is awkward,' he replied. 'And the reason I am here. Your father offered me a place to stay for a while – just until I feel able to face my family. It must seem like cowardice to you, but I am afraid I couldn't bear it at the moment.'

I looked into his eyes, saw the suffering and doubt and felt almost protective towards this man, who was a stranger to me and some years my senior.

'No, not cowardly at all. I think I understand. You must feel so strange, as if there is nowhere you truly belong. It would be very uncomfortable living with people who know you, but of whom you know nothing. They would be bound to speak of things you should know and be embarrassed when you could not remember.'

'It is easier to be with strangers,' he said, acknowledging the truth. 'How strange that you should see it at once. Philip understood that too – that is why he offered me a bolt hole.'

'I am glad he did,' I said. I felt that he was fine and good, a brilliant example of all that made up the backbone of England. In my youth and innocence I was very idealistic and very proud of my country's stand for justice. Because that was what Papa said the war was about – honour and justice. 'You are so brave, Captain – all our men have been very brave.'

'Have we?' He pulled a wry face at me. 'I have no memory of anything – except in flashes. Sometimes I hear guns and screaming . . .' He pulled himself up. 'Forgive me. I should not speak to a young girl of such things. I shall give you nightmares and your father will never forgive me.'

'I am not such a silly child as you imagine!' I replied with spirit, then as I saw his grimace, 'Are you feeling very ill, sir? Would you like me to fetch a manservant, since you decline to let me help you?'

'Give me your arm then, if you are determined.' He slipped his arm through mine and I felt his weight drag on me as we walked.

'Why did you not ask for someone to fetch you? You must have had a long walk from the village.'

'I was given a lift as far as your gates by an obliging farmer,' he replied. 'He would have brought my trunk, but the guard had arranged that already, though he was unable to arrange the same transport for me. I suppose I could have telephoned from the station, but I did not wish to be more trouble than need be.'

'It would not have been any trouble,' I assured him. 'Papa has a very grand automobile, which no one else uses. However, Mama has her carriage and there is always the governess's trap. Someone would have fetched you, had you asked. You were very foolish not to do so, even the length of the drive is tiring when you are not feeling well.'

'Yes, I see that now.' For a moment a smile of amusement lurked in his eyes. I thought how handsome he would be if he smiled more and if his skin looked less grey. 'I shall remember in future, Miss Allington.'

'I might permit you to call me Julia,' I said, teasing him a little because I wanted to see him smile again. 'When we know each other better, that is.'

'Shall we know each other better?' he asked, and the bleak expression was back. I remembered that he had no knowledge of himself and began to apologise, but he shook his head, a lock of dark hair falling forward over his brow from beneath his cap. 'No, please do not, Miss Allington. You must treat me as you would anyone you know. I am not to be made an invalid – the doctors said it was the worst thing that could happen. I am quite well actually. I simply cannot remember anything before waking up in an English hospital.'

Once again, I felt tremendous sympathy for him. His manner proclaimed him a gentleman. My father trusted him implicitly or he would not have sent him here. I thought he would be a very pleasant and interesting guest.

We had almost reached the house now. Built in the time of Queen Anne, it was a pretty, rambling house with a thatched roof, leaded windows and buff coloured stone walls. Not a mansion, but a warm and comfortable family home some ten miles inland from the Cornish coast.

4

My mother came out of the front door to meet us and I knew she must have seen us from one of the windows overlooking the drive. She was dressed in a dark green gown that set off her wonderful colouring. Papa loved her in green and she wore it often to please him. She smiled at us, the warmth of her personality flowing out to embrace us both.

'You are Captain Hamilton, of course,' she said and her expression was serious as she saw how weary he was. 'You look tired, Captain. Please come in and rest. My husband told me you were coming down and your room is ready for you.'

Mama had taken his other arm, as she drew him into the house his weight was transferred to her. I released myself, letting them go on together, but then as they reached the bottom of the stairs I ran up to them, reaching out to him.

'Please take this,' I said, offering him the rose I had plucked. 'The perfume is so sweet. It will make you feel better just to smell it.'

He smiled at me and accepted the offering, then glanced up at the staircase, which was clearly presenting a formidable challenge. I stepped back and watched them make the slow ascent to the landing above. He was Mama's responsibility now. Papa had sent him to us because he needed to be loved and cared for, and in this house everyone was loved. If anyone could help him to live again, it was my mother.

I was glad he had come to visit us. Surely we would become companions and friends during his stay? I had many friends. I saw no reason why Captain Hamilton should not become one of them.

I was changing into a pale apricot tea-gown when Mama came to my room early that afternoon. She stood looking at me for a moment or two, her smile affectionate and approving.

'You wear that shade so well,' she said. 'Your hair is such a pretty colour, Julia – honey blonde I think would describe it best, and your eyes are azure, like the skies on a summer's day in France.'

'Do I look like my father?' I asked.

I knew that Papa was not my father. He was Mama's second husband. My own father had died in a riding accident soon after their marriage and Mama came to England to be with her grandmother, who had lived on the coast some ten miles or so from our house. I sometimes thought I remembered Great-grandmother Ruston, though I wasn't sure. She had died when I was still a baby.

It did not hurt me that I was not Papa's true child, for he had proved often enough that I was his daughter in all but blood. No one could have been more loved than I and I knew I was fortunate to have such a family.

'Yes, you are like Gérard . . . at least sometimes,' Mama said and for a moment there was sadness in her eyes. 'But I often think you resemble my own mother, who was very beautiful.'

'You are beautiful, Mama.'

'I look like a gypsy,' she said. 'Or at least, I did as a young woman. I have acquired a little style these past few years, I think.'

Mama was the picture of elegance in her pale green silk afternoon gown. Her hair was swept up in a roll at the back of her head, though I knew Papa preferred it to hang loose around her shoulders. She did not often wear it loose, except when they were alone together. They were still lovers, still very much in love. You could see it in their eyes when they looked at each other.

'You don't mind that I am going out this afternoon?' I asked. 'Had I known we were to have a guest I would have told Marina that I could not have tea with her. She has a few friends staying she wants me to meet, but I could always telephone and say it isn't convenient.'

'Of course you must go,' Mama said. 'Captain Hamilton will probably stay in his own room for most of the time – at least until he begins to feel better. He has been very ill, Julia. We must all be very patient and kind to him.'

'Yes, of course, Mama. I like him. He has nice eyes.'

'Has he?' She looked surprised. 'I hadn't noticed. All I know about him is that he is being awarded the Victoria medal for bravery on the battlefield. I understand that he single-handedly rescued a young soldier who had been caught on the wire and was badly wounded. He was shot just as he was carrying the

6

soldier back to his own trench and has been unable to remember anything since he recovered consciousness.'

'He told me he had lost his memory,' I said, 'but not how he was wounded. He must be very brave, Mama.'

'It was not the first time he had risked his life for others,' Mama continued with a frown. 'On another occasion he went out and brought back a lost patrol, and he has been recommended in dispatches several times for courage under fire.'

'No wonder Papa sent him here,' I said. 'He must be a very special man. Do you not think so?'

'Yes . . .' She nodded but looked thoughtful. 'I am not sure what it is about him, Julia, but I sense something . . . something that goes deeper and further than his experiences in the war. I think he has an old soul, by which I mean that he has suffered far more than any of us understands.'

I was respectfully silent. Mama had known suffering herself. I could not argue with something I did not understand, but to me Captain Hamilton was simply a brave soldier who had gone beyond the call of duty to rescue his comrades.

'I expect he feels very strange because he cannot remember who he is,' I said. 'It must be awful not to remember your family, Mama.'

'Yes, though some people prefer to forget,' she said, and then shook her head as I looked at her. 'No, I am merely thinking aloud. Do not let me hinder you, Julia. I merely came up to see if you were nearly ready. I shall order the carriage for you now.'

'Thank you,' I said. 'Marina is excited because she has a friend of her brother's staying. They have both been training for the RFC and after this leave they will be sent to Belgium to begin flying missions over France.'

Mama nodded. 'So many gallant young men,' she said. 'Let us hope that both Johnny and this other young man will return safely. We have already lost too many pilots in this terrible war – to say nothing of the terrible losses in the trenches.'

'Yes, Mama, I know,' I said. I pinned a fresh rose to my gown. 'There are still some of your roses blooming in the garden, even now in the middle of winter.'

She smiled. 'Yes, of course, as you know, we sometimes

7

manage a few buds for the Christmas table,' she said. 'We are fortunate in Cornwall to have a mild climate, Julia. It was sweet of you to give your other rose to Captain Hamilton, but now you must finish getting ready or you will keep your friends waiting.'

I was thoughtful as Mama left me alone to finish my toilette. She seemed to be a little doubtful about Captain Hamilton, though I could not understand her reasoning. He was certainly a gentleman, and a brave soldier, so why had I felt she was warning me not to become too attached to him?

'Oh, do look at him,' Marina Carstairs whispered in my ear as she drew me into their drawing room. 'Isn't he divine? Truly divine!'

The Carstairs were very wealthy and this house was huge; much bigger than Papa's and expensively furnished, but not as pretty or comfortable as my home. I glanced across the large room to the young man she was indicating.

He was tall, lean, had very dark hair and eyes that looked almost black from this distance. I thought he must be about nineteen, and his laughter was infectious. He obviously enjoyed life and appeared to radiate energy. When he realised we were there, his eyes seemed to light up with amusement, and I knew he had guessed what Marina was saying about him.

Marina was one of my closest friends; a bubbly, pretty girl of eighteen with curly dark hair and blue eyes. We had shared a governess for some years, and went to each other's parties. Marina had had a coming-out ball at the Carstairs' London house earlier that year, and I had attended, though I was still only sixteen.

'I couldn't have my dance without you, Julia!' she had said when it was suggested I was too young to attend. 'Besides, all the guests are people you know, and if they aren't, you won't be silly enough to fall in love. You are too young to become attached to anyone just yet. You want to have lots of fun before you get married. I intend to!'

Now her hand was on my arm, exerting pressure as she waited for my reaction. 'Is he your latest flirt?' I whispered back as the stranger grinned at me. 'He's very handsome.'

'Oh, yes, isn't he?' She smiled at me wickedly. 'But I'm going to be very kind and let you have him, darling Julia. I'll let you into a secret – I'm in love and I'm going to be engaged at Christmas.'

'Really?' I stared at her in surprise. 'Who is he? Do I know him?'

'Lord Rochfield's third son,' she said, her blue eyes glowing with happiness. 'You must have met him at my dance.'

'Yes, I remember. He is a little older than you, Marina.'

'That is why I adore him,' she said and hugged my arm again. 'Paul is so sophisticated – so charming, and he has a lovely house in London. We shall spend most of our time there when we are married. He is a civil servant attached to the War Office.'

'I am so happy for you, dearest.' I smiled at my friend, glad that she had found someone she could really love and admire.

'Come and meet Brent Gregory,' Marina said. 'He is from America, but his mother was an Englishwoman. His family are in banking and he was expected to follow suit, but he got bored with college and decided he wanted some excitement so he came over and joined the Royal Flying Corps.'

I allowed my friend to introduce me to Flying Officer Gregory. We shook hands, and then he invited me to call him Brent.

'Everyone does,' he said. 'May I call you Julia? Or would you think that too forward of me?'

I laughed. Mr Gregory's manner was very engaging, though also more direct than I was used to. I wondered if it was because he was an American.

'I suppose if I am to call you Brent it is only fair that you should call me Julia,' I said, teasing him a little because I had liked him immediately. 'I do not usually permit strangers to do so but . . .'

'You are willing to make an exception in my case,' he said and gave me one of his flashing smiles. 'I do hope so, Julia. You see I only have three days leave and I don't want to waste a moment of them. I want to get to know you as quickly as possible, so that you will think about me when I've gone.'

'What makes you imagine I shall want to think about you?'

'But you will, won't you,' he said. 'I knew the moment you walked in that we were going to be good friends – maybe more.' He saw my frown and pulled a wry face. 'There I go – rushing things. I'm always in a hurry. My father says haste should be my middle name. I never have time to think before the words come rushing out.'

'Are you always this direct?'

'Always – do you mind?'

'No – it's refreshing,' I admitted. 'But I like to take my time about making friends. We do things differently down here in Cornwall – there is always plenty of time, you see.'

'You need time with those devilish twisting lanes of yours,' he said and pulled a wry face. 'I came down by car and it took me ages to find this place. I kept getting lost and every time I asked the way I was told something different.'

'You were probably having your leg pulled. We do that sometimes – to foreigners,' I smiled as he frowned. 'That's anyone from across the Tamar. Not just Americans. If you come from another county you are a foreigner in Cornwall.'

'I see . . .' He looked at me from narrowed, searching eyes. 'I think you like to tease a little, Julia.'

'Yes, sometimes.'

'I shall have to be on my guard, then.' He hesitated. 'How do you feel about coming for a drive with me tomorrow – or is that pushing it a bit far?'

'Oh, I couldn't – not without a chaperone!'

'Isn't that a bit old-fashioned for 1917?' He frowned as I laughed. 'You're doing it again, aren't you? Teasing me?'

'Yes and no,' I replied. 'My mother would have to meet you before I went driving with you. If she likes you, she will let me go with you – without a chaperone.'

'So how do I get to meet Mrs Allington?'

'You come to visit us at home tomorrow – for lunch if you wish? Perhaps Marina and Johnny will come, too.'

Johnny had gravitated towards us. 'Are you trying to cut me out?' he asked Brent with a mock scowl. 'I'll have you know Julia is practically engaged to me.'

'No, she isn't,' I replied, pulling a face at him. 'I know you too well, Johnny and there's no way I'm ever going to marry you – you are too argumentative.'

'Julia has invited us for lunch tomorrow,' Brent said. 'You're coming, aren't you? I want to take Julia driving.'

'We'll both take her,' Johnny replied. 'Her mother will never allow you to take her alone, Brent. I wouldn't anyway. He is a shocking flirt! Be careful of him, darling Julia. You would do much better to ditch him at once and marry me.'

Brent pulled a face at him and I laughed. I was enjoying this meeting with Johnny's friend. Johnny would be so amazed if I agreed to marry him. He would probably run away as fast as he could. We were the best of friends, but we should never be lovers.

'We'll all go,' I said. 'Marina, too. Then I'll have plenty of chaperones . . .'

'Are you enjoying yourself?' Brent asked, glancing at my face.

'Wonderful . . . it's so exhilarating!'

It was fun being driven in Brent's car. It was a very smart Briscoe touring car with a special V8 engine, so Brent told me and extremely fast, modern and sporty – not in the least like Papa's grand automobile. Brent had given me a cape to cover my gown, and I had needed it for the mud of country roads spattered us as we rushed along at what my mother would have considered highly dangerous speeds.

We had in the end ventured on our drive alone, because Marina's brother had his own car and he had driven over with her. Johnny told me it was because he did not trust Brent's driving and begged me not to risk going with him, but not within Mama's hearing, of course.

Mama had welcomed Brent as she did all my friends, with a smile and the warmth that always radiated from her. She might not have been so pleased had she witnessed the way Brent took corners at dangerous angles and almost swerved into a hedge to narrowly avoid an oncoming farm wagon. He stopped the car soon after that, and helped me out. We had parked at the edge of a sweep of open land.

'I'm sorry about that,' Brent said, jerking his head to indicate the road behind us. 'It's these damned roads. They make me feel claustrophobic. I'm used to wide spaces at home.'

'You mean like the moors?' I looked at him, noticing the impatient expression in his eyes. What a very unsettling young man he was!

'Yes, sort of, but bigger. America is a big country, Julia. The roads just go on and on for ever – straight, open and free.'

'Isn't that just a little boring?' I arched my brows at him, a little annoyed at the implied criticism of my beloved Cornwall. 'Our landscape is a bit bleak just here, but much of it is beautiful in the spring and summer.'

'I'm not sure if you're teasing me?' His eyes narrowed; suspicious and slightly angry. 'Oh, what the hell!'

Before I realised what he meant to do, Brent reached out and grabbed me, pulling me close to his chest. I gazed up into those dark, intense eyes. I should of course have been angry at his behaviour, but somehow I wasn't.

'God,' he whispered huskily. 'Those eyes! I've never seen such eyes – like a cool green mountain pool!'

Then he bent his head and kissed me. At first it was just a gentle, exploratory caress of his lips on mine, but then it deepened, his arms tightening as his tongue invaded, flicking at the sensitive inner flesh of my mouth; teasing, pleasing. When at last he drew away, he seemed slightly dazed, a little bewildered – as if something he hadn't expected had hit him between the eyes.

'What is it?' I asked. 'Are you cross, Brent? Did I do something wrong? I've never been kissed like that before. I wasn't sure what to do.'

'You could never do anything wrong,' he said, his voice sounding odd, choked. 'How old are you, Julia?'

'Seventeen.'

'Damn! Damn! Damn!'

'Now you are angry – why?' I looked at him uncertainly.

Brent laughed and raked his fingers through his springy dark hair. 'I'm angry because I'm a fool,' he said. 'I took advantage of a sweet, innocent child and I'm the one who got burned. It just serves me right!'

'What do you mean?' I stared at him, torn between laughter and amazement as I brushed a strand of fine hair from my eyes.

'I've fallen in love with you,' Brent replied, a rueful expression on his ruggedly attractive face. 'And it was a very stupid thing to do.'

'Because you are going away soon?' I asked, not understanding.

'Because of that, and because you are too young, Julia.'

'I am not a child!' I retorted. 'And seventeen isn't too young to be kissed. Marina is only eighteen and she will soon be engaged – at Christmas.'

'And married perhaps six months later? If she's lucky, that is.' He groaned and made faces that drew a laugh from me. 'I told you I was impatient, Julia. I want to sweep you up in my arms and carry you off – to make you my wife this minute.'

'Don't be silly, Brent,' I murmured and giggled. This was so wicked of me. Mama would be shocked that he had kissed me and I had made no attempt to stop him. It was very naughty of me, but it was also very amusing. 'That sort of thing doesn't happen in real life, only in storybooks. You like me, but you don't know me. You can't possibly be sure that you want to marry me.'

'But I do,' he said and his eyes had turned almost black with the intensity of his emotion. 'That's why I swore, Julia. I know I can't carry you off just like that. Your family wouldn't hear of it. They would insist on a long engagement and make us wait for years.'

'I wouldn't come with you even if I was allowed,' I told him. 'I like you, Brent. Very much as it happens and I enjoyed our kiss. I'm glad you gave me my first kiss. I shall always cherish the memory, but I don't want to marry anyone just yet.'

Brent took my hands in his, holding them so tightly that it became painful. His gaze seemed to burn into me, as if he wanted to possess my very mind.

'Wait for me, Julia,' he said and he sounded almost desperate. 'Don't forget me. Whatever you do – whoever you meet – keep your heart for me. Please? We were destined for each other. I know it and you will too, one day. I promise you that you will love me.'

Just for one moment I was tempted to give my promise. My heart was beating wildly and I could not help feeling carried away by the fierceness of his passion. Yet a small sensible voice at the back of my mind told me this was foolish. It was far too soon! I pulled my hands from his.

'I shall not promise you anything,' I told him with a little toss of my head. 'You are too impatient, Brent. I think we shall be good friends and I will write to you, but please do not say such foolish things.'

'Do you promise not to forget me?' he demanded. 'I'm not much good at writing letters, Julia, but I will try to answer yours.'

'You must if you want to be my friend.'

'I want to be much more than that!'

'Then you must begin by learning to be patient,' I teased him. 'Now I think it is time you took me home, Brent.'

'May I kiss you again?'

'No, not yet. Perhaps another day . . . when we know each other better.'

'Then I may come again tomorrow?'

'Every day until you leave.' I smiled at him and touched his hand. 'I do like you very much, Brent. I want you to know that. One day it may be more but you must not rush me. I want to know everything about you. Tell me about your home and your parents, please?'

'Very dull,' Brent said, pulling a face as he helped me climb back into the car. 'At least, my father's people are – bankers and very stuffy. My mother was different. She was English. I remember she used to laugh a lot. Father wasn't as stuffy or as dull when she was alive.'

'I'm so sorry you lost your mother,' I said. 'What was her name before she married?'

'Emily Ruston,' he replied. 'I think I may have some relatives in this part of the world. My mother was an only child, but her father had a brother. So the relationship would be distant . . . What?' He looked at me curiously. 'What have I said?'

'My great-grandmother's second husband was called Ruston. Isn't that strange? They lived on the coast some ten miles or so from here.'

'That's interesting.' Brent smiled. 'We might have some connection by marriage – though not by blood. Unless he was your mother's father?'

'Oh no,' I said. 'My mother's own name was Heron before she married. There could be no blood relationship, but our families might be connected in some way.'

'We must ask Mrs Allington,' Brent said. 'She might be able to tell me if I do have any relatives in this part of the country.'

Two

B rent asked Mama over tea that afternoon if she had ever heard of his grandfather. She looked at him in silence for what seemed a long time, then shook her head.

'I have no idea whether your grandfather and my grandmother's second husband were related,' she said. 'But if they were . . . no, there are no living relatives that I know of.'

Something in her manner was a little odd at that moment. She seemed uneasy, and I sensed that she was not telling Brent the whole truth, yet there was surely no reason for her to lie to him.

'It was just a long shot,' Brent replied carelessly. 'One of these days I'll chase it up. Mother always wondered if her uncle had married and had a family. I should like to know just to satisfy myself.'

'Max and Anne Ruston had no children,' Mama said, and there was a closed expression in her eyes.

'In that case, there are no relatives if he was my grandfather's brother.' Brent nodded cheerfully. 'Grandfather's property came to me when my mother died. A firm of English solicitors handles it all. I've never bothered to look at it, but I may decide to settle here one day.'

'Surely your father will expect you to go home when this is all over?' Mama asked, frowning slightly. 'I think Marina told me he is in banking and wanted you to carry on the business.'

Brent glanced at me. 'Well, that depends on many things, Mrs Allington. My father has another son. Billy isn't old enough to know what he wants just yet, but he may follow in the old man's footsteps. I doubt I shall. Even if I don't stay here, I have no wish to spend the rest of my

16

life in an office. I might breed horses, either here or in Ireland.'

'How very interesting,' Mama said and sipped her tea.

'Where is Captain Hamilton?' I asked. I had the oddest feeling that Mama did not like Brent and that made me uncomfortable.

'He went for a walk,' she replied. 'I told you it was unlikely that he would want to mix in company for a while. You must not expect him to fall in with your wishes like your other guests, Julia.'

'Who is Captain Hamilton?' Brent asked.

'A friend of Papa's,' I told him. 'He was badly wounded in France and Papa sent him here for a rest.'

Brent nodded, his dark eyes intent on my face and watchful.

'We must be going,' Marina announced. She went to kiss my mother's cheek. 'It was lovely to see you again, Mrs Allington. Mama will send you a dinner invitation soon.'

'It was good of you to visit us, my dear,' Mama said. 'And you, Johnny.' She rose as he approached her and kissed him on the cheek. 'Take care of yourself, my dear.'

'Rather! It's going to be the best fun ever.'

'Yes, of course.' Mama turned to me. 'See your friends off, Julia. I have some letters to write. Please excuse me. Take care of yourself, Mr Gregory. I wish you good fortune in whatever you choose to do.'

Brent had sprung to his feet the moment she stood up. He offered her his hand and grinned at her. 'You will be seeing me again, Mrs Allington. Julia has kindly offered to write to me while I'm over there.'

'Has she indeed?' Mama smiled, though I wasn't sure she was pleased by the news. 'My daughter can be very impulsive, Mr Gregory. You must remember that she is very young.'

'Mama! I am seventeen.'

'Very young,' my mother repeated. 'Young women tend to change their minds easily. Do not place too much reliance on a promise given after such a short acquaintance, Mr Gregory.'

My face was hot as Mama nodded, smiled and walked from the room. I was a little hurt by her words. It was clear to me

17

that she did not like or approve of Brent, and I felt that she was being unfair to him. He had surely done nothing to arouse her distrust.

Brent lingered as Marina and Johnny took their leave of me. His expression was rueful as he looked at me.

'Your mother doesn't like me, Julia.'

'I think she is just protecting me,' I said unhappily. 'I've never had a particular male friend before, Brent.'

'Am I a particular friend?' he asked hopefully.

'Yes . . . perhaps.' I gazed up at him. 'I think you might be one day.'

Brent grinned. 'I'm going to have to learn patience, aren't I? Your mother is right, Julia. You are very young.'

'But not a child,' I retorted. 'Come and visit me tomorrow. Please?'

'Wild horses wouldn't keep me away!'

I laughed, reached up on tiptoe and kissed his cheek. 'You are fun, Brent. I like you very much.'

Brent didn't answer. I watched as he drove away. His kiss and declaration of love had been exciting, but slightly unreal. I did not believe he could possibly mean them seriously. One day perhaps we might fall in love, but not yet. No, he was simply teasing me the way Johnny always did.

Just before I turned to go back in the house, I caught sight of Captain Hamilton walking slowly towards the house. For a moment I hesitated, but something warned me not to go to him. He had wanted to be alone, and I must respect his wishes. He might resent it if I bothered him with my attentions.

'I should not become too attached to Mr Gregory if I were you,' Mama said to me when I came down to the drawing room after changing for the evening. 'He is a pleasant young man, of course, but not to be taken too seriously, Julia.'

'Why didn't you like him, Mama?'

She wrinkled her brow. 'I did not dislike him,' she replied. 'But I think him unsuitable. He comes from a good family, particularly on his father's side, but his behaviour and attitude are that of a man who does not wish to settle. He is still young, of course. I would prefer someone a little older for you, my dearest. A good, gentle man to take care of you and cherish you.'

'Someone like Papa?'

Mama laughed and acknowledged the hit. 'How foolish I am! You are far too young to think of marriage. When you are older I am sure you will choose wisely, my darling.'

'Brent is just a friend, Mama. You do not mind that I promised to write to him?'

'As a friend – no, I do not mind. I have never interfered over your friends, Julia.'

'He is going to war,' I reminded her. 'We don't know if he will return. I wanted to give him something to look forward to, that's all.'

Her eyes were thoughtful, sombre. 'You are quite right, Julia, and very sensible. Certainly not a child.'

'No, Mama. I may be young but I am old enough to know my own mind.'

She seemed about to say more, but at that moment Captain Hamilton walked into the room.

'I was feeling better,' he said into the slight silence. 'Would it be convenient if I dined with you both this evening?'

'We should be delighted,' Mama replied. 'You must do whatever suits you, Captain Hamilton. This is your home for as long as you wish to stay with us.'

'You are very kind.' He smiled but his eyes retained their sadness. 'Miss Allington, good evening. I hope you had a pleasant day with your friends?'

'I went driving,' I said. 'It was great fun. Do you drive, sir?'

'Yes. I learned when I was at Oxford,' he said, then frowned. 'Good grief! I imagine that is the truth, though I have no idea where it came from. I cannot remember being at Oxford or learning to drive, but I believe I can.'

'That is a good sign,' my mother said. 'Your memory may return gradually, Captain Hamilton. You must be prepared for lots of little surprises like that one.'

'Yes . . .' There was a haunted air about him at that moment; a lost, unhappy expression in his eyes that made my heart go out to him. 'Yes, I suppose I must be prepared for anything.'

At that moment I wondered if there was something he had wanted to forget – before the war, before he was wounded – and I also wondered if he sensed that himself. Was it perhaps the source of the fear I had seen in his eyes when we first talked?

I dismissed the thought immediately, chiding myself for having had it. This man was a war hero and it was wrong for me to think such a thing even for one second!

During dinner Mama and Captain Hamilton talked about gardens. He had discovered her secret place. Of course it was not really secret, but it was hidden from view by high hedges, which made it a very private, tranquil place.

'I imagine it must be glorious in spring and summer. All those wonderful roses, orange blossom and spiraea – a mass of white.'

'Yes, it is a wonderful sight,' I told him enthusiastically. 'And Mama has the most wonderful scented lilies, which are white, too, and grow very tall.'

His eyes were thoughtful as he looked in my direction. 'Which is your own favourite flower, Miss Allington?'

'Roses – white roses,' I replied and blushed as his eyes seemed to become warmer.

'Like the one you gave me? It was a precious gift – a rose in winter.'

I nodded but made no answer. When he looked at me that way I felt odd, a little breathless, almost dizzy. I admired him immensely, but I was also slightly nervous of him – aware of my naivety. With Brent, I was on even ground, well able to hold my own, but this man had the advantage. He must know so much more than I did, which was another foolish thought when he had lost his memory.

Yet he was a highly educated man. As he talked to Mama about her garden and various plants that he had admired, I realised that he knew quite a bit about them. He spoke instinctively, using the Latin names of several, and talked about their habits as though he were something of an expert on the subject.

It was a while before I realised that my mother was skilfully drawing him out, forcing him to use his knowledge without his being aware of it. From the topic of gardening she led him on to old and beautiful houses and their history, and from there to the politics of the last twenty-odd years. He answered her questions easily, gave opinions which were clearly well founded and long-held, and it was only when Mama suggested that we should all retire to the drawing room for coffee that he smiled and acknowledged what had happened.

'Philip told me you could work miracles,' he said. 'I had no idea that I knew so much about plants until this evening, though my walk round your garden had stirred memories I could not name. Thank you, Mrs Allington. You have given me a part of myself back again.'

'I am sure you will remember everything in time, sir. The memories are there, stored like facts in a gardening book. As you need them they will come back to you providing you let them come and don't force out what still remains hidden.'

'How wise you are,' he said. 'I was lucky that Philip took pity on me languishing in that wretched hospital. Your husband is a tireless worker for our wounded, Mrs Allington. You must be very proud of him. It is his influence that has secured many comforts and a degree of understanding for men like me.'

'I am always proud of Philip, whatever he does,' Mama replied. 'He has no need to work, of course, but as soon as he knew war was likely he made himself available for voluntary work, and he sits on various committees. I know that he reports personally to an important government minister, but the details are, of course, confidential.'

We had both followed her into the drawing room. She sat down in her usual chair by the fire and Captain Hamilton took a seat on the comfortable sofa placed at angles to it. The colours of the room were soft shades of autumn, restful and relaxing for a winter's day. I went to perch on a seat in the window, curling my feet beneath me so that I could watch them from a small distance and observe.

'Now, will you have tea or coffee?' Mama asked. 'I have begun to rather enjoy coffee in the evenings, but it does not suit everyone. Julia prefers tea, don't you, darling?'

'Coffee at night gives me weird dreams.'

'Then perhaps I shall have tea, too,' Captain Hamilton said, glancing my way for a moment. 'Dreams can be unpleasant and puzzling, I find.'

Again I caught that haunted expression in his eyes. What had he glimpsed in his dreams that frightened him? Did he see wounded men with shattered limbs; was it dreams of the war that disturbed his sleep, or was there something else? Something he did not want to face even as he slept?

I drank tea that evening, but I still had dreams. At first they were pleasant. I was driving with Brent and it was great fun. I was laughing and he was teasing me. Then we were at the edge of a yawning chasm; below us lay jagged rocks and a rushing torrent of white water.

'Marry me,' Brent said, his face suddenly strained and tense. 'Marry me, Julia, or I shall jump into the rapids and drown.'

'No!' I cried. 'I cannot marry you, Brent. I love someone else.'

And then Brent seemed to fade into the distance and vanish like the white spray below. I glanced over the edge and I could see him being tossed over those wicked rocks, his face battered and bleeding, yet still I heard his voice begging me to marry him.

'No . . . No, I can't,' I whispered. 'Don't die, Brent . . . don't die for loving me . . . please.' And then I woke with a start.

I lay in the dark shivering for a few moments. The nightmare had been so real, so horrible. I felt frightened and upset, and I knew I should never sleep.

Leaving my bed, I pulled on a warm but shabby dressing gown over my nightdress and slid my feet into slippers. Then I went out into the hall. The house was very quiet and still. I carried a small oil lamp with me to light my way because I did not want to flood the house with bright light and perhaps wake others.

Downstairs, I made my way to the kitchens. I was no stranger to them, for my mother encouraged me to understand the way the house was run, and as a child I had spent many happy hours sitting at the large pine table with Cook, eating biscuits warm from the oven.

I found a glass of lemon barley water and carried it to Papa's library, where I curled up in a deep armchair and began to sip my drink by the embers of a dying fire. When the door opened and someone entered I thought at first my father had come home, but then I saw it was Captain Hamilton.

He hesitated, looking at me awkwardly for a moment. 'Forgive me,' he apologised. 'I could not sleep and came looking for a book.'

'I had a bad dream,' I confessed. 'I did not want another so I came down to fetch a drink. I like this room. I quite often sit here if I cannot sleep.'

'And now I have intruded on your private place.' He turned as if to leave, but I spoke his name and he looked at me again. 'You wished to say something, Miss Allington?'

'Only that there is no need for you to go. Please stay and find your book. Papa has wonderful books. He is a great collector. Many of them are valuable, though he keeps those in a locked cabinet since an over-zealous maid damaged something that was extremely rare.'

'That was unfortunate.' Captain Hamilton sat in the chair opposite me. 'Was your father very angry with her?'

'Oh no. He blamed himself for leaving the book lying around. He said the girl could not be expected to understand what she was dealing with. Papa is very fair-minded. Even when Phil broke the library windows when playing cricket, he merely advised my brothers to play their games further away from the house.'

'An exceptional man.' Captain Hamilton smiled at me. 'You are very fond of your father I believe, Miss Allington?'

'Oh yes, very,' I replied. 'I love all my family, of course, but I sometimes think I love Papa best. I should not, should I? It is wrong to favour one person too much, isn't it?'

'Perhaps. But also very human, don't you think?'

'Papa says that obsessive love can be dangerous.' I screwed up my forehead in a frown. 'I am not sure why, but I think it has something to do with Mama. Something that happened years ago. I believe she had a friend who behaved badly out of a mistaken sense of caring too much, but I have not been told the whole story.'

'I imagine it would not be hard for someone to become obsessed by Mrs Allington,' he said. 'She is an exceptional woman – very beautiful and extremely understanding.'

'Yes, isn't she?' I gave him a look of approval. 'Everyone says that about Mama. All my friends admire her.'

'And what do you friends say of you, Miss Allington?'

'Oh, most of them think I am an impossible tease,' I replied, giving him a wicked look. 'It comes from having younger brothers of course. I had to learn to keep them in order. Besides, I think one should be happy if one can, don't you?'

His expression was thoughtful as he looked at me. 'I am certain that is the desire of most humans, though seldom achieved in my experience – though possibly in the company of a delightful child such as you, Miss Allington, it might be obtainable.'

'I am not a child,' I said crossly and rose to my feet. 'Brent doesn't think so. He kissed me this afternoon and he wants to marry me.'

'Forgive me.' There was a glimmer of amusement in Captain Hamilton's eyes. 'I did not mean to offend you, but you seem very young to me.'

'Yes, I suppose I do. Mama said you had an old soul.'

'Did she?' He nodded. 'Your mother sees a great deal.'

His tone was odd, distant, and I was afraid I had offended him.

'It was not meant as a criticism. I hope I haven't made you angry?'

He shook his head. 'No, Miss Allington. No offence – either towards you or your Mama. I shall forgive you if you will forgive me?'

'You are forgiven,' I said and laughed. 'Everyone thinks I'm still a child because I tell them what I think. Papa says I am too impulsive and confiding, but why should I pretend to be something I am not?'

'There can be no reason,' he said and his smile had returned. 'I believe you are quite perfect as you are, Miss Allington.'

I felt the heat in my cheeks. 'Oh, no, I am not perfect,' I denied. 'Far from it – as Mama would tell you. But for being nice to me I think I shall allow you to call me Julia.'

'Indeed? I am honoured.' His eyes teased me gently. 'Would you like to call me Charles?'

'Oh no, that would show a lack of respect,' I replied quickly. 'Mama would think me rude.'

'Of course. I am much older than you, Julia. They tell me I shall soon be thirty – a very great age when you are seventeen.'

'Now you are being very wicked,' I protested and giggled. 'You are not old at all – Marina would think you very romantic. Her husband-to-be is older than you are.'

'Marina was one of the friends you entertained yesterday? I heard you all laughing together.'

'Yes. She is my best friend, but I have lots more. Papa knows everyone for miles around. We have visitors most days, especially when he is at home.'

'You are fortunate to have so many friends.'

The shadows in his eyes reminded me of his loneliness, and I realised how terrible it must be to lose all memory of one's friends and family. Impulsively, I put down my glass and moved towards him. Still feeling sympathy for him, I reached up and softly kissed his cheek. 'You do have friends who care for you,' I said. 'Mama and Papa – and me. You are not alone, Charles.'

Blushing furiously as he stood absolutely still, making no reply, I retreated and then fled from the room. I was overcome with embarrassment at what I had done. How shockingly forward I had become! In the space of a few hours I had allowed one man I hardly knew to give me a passionate kiss on the lips, and I had kissed another!

I was hot with shame, but just before the library door closed behind me I heard Captain Hamilton say the words that eased my embarrassment a little.

'Thank you, Julia.'

I could not stay. I had stepped over some kind of boundary and I knew that something had changed irrevocably.

Brent came to visit us alone on both of the following days of his short leave. Mama was polite to him, but the warmth she usually extended to all my friends was missing. I wondered about that, and I was sad because she did not seem to like Brent. I could not see that he had done anything to arouse her antipathy – except for that kiss, which she did not know about and was as much my fault as his.

I had not tried to stop him kissing me. Indeed, I had enjoyed and encouraged it. However, he did not attempt to kiss me again. I was not sure whether I felt disappointed or relieved. I liked Brent very much, but I was not sure I wanted to fall in love with him. He was just a special friend.

When the time came for us to part, he looked at me with such longing in his eyes that it hurt me because I could not promise what he wanted.

'You won't forget me, Julia?'

'No, of course not. We are friends. I've told you I shall write – if you want me to?'

'Yes. I may not reply often.' He raked impatient fingers through thick hair. 'I'm not sure about letters getting from there to here, but keep writing to me whatever happens. Promise?'

'Yes, I will promise you that, Brent.' I was relieved that I could give him this at least.

'Thank you.' His grin was like a ray of sunshine breaking through the clouds. 'You're a wonderful girl, Julia. It has been a privilege for me to meet you. Whatever happens in the future, I'll always remember that kiss. A lot of girls would have been outraged – or pretended to be.'

'It was nice,' I told him, then reached up to kiss his cheek. 'Don't be too much of a hero, Brent. I want to see you here again one day.'

'I'll be back,' he said. 'That's a promise, Julia. Keep thinking about me.'

He started his car, waving cheerfully to me as he drove away. I watched him go. I was a little regretful and I prayed that he would be safe. So many young men had died in the RFC. I hoped that Brent would not be one of them.

I was feeling sad as I went inside the house. Until the last few days the war had seemed distant. It was something I read about in the newspapers – something my parents discussed over dinner, but removed from me and my everyday life. Now it had become all too real.

Papa came home in the middle of the next morning. He had brought exciting packages for his two 'favourite girls', and he hugged us both, taking time to ask what we had been doing while he was away. He then spent some time in his library talking with Captain Hamilton.

'Your father has arranged for an eminent psychiatrist to visit Captain Hamilton here,' Mama told me later. 'It will be more comfortable for him than going to a hospital, and the doctors feel he needs to be able to relax.'

'Yes, Mama. He is so troubled by his loss of memory, but he seems a little happier since he settled with us. Do you not think so?'

'Yes, I do,' she agreed. 'I feel much better about him now that your father is home. I understand so much more than I did . . .'

I looked at her expectantly but she did not elaborate and somehow I could not ask questions. It was not my business to inquire into Captain Hamilton's past.

Now that Brent was no longer a constant visitor my life had returned to its normal pattern. I spent some hours each day helping Mama. There were flowers to arrange, dinner invitations to write and books to be read aloud when we sat together in the afternoons. I walked often, practised at the pianoforte and did a little embroidery when I had nothing else to do, and of course most days someone would visit us for tea.

Marina and her parents came to dinner two evenings after Papa's return. I saw at once that my friend was impressed with Captain Hamilton.

'He is rather magnificent,' she whispered to me as we followed her mother and mine into the drawing room, leaving the gentlemen to their port and brandy. 'Rather mean and moody and a real war hero! You must find him so exciting to have as a guest in your home.'

'I like him,' I replied. 'He teases me sometimes, and his eyes are so sad. I feel as though I want to comfort him.'

'You are falling in love with him!'

'No, of course I'm not,' I denied, my cheeks warm. 'I admire and respect Captain Hamilton, that is all.'

'I was just teasing,' Marina said and gave me an odd look. 'I shouldn't fall for him if I were you, Julia. I think he might be dangerous to love.'

'What do you mean?' I stared at her in surprise.

Marina shrugged. 'I'm not sure. It just came out – instinct I suppose. Oh, I don't know, Julia. I simply feel he isn't the right one for you. Brent was far more your type.'

I laughed and gave her a wicked look. 'He kissed me and told me he wants to marry me!'

'He didn't!' Marina went into a fit of giggles. 'What on earth did you say?'

'I told him we didn't know each other and refused to promise anything – except that I would write to him.'

'Good for you!' Marina cried. 'What a terrible flirt! I cannot imagine how he could suggest such a thing on first acquaintance.'

'He was very serious,' I said, a little offended that she found it so unbelievable. 'I think he meant it – at least when he said it.'

'Well, exactly!' Marina said. 'He probably means it every time he meets a pretty girl. You are very pretty, Julia.'

'Thank you.'

I was a little subdued by my friend's remarks. Brent had seemed so intense, so serious in his declaration of love that I had almost believed him. I could very easily have given my promise to wait. I was glad now that I had not.

'Julia. Will you play something for us?' Mama asked, interrupting my flow of thought.

'Yes, of course.' I smiled at her and went over to the piano-forte, beginning one of her favourite pieces from Chopin.

I was engrossed in the beautiful music when I happened to look up. Captain Hamilton had just entered the room and was staring at me. The expression on his face was wistful . . . as if he were reaching out for something he was desperate to find.

Then our eyes met and he smiled. My heart missed a beat before racing madly on. I was shocked as the heat rose in me and I knew suddenly why I had not given my promise to Brent. Something had held me back, even when I had been in his arms enjoying his kiss.

28

Marina's teasing words had been more prophetic than she knew. I was attracted to Captain Hamilton, and the feeling his smile had aroused in me that evening was not merely sympathy.

For four days following that evening I did my best to avoid Charles Hamilton's company. It was impossible to do so completely, of course, for he was taking all his meals with us now. He was always polite, going out of his way to exchange a few words with me, though I gave him little encouragement.

On the fourth day, however we met in Mama's garden. I had gone to pick some winter-flowering greenery and I discovered him near the bush, which still had the special white roses blooming. Hesitating, I almost walked away, but then he turned and saw me.

'Please don't go, Julia,' he said. 'Have I done something to offend you? I have a feeling that you have been keeping your distance of late.'

'No . . . Yes, I have a little,' I confessed. 'I was very forward the other night in the library.'

'I wondered if that might be it.' He smiled at me. 'Please do not let a moment of impulse spoil our friendship. I was grateful for your kindness.'

'I would not want to be a nuisance to you. I know I am a child in your eyes.'

'No, you are not a child,' Charles replied. 'At first I thought so, but I have since realised I was very wrong. You are young and very lovely, Julia. You are also a woman.'

I almost ran away from him then. My heart was thumping as if I had been running very hard and I was frightened. This was all happening so fast! Falling in love was a strange and terrifying thing for me.

'Do you think we might walk together?' Charles asked. 'I think the air here must suit me. I am stronger than I was when I arrived.'

'Yes, I have noticed you move more easily,' I replied. 'I shall enjoy walking with you, Charles.'

I had decided I would call him by his name when we were alone like this. We had stepped over the boundaries of age

29

and respect and were meeting as equals now. Two people who liked each other and wanted to learn more of one another.

'Tell me about you, Julia. What you like . . . what you want from life?' Charles invited as I fell into step beside him.

'I like so many things,' I said, my mind searching for ways to entertain him. 'Music and books, walking in the garden, visits to the sea, dancing and eating good food. But mostly I enjoy people. I love talking to them, hearing what they have been doing . . . oh, everything!'

'In fact, you love life,' Charles said and there was that faint air of amused indulgence about him. 'It is refreshing to find someone who is so easy to please. Anyone would find you an intelligent, pleasing companion. I am not surprised that your young American friend wanted to marry you.'

'Oh, Brent was probably only teasing,' I said. 'I dare say he will want to marry someone else next week.'

A little voice in my head told me that wasn't fair to Brent, but I shut it out. It was somehow important to me that Charles should not think I had taken it too seriously.

'I expect love comes in many guises and shapes. Not all of them pleasing or fulfilling.'

Charles's remark disturbed me a little. He sounded as though he spoke from bitter experience. Yet he could not, for he could remember nothing of his personal life. Other things were coming back to him piece by piece. As he walked he spoke of his love of art and form.

'A beautiful painting has the power to move me to tears,' he told me. 'I believe in the past I was an amateur artist of sorts. Apparently, there was a small exhibition of my watercolours held in London before the war.'

'Oh, you must begin again!' I cried enthusiastically. 'I have no such talent, of course, but Mama paints a little when she has time. You must ask her to lend you her colours until you have your own.'

Charles looked at me thoughtfully. 'What shall I paint?'

'Mama's garden, or the house,' I said at once. 'Oh, anything at all. If you are doing something you truly love you may find memories of another time gradually return.'

'Philip said much the same to me last evening,' Charles

replied with a little frown. 'He has been doing some research on my behalf. A doctor is coming to see me quite soon.'

'Yes, I know. Mama told me.'

'I was not certain I wished to see him, but I think I must. I ought to try and find a normal life, don't you think so, Julia?'

'You owe it to yourself to take up your own life,' I agreed. 'But I hope that won't mean you have to go away too soon?'

'Oh, no, I shan't do that,' Charles said. 'My mother came to see me in the hospital. She thought it was my duty to recover my health for the sake of the family . . .' His brow wrinkled in thought, which was clearly not particularly pleasant. 'My father is Lord Hamilton, you see, and apparently he had a stroke some months back. He is confined to his bed most of the time and is not expected to live more than a year or so at most.'

'Oh, I am so sorry, Charles.'

'Yes, I was sorry. I have no feelings about it, Julia. That upset me. I should feel grief, shouldn't I? It was one of the reasons I felt I could not go back there just yet.'

'I should be devastated if anything like that happened to Papa.'

'Of course,' Charles said. 'I actually rather disliked Lady Hamilton. Wasn't that terrible of me?'

I stopped walking and gazed up at Charles as he confessed his guilty secret. No wonder he had seemed haunted at times.

'It would be bound to make things uncomfortable for you if you went home feeling that way.'

'Yes. Very.' He looked rueful. 'A son should not dislike his mother. I felt it was very ungrateful of me when she had travelled all the way from Rondebush to visit me in London. I had the distinct impression that she did not quite believe in my loss of memory – she thought I could remember her if I chose to do so.'

'Surely not? The doctors must have told her of your condition?'

'I suspect that Lady Hamilton is a woman of strong opinions.'

From the expression in his eyes at that moment I guessed that the meeting between mother and son had not been particularly

31

pleasant, and I wondered what kind of a woman would try to impose her will on a man who had clearly been extremely ill.

'Then I am very glad Papa sent you to us, Charles.'

'So am I, Julia.' He smiled down at me. 'More than you will possibly ever know.'

Something in his tone at that moment made my heart beat faster. I believed that Charles was beginning to like me as much as I liked him.

Three

A nd so our walks began. Each day for the next eight days, Charles Hamilton and I spent at least two hours together. The weather was crisp and cold, but there was very little rain to keep us indoors and spoil our pleasure.

Charles told me he had borrowed Mama's paints and was experimenting.

'The rosebud you gave me has bloomed and faded,' he said. 'But Mrs Allington permitted me to pick another rose and some winter-flowering shrubs to go with it. I thought a simple still life to start me off. I may not be able to paint at all.'

'But of course you will,' I said confidently. 'Papa told me he has seen some examples of your work. He thinks it is good.'

'And so it must be, of course.' Charles laughed at my enthusiasm. 'How totally you give your love, Julia. Any man loved by you would indeed be fortunate.'

I blushed and looked away. Sometimes Charles made me feel so naïve – so very childish – and yet at other times I sensed something very different. There were moments when I believed I was becoming important to him. I felt that he needed me, and at times the look in his eyes was that of a man gazing at a woman he desires – a hungry yearning that he was trying to subdue, but could not.

Was Charles falling in love with me? I knew that he must have known other women in the past; beautiful, sophisticated women who would have been a match for him in intellect and experience. I knew so little of the world. How could I possibly hope to hold the interest of such a man for long?

I was a little in awe of this man, who besides being a war hero was obviously my superior in education and birth. Yet, we were companions during those first tentative days, and I was sure Charles was happy with me.

The day before the psychiatrist was due to arrive I sensed that Charles was nervous. He looked at me oddly several times until at last I was driven to ask him what was wrong.

'Supposing I do recover my memory, Julia? Supposing I don't like the person I used to be?'

'I like the person you *are*, Charles,' I told him. 'Can it really matter if some of your memories are not as pleasant as you would like them to be? You can always be a better person in the future, but I cannot imagine you have ever done anything truly bad in your life. I couldn't like you as much as I do if you weren't essentially a nice person.'

'Oh, Julia, Julia!' he said and he was smiling now, the shadows banished. 'How good you make me feel – and how foolish. I see I have been worrying for nothing. You like me, therefore I must be good and decent.'

'Don't mock me,' I said, slightly hurt by his amusement.

'I wasn't mocking – or only at myself, dearest Julia.' He gazed down at me and his eyes were the colour of wood smoke, soft and free of the doubts that so often haunted him. 'You have been so good for me. I think you have woven a spell around me, little witch.'

'Then I shall cast another and make you well,' I said. 'All your memories will be happy ones and we shall always be friends.'

'Perhaps we might be more than friends,' Charles said, then shook his head. 'No, that is unfair of me. I am too old for you. And too weary. You should have a young lover. Someone who will make your heart race with excitement.'

'You make my heart do odd things, Charles.'

'Do I, my little one? Then I must think very carefully of the future, must I not?'

I was too shy to ask him what he meant and he did not elaborate.

The next day Charles spent three hours alone with the psychiatrist. I was frantic with worry the whole time. If Charles regained his memory he might go away. He might decide that I was not the kind of person he liked to know –

he might even remember another woman he had loved. She would be more his age; beautiful, clever, sophisticated. Then I should lose him.

I was in Mama's garden picking some roses and greenery when he found me. I heard him call my name and turned to see him walking towards me. My heart raced and then stood still at his first words.

'I shall always remember you standing there with a rose in your hand, Julia.'

'You are going away?' The disappointment swept over me and it was more terrible than I had imagined.

'Mr Rosendale wants me to visit his clinic for some tests,' Charles said. 'He is a little worried that I am still having headaches.'

'Are they very bad? You haven't told me before.'

'Sometimes they are bad,' he admitted. 'At the hospital they said it was a matter of time, but Rosendale wants to do some tests. He also thinks I should pay a brief visit to my home, to see if it will trigger my memory.'

'But you did not want to go back there . . .' I was afraid that if he did I should never see him again.

'I shall come back,' Charles said and I knew that he had read my thoughts. 'Philip has asked me to spend Christmas with you and I shall. If you want me to, Julia?'

'Of course I want you here for Christmas!'

'Then I shall be here.' He took my hands in his. 'What I am about to say is not entirely fair, Julia, but do you think we might suit one another? Not just yet perhaps, but in a few months or a year's time?'

'Are you speaking of marriage?'

I was surprised, excited and thrilled that he should consider making me a proposal of marriage.

'It is unfair of me,' he said. 'You are on the threshold of life, Julia. You have so much to see – so much to experience.'

'Could I not discover these things as your wife?' I asked, gazing up at him eagerly. 'You could teach me all I need to know to be a proper wife to you, Charles.'

'Oh, my sweet girl,' Charles cried. 'Don't you see? It is you who have begun to teach me the truth of life. Until I came here I was close to despair. The darkness in my mind was unbearable. Had it not been for your father and some of the doctors at the hospital I might well have been driven to take my own life. Indeed, I saw little reason to live, but you have made me remember some of the good things. You and your parents are a reminder that life can be sweet.'

I laughed as I met his gaze. His time with Mr Rosendale seemed to have done Charles good. It was as if he had managed to shake off some of the shadows that had hung over him. I believed this was the real Charles – the man he could be when he was truly well again.

'I love you, Charles Hamilton,' I told him. 'I don't need months or a year to know that you are the man I want to marry. Mama will say that we must wait, of course. Mama always wants to protect me, but I think that Papa will not make us wait too long.'

'You precious girl,' Charles said and bent his head to mine. His kiss was sweet and gentle, drawing a response from me. Yet he did not pull me close to him, nor did his mouth demand more. He was tender, loving and unselfish. 'I shall return to you a few days before Christmas and then I shall speak to Philip.'

'Oh, Charles,' I cried, my heart leaping. 'I wish you did not have to leave at all.'

'I've given my word,' he said. 'Besides, I must do all I can to become well again, Julia. I do not want you to marry an invalid.'

'You are not an invalid,' I said. 'Every day you grow stronger. By the spring you will be completely better.'

'I shall try to be,' he promised. 'Perhaps by then your Mama will agree to our wedding.'

'Oh yes,' I said. 'She must! I am sure she will.'

I did not want to wait for months and months. I was certain that I loved Charles, sure that I wanted to be his wife. My mother would worry at first, but in the end she would agree because she would know it was for my happiness.

I wrote to Brent Gregory that evening. He had asked me to continue my letters whatever happened and I saw no reason

36

to disappoint him. Brent was my friend. I loved Charles and I had promised to marry him as soon as possible, but that did not mean I could not have friends.

I made no mention of my hopes for the future, but I did tell Brent that I was becoming fond of Charles. It was kinder to prepare him rather than spring the news of my marriage on him out of the blue.

When Charles left the next day I was sad, but I knew he would return. I had no doubts whatsoever that he loved me. He would return in time for Christmas, speak to Papa, and we would marry in the spring.

'There are two letters for you this morning, Julia.' Papa brought them into the parlour where I was arranging some flowers for my mother. There were just five days left before Christmas and we were expecting my brothers home at any moment. 'Is one of them from Captain Hamilton?'

'Yes, Papa. How did you know?' I asked, a little surprised.

'Because he has also written to me.' Papa smiled at me. 'And who is the other one from, may I ask?'

'Of course, Papa. You may read the letter if you wish. It is from Flying Officer Gregory. Brent is a friend of Johnny and Marina and also mine.'

'You met him while I was away in London, I believe?'

Something in his tone told me that Mama had spoken to him concerning Brent. I wondered why my friendship with the young American had disturbed my mother, but in another moment I forgot the small mystery as my father continued.

'Captain Hamilton tells me that his tests are finished,' Papa said. 'He has decided to visit his home for two days, and then he will join us until after New Year. He writes that he has something important to discuss with me. What do you think that could be, Julia?'

I knew that he was teasing me and blushed, hardly daring to meet his eyes. His next words were very surprising to me.

'Your mother was even younger than you are now when I first saw her, Julia. I fell in love with her instantly, though it was some years before she began to love me. Indeed, several years passed before we met again. I see no reason for you to suffer a similar experience.'

My eyes flew to his and I knew that somehow he had guessed my secret. 'How did you know, Papa?'

'Charles let his feelings for you show once or twice and I saw the truth in your face immediately. You have a very expressive face, my dearest. Your Mama thought it might be otherwise, that there was someone else you liked as much or more, but I told her I believed you and Charles were in love.'

'Do you mind, Papa? I know I am only seventeen.'

'But Charles is older and a good man. I believe he will look after you.' Papa looked thoughtful. 'You *have* talked about things, Julia? You do understand that there may always be gaps in Charles's memory? He has been through a great deal one way and another.'

I met his gaze steadily. 'Yes, I know, Papa. I believe Charles needs me. Perhaps by loving him I can help him to find himself again.'

'Your mother will need a little persuading but perhaps by the summer we may have convinced her that you will be safe with Charles.'

'Could we not persuade her by the spring?'

Papa's mouth quirked mischievously at the corners. 'We shall see what happens, my impatient daughter. I may be mistaken. Captain Hamilton may not ask for my permission to court you, Julia.'

'Oh, Papa!' I cried. 'You know he will.'

'You have only a few days to wait, Julia. I am certain that he will be here before Christmas – the rest will then be revealed.' My father gave me an indulgent look.

I nodded but made no answer. Papa's manner had told me all I needed to know. He approved of Charles Hamilton, and he would support our desire to marry. Even if Mama was a little anxious for my sake she would listen to Papa as she always did, which meant that by the summer at the latest we could be married.

I had a warm feeling of contentment. It was true that Charles and I scarcely knew one another, but we would make a journey of discovery together and that journey would be wonderful.

My brothers arrived home two hours before Charles was due. He had sent a telegram that morning, and Papa had driven to the station to meet him. By the time they returned together, Phil and Lawrence had turned the house into chaos.

A huge fir tree had been set up in the drawing room, its powerful scent pervading the house. My brothers were loudly disputing the placement of every candle and glass bauble. I had been pleased to see them when they returned, but I was beginning to tire of their noise. It was a relief to leave them to their squabbles and go out to meet my father and Charles as the car drew up outside the house.

Immediately, I sensed that they were pleased with one another, and as Charles came towards me there was a look of satisfaction in his eyes. He looked so handsome and confident as he swept me up in his arms, holding me and kissing me briefly on the lips.

'Wonderful news! Philip has agreed to our engagement this Christmas,' he said. 'The wedding may have to wait until the summer, but we shall not mind that, shall we, my darling?'

'No, of course not. As long as we can see each other often.' I looked at him anxiously, my eyes searching his face as I discovered signs of tiredness. 'How are you, Charles? Are your headaches better now?'

'I haven't had one for more than three weeks, but Rosendale gave me a few powders in case they come back. He had thought there might be some physical cause for them – and my loss of memory – but now he thinks that both symptoms are merely due to trauma. He is certain I shall recover my memory soon.'

'That is good news, Charles.'

'Yes.' He touched my cheek, sensing my concern. 'The visit home wasn't too bad, but I think I shall not go down again until we are married. I intend to divide my time between London and Cornwall.'

'You intend to return to London?'

We had progressed into the house as we talked. Hearing the noise of my brothers' squabbling, I drew Charles into the smaller front parlour where we could be alone. It was a warm, comfortable room that both Mother and I used often, littered with our books and needlework.

'Do not look so distressed,' Charles said and took my hand. His look was warm and indulgent, very like Papa's. 'Now that I have been passed as more or less fit for duty, I have been offered a desk job in town. I feel I ought to take it, Julia. I shall not return to the fighting, of course, but there is still a war going on. I can be useful, and I believe working may help me return to normal life.'

'Yes, I understand.' It would stop him brooding too much about his lost past. 'I shall miss you, but you must do as you think best, of course.'

Charles laughed at my obvious disappointment. 'No, my dear girl. You will not miss me, because Philip has agreed that you shall come to London for an extended visit. You may spend time at the dressmakers and museums – just as you would if you had gone there for the Season – and I shall take you to the theatre and parties. I doubt there will be many large balls this year, but we may find that some of my acquaintances are holding small dances. I think that we shall find life goes on despite the war.'

'Oh, Charles!' I gazed up at him in delight. 'How good both you and Papa are to me.'

'Why should we not be?' he asked. 'I have not showered you with expressions of my affection, Julia, that is not my way, but you are very precious to me. And to your Papa, of course.'

I blushed, finding it difficult to meet the warmth of his look. How swiftly love had changed my world. Only two months earlier my heart had been untouched by passion, and now I was almost engaged to be married. I released my hand and moved away from Charles.

For one fleeting moment I thought of another proposal, and of another, impatient, passionate young man, but Brent had merely been flirting with me that day. I had thought of it several times and I was sure now that Marina was right.

Brent had written to me twice since he left to join the RFC unit in France. His letters were full of the RFC and the missions he had already flown. I was sure that his declaration had been

40

impulsive and meant nothing. When I next wrote I would in fairness tell him of my engagement. I would offer to remain his friend, but the decision whether or not to continue writing must be his.

'What are you thinking?' Charles asked. 'You seemed far away then.'

'Oh, nothing.' I raised my head to look at him. 'I am so happy, Charles. I never knew I could feel this way.'

'Nor I, my darling.' He came towards me, took my hands in his again. 'I am older than you, and nowhere near good enough for you, but I shall strive to make a good life for us. If my memories never return we shall make others together.'

'Yes. Yes, Charles. You must not worry about the past. It is only the future – our future that matters.'

He nodded, hesitating for a moment as though there was something in particular he wished to tell me, then he seemed to change his mind. Letting go of my hand, it was his turn to move away.

'You are right, Julia. Whatever happened in the past is over. We cannot change it. The future belongs to us. We shall make of it what we wish.'

His back was towards me as he picked up a book someone had been reading earlier and glanced at it.For a moment I felt a tiny trickle of ice at the nape of my neck. What was causing those shadows I had glimpsed in Charles's eyes? What had he decided not to tell me?

Then he glanced round at me and the shadows were gone. I could not even be sure they had ever been there. He was smiling at me.

'I have two gifts for you, Julia,' he told me. 'Shall I give them to you now or wait until Christmas Day?'

He was just like Papa! Too excited to wait. He wanted to give me his presents at once.

'Is one of them a ring?' He nodded and I laughed. 'You may give me that now. Keep the other for under the tree, please.'

Charles took a small blue leather ring box from his jacket pocket. He opened it to show me what was inside, and I gasped with pleasure as I saw the square emerald surrounded by large white diamonds.

41

'Oh, it is beautiful,' I said. 'Thank you so much, Charles.'

'Give me your left hand,' he commanded and I did so. I was thrilled as he slid the ring on to the third finger. 'The ring is new, bought specially for you, my darling. No other Hamilton bride has worn it.'

'I love it – and you.' I lifted my face for his kiss, which was warm and tender.

As our kiss ended we heard giggles and a scuffle behind us. We turned to discover that my brothers were watching us. Phil and Lawrence were eager to meet a real war hero. They were a little in awe of him initially, but also very curious about the fact that he had been kissing their sister.

'You're engaged,' Lawrence cried as he saw my ring. 'Good grief! I didn't think you would marry for ages, Julia. You're only a baby.'

'Well, I don't suppose we shall marry for some months,' I replied with what dignity my brother had left me. 'And *you* are the baby of our family, Laurie.'

'Don't squabble,' Phil said, assuming a lofty air. He looked directly at Charles. 'Papa says you were in France, sir. I should like to hear about your experiences if you have time. I hope to join the army as soon as I'm able.'

'You can't for at least another two years,' I told him. 'Besides, Papa wants you to go to college.'

'I should imagine the war will have ended by then,' Charles said. 'If I were you I should concentrate on gaining a good education. War isn't as much fun as you might imagine.'

'Do you really think it will be over soon?' Phil asked, looking disappointed.

'I hope and pray it will,' I replied without waiting for Charles to reply. 'Go along, both of you. You can talk to Charles another day.'

My brothers hesitated, clearly fascinated by my fiancé, but Phil gave Lawrence a little push and they went off together. We could hear them arguing as the sound of their voices receded into the distance. I turned to Charles impulsively.

'I am sorry Phil asked so many questions. Both my brothers are fascinated by the war and I don't suppose they understand for a moment what it is really like out there.'

'I didn't mind,' Charles replied. 'Oddly enough, I've begun to remember certain things that happened out there. It's the stuff of nightmares, Julia. Your brothers are well out of it, believe me.'

'They are too young to realise their good fortune. I know Mama is so relieved that they are not old enough to join up.'

'Yes, she must be.' Charles looked slightly rueful. 'Your Mama may well think you too young to be engaged, Julia.'

'Papa will convince her,' I said confidently. 'Mama always listens to him. Besides, she likes you, Charles. And I love you. Mama will be happy for me.'

Papa had prepared my mother for our engagement. She kissed us both when we joined her for tea that afternoon and wished us happiness.

'Julia is very young,' she said to Charles. 'But by the summer you will have learned to know one another, and if you are both still of the same mind I shall be happy to see you wed.'

'You are very kind, Mrs Allington.'

'Thank you, dearest Mama.' I hugged her. She smelled of the soft perfume she always wore

'Perhaps you should call me Jenny,' she said to Charles and smiled at him after returning my hug. 'Since we are to be family I think we should dispense with formality, don't you?'

'I should be honoured if you will return the favour and call me Charles, Jenny.' He accepted the fragile teacup from her hand.

I sipped my tea, feeling a little surprised that Mama had not resisted the idea of my marriage more strongly. Even though she was insisting that the wedding should not be before the summer I sensed that she was pleased with my choice.

Had she believed I might favour someone else? And why had she taken such a dislike to Brent Gregory?

It was a small mystery, but it no longer mattered. I had given my promise to marry Charles. We were in love and the memory of Brent's kiss had faded from my mind. It had been my first kiss but it meant nothing.

I had so much to look forward to now; Christmas with Charles and my family, and all the excitement of sharing my news with Marina. Her parents were giving a small dance for her on New Year's Eve to celebrate her engagement, and now Mama was talking of a party for us.

'I thought just a few intimate friends,' Mama said. 'It will be easier for Charles if he meets your friends gradually, Julia. We must remember that he has been ill.'

'Yes, of course.' I gazed up at him anxiously. 'You must not tire yourself, Charles.'

'You are both kindness itself,' Charles replied. 'But I do not wish to deprive Julia of any pleasure. We shall begin to mix in society both here and in London. I have been told it is the best way to recover my health – and my memory.'

'Then we shall have a family Christmas and hold a party a week after Marina's dance,' Mama said.

Christmas Day was as enjoyable as ever. My parents had always made it a special time for my brothers and me. We sang carols, went to midnight mass on Christmas Eve and drank hot, spicy punch when we came home, stamping our feet with the cold.

Christmas Day was one of rejoicing. Good food, presents under the tree after lunch and games that everyone took part in. Charles gave me a pearl necklace with an emerald clasp to match my ring. He said nothing about it being bought especially for me, as he had done when giving me the ring. There was no need. I would not have minded had it been a family heirloom. Why should I? I was content knowing that Charles loved me and I loved him.

Each day was as pleasant for me as the one before it. Charles and I talked about so many things. He seemed to remember a little more as time passed, though never his own past or his family – the things he had done in childhood and as he grew to manhood were as much a mystery to him as ever.

However, he did talk to me now of his feelings about the war.

'I remember lying in the trenches,' he told me once as we were walking in the gardens. 'It was wet and the mud clung to my boots and clothes. I hated the smell of it. Then the screaming started . . .'

'Oh, Charles.' I looked at him anxiously. 'It must have been so awful for you – for all of you.'

His eyes were gazing into the distance, and I knew he was haunted by the terrible memories.

'I knew a soldier was caught on the wire. I couldn't stand the screaming anymore so I went out and got him . . . that's all there was to it. I just couldn't listen to it a moment longer.'

'You were very brave, Charles.'

'No – not brave.' He frowned. 'I cannot bear suffering, Julia. Not in animals or in people. I would rather they were dead . . .'

That seemed an odd thing to say, for a man who had risked his own life to carry a wounded soldier back to the trench.

'But you carried him back – that soldier was wounded and you saved his life.'

'So they tell me,' Charles said. 'I remember nothing of what happened after I went out there to fetch him.'

'You saved him,' I said. 'And then you were wounded. Papa told me about it.'

Charles nodded but changed the subject. He began to talk about his painting. He had started a watercolour of the house. If it turned out well he intended to give it to Mama as a gift.

'I should like to paint you, Julia,' he said. 'Would you sit for me?'

'Yes, of course,' I replied. 'If you are sure you really want me to.'

'Oh, yes,' he said and touched my cheek gently with his fingertips. 'I am quite sure. I want to capture that innocence – before it goes. You have changed a little already. I would like a portrait of you as you are – as you were that very first day. When you gave me your rose.'

I gazed up at him, my heart almost bursting with happiness. Surely his desire to paint me was proof of his love if I had needed it – which of course I did not.

I felt secure in the affection of my family and my fiancé. I was truly loved and the future beckoned brightly. What more could I want?

Charles was sitting on a stone bench in Mama's garden. I had been looking for him all over the house. It was a damp, foggy morning and I'd thought it too unpleasant for walking.

His back was towards me as I crept softly up on him, hoping to surprise him, but suddenly he made a moaning sound and began to cry out.

'Murder! It was murder . . . no right. You had no right . . .'

I hesitated, feeling shocked and uncertain. Charles had begun to shake and shudder uncontrollably, strange cries and mutterings coming from him. It was as if he were having some kind of a fit. He must be ill!

I ran towards him, fearful for him. 'Charles! Charles my dearest – what is it? What is wrong?'

He stared at me with feverish eyes and I knew he was not seeing me at all, but some tortured vision of his own. He was clearly caught up in a kind of nightmare that had for the moment taken over his senses.

'Get away,' he muttered. 'I don't want to look at you. Get away before I kill you! You deserve that I should . . .'

'Charles?' He had risen to his feet, was towering over me in a threatening manner. 'What are you saying? What are . . . ?' I took hold of his arm as he seemed in such a ferment of agony that I feared what he might do. 'It is me – Julia.'

Charles jerked his arm as if to shake me off, bringing it back so violently that I was sent flying, missed my footing and fell to the ground. I gave a yell, more out of shock than pain as he towered above me.

'Charles! It's Julia. It's Julia . . .'

Whether it was my scream that broke into his tortured thoughts I do not know, but he stopped and stared at me. For a moment his eyes were blank, as though he did not know me, then they cleared and a look of horror came to his face.

'Julia? What happened?' He held out his hand, helping me to rise. 'Did I hit you? Oh, my God! Forgive me. What did I do to you?'

'I was trying to calm you,' I said. My heart was still racing. It had been frightening for a few moments. 'You had some kind of a fit, Charles. I think you must have been dreaming of the war. You said it was murder and you were threatening to kill someone.'

'Was I? Good grief!' He looked alarmed. 'Did I knock you down? I am so very sorry, Julia. I had no idea what I was saying or doing. You must believe I would never deliberately harm you?'

'I know that, darling.' He looked so dreadfully upset that I laughed and kissed his cheek. 'It wasn't your fault. I took hold of your arm. You just tried to throw my hand off and I stumbled – that's all it was.'

'I would never forgive myself if I hurt you. I thought I was over all that business or I wouldn't have . . .'

'Please don't be upset,' I said quickly. 'I didn't know what to do, but if it ever happens again I'll just wait until it is over. Don't worry, Charles. It may never happen again, and if it does I'll call for help.'

The incident had distressed Charles far more than it had me. He kept looking at me throughout the remainder of the day, and he must have apologised fifty times. In the end I got a little cross with him.

'For goodness sake stop worrying over an accident. I wasn't hurt. I'm not even upset, Charles. I love you and I want to share everything with you – the bad as well as the good.'

'I adore you,' he said and kissed me. 'If I thought I could hurt you, I . . .'

'Charles! No more. You didn't hurt me. You never would.'

'Sorry.' He gave me a rueful look. 'It is just that you mean so much to me. I couldn't bear it if you stopped loving me.'

'Well, I shan't, so you can stop fussing. I am perfectly happy. There is nothing to worry about.'

The subject was dropped, but I knew Charles was anxious. The incident had cast a slight shadow over our happiness, but I was determined that it should not spoil things. I wanted to be happy and I was.

I discovered when we met at her dance, that Marina was also very happy. We spent a few minutes talking privately when we went upstairs to refresh ourselves between dances.

'I like Captain Hamilton,' she told me. 'I was wrong to say what I did the first time I met him; he is exactly right for you, Julia. Brent was lots of fun, of course, but too young for you, dearest. Johnny says he's a terrific pilot, though, the best of all of them in his unit. Some of the others who joined with them have already been killed, but Johnny and Brent seem to bear charmed lives.'

'I'm so glad,' I said. 'I wrote to Brent yesterday and told him I was engaged at Christmas. I don't suppose he will write to me again.'

'There's really no point, is there?' Marina patted her hair. 'Shall we go down now?'

'Yes. You are coming to our party, aren't you?'

'Of course.' She laughed and kissed me on the cheek. 'We shall probably be in London together soon – buying our bridal clothes. I'm so excited, Julia. I just can't wait!'

Marina's wedding was to be held at the beginning of May. Her parents had decided there was no point in a long engagement, but she was older than me and had known her fiancé for some months. At this time I had no idea when my mother would agree to my marrying Charles.

Of course Mama was right to make us wait. I had known Charles for such a short time, but I was sure I would be happy as his wife. Sometimes I wished that we could marry immediately, but at others I was content to wait.

We were getting to know one another. Charles was always so loving to me, so tender. Why should I be impatient?

And so the days drifted by until it was time for Charles to return to London.

'Please don't come to the station with me, Julia,' he said as he kissed me goodbye that morning. 'I want to remember you here where you belong, in this beautiful place.'

'I belong wherever you are, Charles,' I reminded him.

'You will soon be with me in London,' he said, trailing his fingers down my cheek. 'My lovely girl. In a few more months we shall be together for the rest of our lives.'

'Yes, I know. It's what I want with all my heart.' I reached up to kiss him. For a moment his arms closed about me and his kiss was hungry . . . passionate. 'I love you so much, Charles.'

'And I love you.'

48

I watched as he drove away with Papa. I was sad that we must part so soon, and yet I understood that Charles needed the challenge of the job he had been offered. Perhaps at work he would begin to remember those things that were still hidden from him.

It did not occur to me for some days after his departure that Charles had made no mention of introducing me to his family. I was not even sure he had told them that we were to marry in the summer.

Four

It was a week after Charles had gone up to London when the letter came. I recognized Brent's handwriting immediately and my hand trembled a little as I opened it. Would he reproach me for finding a lover so soon after his own passionate declaration?

His letter did not mention it, and I could not be certain he had received my letter, as it was possible that it had gone astray. His own letter contained shocking news, which brought tears to my eyes. Marina's brother had been shot down and killed. Even as she had been telling me that Johnny bore a charmed life he must have been preparing for the mission that was to rob him of the future. I was shocked, hardly able to believe that Johnny was dead. How could it have happened so swiftly?

'Oh, Mama,' I wept as I showed her Brent's letter. 'Poor Marina – and her parents! Whatever must they feel? Do you think I should go over – or telephone Marina?'

Mama frowned as she read the letter. 'This is terrible news, Julia. The family can hardly have heard it themselves much before this. I think we must wait for them to contact us – at least for a day or two.'

'Yes, I suppose so.' I looked at her with misty eyes. 'I am so glad Phil isn't old enough to go. Poor Johnny. He was so young – always teasing me. He kept asking me to marry him . . .' Tears trickled down my cheeks. 'I always laughed at him – now he is dead. It hurts to think that he will never come home. I feel so sorry for him and his family.'

'Johnny was your friend,' Mama said, looking sad. 'This is the first time you have lost someone you care for and it is a very painful experience. You must expect to grieve for him, Julia. I am very glad you were not engaged to him – or this

50

other young man. I fear for the lives of all our brave pilots out there.'

'I thought you did not like Brent, Mama?'

'I neither liked nor disliked him,' Mama said and seemed thoughtful. 'I merely felt he was not a suitable young man for you. And I was right, wasn't I, Julia? You have Charles now and he loves you.'

'Yes, Mama.' I was silent for a moment. 'Do you think Marina's wedding will be postponed?'

'I should imagine not. There is really no point in her going into full mourning, especially as everything is arranged. However, her mother will not wish to take her to London as they had planned. I think it might be a good idea to invite Marina to come with us – if she feels up to it, of course.'

'Oh, yes, that would be much better for her,' I agreed at once. I wanted to be with Marina, to do what I could for her.

'She may not want to attend dances or parties, of course, but shopping and quiet dinners might be just the thing to take her mind from her very natural grief. And her fiancé will be in town some of the time so that will be nice for her.'

'You must ask Mrs Carstairs, in a week or two, Mama.'

'Yes, I shall.' My mother glanced at Brent's letter again. 'Is it your intention to keep up this correspondence, Julia? Have you told Flying Officer Gregory of your engagement?'

'Yes, Mama. I cannot be certain he received it, of course. I believe letters do sometimes go astray out there.'

'You must certainly reply to this,' Mama said. 'But then I should end it if I were you. Charles might not approve.'

'Brent and I are simply friends, Mama. I did promise him I would write while he was away and flying with the RFC. It would be unkind of me to stop if he wishes to continue. I am sure Charles would understand.'

She was still doubtful. 'Well, I suppose there is no harm in the circumstances, but I think you ought to mention the friendship to Charles. If he doesn't approve then you must stop.'

I nodded but made no reply. I would mention Charles often in my letters to Brent, and I would tell Charles that I was writing to a friend in the RFC. Surely there could be no objection? I felt

51

more than ever obliged to keep my promise now that Johnny had been killed.

He and Brent had been close friends. I could tell from what had been left unsaid in his letter that he was terribly upset by what had happened to Johnny. His own life was constantly in danger. Surely the least I could do was to offer some comfort in my letters?

Marina was naturally devastated by the terrible news. She came over to see me the following day and we sat weeping together in the small parlour, our arms wrapped around each other.

'I can't believe it,' she told me. 'It makes me feel so guilty, Julia – to think I was having fun as my brother was dying . . .'

'You couldn't have known,' I said, holding her close as she sobbed out her pain and grief. 'It wasn't your fault, Marina, and Johnny wouldn't want you to feel guilty. He loved you.'

'Yes, I know.' She took the handkerchief I offered and wiped her face. 'Johnny was always teasing me – the way he did you.'

'We were good friends. I was fond of him, too.'

'As he was of you. I sometimes thought he meant it when he said you should marry him.'

'Oh, I'm sure he didn't. We just liked each other, that's all.'

Marina nodded and blew her nose. 'Papa says the wedding must go ahead as planned, that there would be no point in postponing it, but Mama is sick with grief. She can't possibly take me to London to buy my trousseau.'

'Mama will take you with us. If you want to go?'

She considered for a moment, then gave me a watery smile. 'I think I must go – being with you would be easier. I don't think I can bear to be at home.' She gulped hard. 'There . . . there isn't a body, you know. We are going to have a service, but . . .' The tears began again, trickling down her face and into her mouth.

'Don't think about it,' I said. 'Try to remember Johnny as he was on his last leave.'

Marina wiped her eyes again. 'I do try, Julia. We had fun those last days, didn't we? Brent wrote to me. His letter was so wonderful. I never realised he was capable of writing something so deep and meaningful. I am very grateful to him.'

'His letter to me was quite brief,' I said. 'You must show me yours one day, Marina.'

'Yes, I will,' she agreed. 'It surprised me. I thought he was just a flirt; careless and perhaps a little shallow, but I was quite wrong.'

We sat with our heads touching in shared sorrow, remembering not only those days of Johnny's last leave, but also so many other times we had all been happy together. It was very difficult to accept that Marina's brother would not be coming home again.

Of course we were not alone in our pain and grief. Wives, sisters and mothers all over the country were experiencing the same loss. Once again I could not help feeling relief that none of my loved ones were in danger. I prayed that night to God. I asked that he would keep Brent safe – that he would return home to his family when this terrible war was over.

Papa, Mama and I attended the memorial service for Johnny together. Three weeks after that we left for London, taking Marina with us. Her mother was still too upset to think of making the trip, of course, but she wanted Marina to be fitted for the clothes she needed, and was grateful that she could safely hand her daughter over to us. She trusted Marina's own good sense to tell her what functions were proper for her to attend, and she knew Mama would take good care of us both.

It meant that we ourselves would not attend some of the parties that we might have done, but I really did not mind. I was glad that I had this chance to help my friend through a very difficult few weeks.

Charles came to call the evening we arrived in town, looking very much a man of the world and less tired than he had when we first met. He was sympathetic to Marina, of course, but insisted that he would be escorting me to several parties and functions himself.

'Marina can stay quietly at home with your Mama,' he said. 'You will naturally be with them during the day, but I see no reason why you should not have some pleasure in the evenings, Julia.'

My mother agreed with him. 'It will be nice for you to go out with Charles alone,' she told me. 'Since you are engaged there will be no need for me to chaperone you. I trust Charles to look after you implicitly. Besides, I think I must devote a little time to Marina.'

Marina, too, was happy for me to leave her with Mama some evenings. 'This is your special time,' she said. 'I do not want to spoil it for you, Julia. I had my own season last summer. This isn't precisely the same for you, but you must make the most of your visit. I want you to be happy.'

'If you are sure you won't mind?'

'Quite sure. It is natural that Charles wants to take you out. Besides, your mother will hold a few quiet dinners, and Paul will be here soon. His work takes him away now and then, but he is often in London. And you and I will explore together during the day, Julia. We might go to watch an afternoon showing of the new Charlie Chaplin motion picture. I saw him in something called *The Tramp* when we were here last year. If you would enjoy that?'

'Yes, of course I should. It will be fun and we shall go everywhere together during the day. We can buy lots of pretty clothes together and visit the museums and art galleries.'

Thus began the pattern of our visit. Charles was always busy at the War Office during the day, but he came to the house almost every night. Sometimes he dined with us, and we sat talking or playing cards for an hour or so afterwards. I asked if he would take me to a Music Hall, but Charles did not think them a suitable place for me, even though the King and Queen had attended a performance by Marie Lloyd some six years earlier and given her their approval. I was disappointed by his refusal, but on many nights he did take me out – to the theatre, the ballet and to private parties, also to official functions, where I was introduced to gentlemen he worked with during the day, and their wives.

These were rather dull affairs. The ladies were all much older than me and seemed to lead such busy lives heading committees for various charities. They talked endlessly of the war and their good works, and I was often relieved when the evening was over.

'I'm sorry to drag you to these things,' Charles said to me one evening as we were being driven home in the large black car he had acquired. 'They are a part of my life at the moment, but I'll make up for it tomorrow. We have been invited to a party. I can promise it will be much livelier than this evening.'

'I didn't mind it so much, Charles,' I told him. 'Really. I know I am not as clever or sophisticated as the other ladies there this evening, but I will try to learn. If that's what you want me to do. I can help with the charities for the war effort. Lady Bronsen asked me if I would like to visit a hospital and cheer up the wounded. She said it was just writing letters or reading to men who can't do those things for themselves.'

'There's no need for you to become involved in that sort of thing,' Charles said. 'I wish she hadn't mentioned it to you, Julia. I do not want you to be upset by visiting that place. If you want to help, you can attend fund-raising functions or something of that kind.'

I was silent. Lady Bronsen had seemed more lively than most of the other ladies at that evening's reception. I had enjoyed her company and the idea of doing something useful had appealed to me.

'You are just the sort of girl I'm looking for, Miss Allington,' she had told me. 'Pretty, young and intelligent. Our boys need something to cheer them up – you would certainly do that.'

'I should like to help. If you really think I could?'

'This is my card,' she said, giving me a smile of approval. 'Ask your mother if she will allow you to give us a few hours. We have several rest homes all over the country – one of them quite near where you live actually. We can always do with volunteers, my dear.'

I had put her card into my purse. Charles's objection was probably only out of his concern for me. I would speak to Mama and Marina.

I thought that perhaps my friend would like to spend an hour one afternoon helping men who had been wounded. It might somehow ease her grief for her brother.

'What a wonderful idea,' Marina said when I told her about the hospital. 'Yes, Julia. I should like to come with you one afternoon.'

'You are sure it will not upset you too much?' Mama asked. Marina shook her head. 'Then I can see no reason why we should not all go. I, too, would like to help those poor men if I can.'

'Oh, yes, Mama, that would be wonderful,' I said, pleased that she had not dismissed the idea as being out of the question. It had made me feel a little foolish when Charles had seemed to think I would not be suitable for such a task.

'I shall telephone Lady Bronsen myself,' Mama said. 'We might be able to take something useful with us.'

Mama made the call that same afternoon. She was told we would be welcome whether we brought gifts or not, but books, magazines, flowers and food were always gratefully accepted.

We went visiting the next day, carrying a basket of fruit and a sheaf of papers and magazines. Before we were allowed into the common room we were warned that some of the men were disabled or disfigured.

'If the young ladies feel it would be too much for them it might be better if they did not accompany you, Mrs Allington,' Matron told us.

Marina and I both said we were prepared for anything and wanted to help in any way we could.

'I suggest the two young ladies begin by freshening the flowers for us. After that it is just a case of talking to the patients and asking if there is anything they need. Some will respond, others will not. Do not be distressed if one or two of them are rude. We have to make allowances here.'

A very young and pretty nurse, who spoke with a thick London accent, escorted us after we left Matron's office. Everywhere smelled strongly of carbolic and the walls were painted a dull cream. I thought how awful it must be to have to stay here and felt sorry for the young men who had no escape.

'Don't yer let them boys give yer no cheek,' the nurse said to me and winked. 'They'll try it on somefink wicked if yer let 'em.'

'Oh, I don't mind,' I said. 'I expect they get restless shut away in here. They must desperately want to go home.'

'Some do, some ain't sure what they'll find there when they

do, and some won't be going home ever, poor devils. They ain't whole men no more – not in any sense of the word.'

Her words shocked me. I realised that I was about to encounter far more serious injuries than I had ever dreamed of – even after Matron's warning.

That first visit to the hospital was like a revelation to me. In my protected, sheltered world I had no idea of the reality of war. Charles had been wounded, but the outward signs of his suffering were a slight scar and a limp that was only really noticeable when he was tired – though of course I could only guess at his mental agony. As far as I knew, he had not suffered any more of those odd fits. I was sure he would soon be perfectly well. Whereas some of the men in that common room had suffered terrible injuries, and I soon learned that those still confined to bed were even worse. Not that we were allowed anywhere near the critically sick patients that day.

We were three very new recruits and Matron was not prepared to let us practise on anyone who wasn't already well on the way to recovery. We smiled, changed the water in the flowers, tidied the piles of old magazines, passed cups of tea and biscuits and talked.

I spent most of my time talking to a young soldier who had lost his right hand. He asked me if I would write a letter to his mother for him, and spoke hopefully of going home soon.

'They tell me I need another month here,' he said. 'I sometimes think they patched me up only to let me die of boredom.'

'Oh, surely not?' I said, giving him a teasing look. 'I've seen some pretty nurses here today. I don't think you can be that bored.'

'I'm not bored now you're here,' he said, responding gallantly. 'You're as pretty as any of the nurses, Miss Allington, and you've got time to talk to me.'

'Yes, plenty of time,' I replied with a smile. 'Mama always says I talk too much, but I like being with people. I like to hear what they have to say – what they enjoy doing.'

'I was a clerk in a bank before the war and I enjoyed playing cricket,' he said. 'I shan't be much use for either now, shall I?'

'Oh, I am sure you could learn to write with your left hand if you really wanted to,' I said, determined not to let him see the pity I felt. 'And you can still watch cricket – or be an umpire. You mustn't think there's nothing you can do.'

'Be an umpire?' He looked at me thoughtfully. 'I hadn't thought of that – it's a jolly good idea, miss. I played for the village team, you see, good at bowling I was. Hardly anyone ever wants to be the umpire. I might have a go at that; it would be better than just watching.' He grinned. 'You've cheered me up, Miss Allington. You will come again, won't you?'

'We are staying in London for a few weeks. I'll come as often as I can manage while I am here,' I promised.

'Some of the visitors only come once,' he said. 'It embarrasses them to look at us. They don't know what to say, you see.'

'You will probably get fed up with me talking too much,' I said. 'But I shall certainly come again.'

I was sorry when it was time for us to leave. Marina had found it worthwhile, too. She agreed that she would like to continue the visits while we stayed in town.

'It was distressing to see some of the injuries, of course it was, but I was glad to be of help. And it has made me see that Johnny wasn't the only one . . .'

Her voice broke on a sob. I took her hand and held it carefully in mine. 'You were very brave,' I said. 'I am proud of you, Marina.'

'They are the brave ones,' she said. 'We are so lucky, Julia. I never realised until now how very privileged my life has been.'

She was looking very thoughtful and did not speak much for the remainder of the drive home.

Charles was not pleased when I told him of our visit to the hospital.

'I know you feel it is the right thing to do, Julia,' he said. 'But I wish you had not gone. You are so young and sweet and innocent. I do not want you to change – and it *will* change you. Suffering always changes people. It would have been perfectly adequate if you had joined the sewing guild for women at Claridges Hotel in Mayfair. They have been making clothes for soldiers and the poor since the start of the war.'

'And I am sure they do wonderful work, but there are other ways to help, Charles. Perhaps even more important than sewing. We can't just shut our eyes and pretend it isn't happening,' I said. 'Please don't be cross with me, Charles. I have to grow up and I want to help if I can. Besides, I promised I would go back. I can't break my word – can I?'

He gazed down at me for a moment. 'No, I don't suppose you can,' he said. 'But I would have preferred it if you had respected my wishes and stayed away from that place.'

'I'm not just a pretty picture to admire, Charles. I'm very real and Mama says I am wilful sometimes. I shall try to be a good wife to you, but I do have a mind of my own. I can't always think as you do.'

'No one said you should.'

Charles was frowning and I felt that he was seriously annoyed with me. He did not speak again as we were driven to our hostess's house, and though he was polite and introduced me to all his acquaintances, there was a distinct coolness in his manner.

I was upset because we seemed to have had our first quarrel, and it was partly my fault. I wanted to make things right between us, but I was not sure how. I could not simply agree to what I felt was an unjust demand.

For me it was a long and difficult evening. Some of the guests obviously knew Charles from before the war and he spent ages talking to a rather attractive lady. She was about his own age, very stylishly dressed with long dark hair swept up into a sleek chignon at the back of her head, and I suspected she was wearing rouge and powder on her face. Both her gown and her jewellery were expensive and she was the wife of a baronet who held an important government post.

She laughed a great deal, gazing up at Charles in a flirtatious manner. I found her rather intimidating and I sensed that she thought me merely a foolish child. I knew she was watching me during the evening, though she made no attempt to speak to me other than when we were first introduced.

I asked Charles about her when we were driving home after the party.

'Do you know Lady Watson well, Charles?'

'She tells me we used to be friends,' he said rather vaguely. 'Her name is Anne by the way. I should try to make a friend of her, Julia. She lives quite near Rondebush and we shall probably see something of her when we go down to the country.'

Rondebush was the name of his family home. I glanced at him doubtfully. 'There must be lots of people I can make friends with living near your home, Charles. I am not sure I liked Lady Watson.'

He gave me an odd look. 'Her husband is a useful contact, Julia. There is no need for you to be jealous of her – Anne isn't my type.'

'Why should I feel jealous? You love me – don't you?' My gaze flew to his face. 'Or have you changed your mind?'

'Good grief! Of course not. Why on earth should I?' Charles arched his brows, then gave a short laugh. 'Over that hospital business, I suppose? I'm sorry if I was a growly bear earlier, darling. I'd had a difficult day at work and I've had a couple of headaches again recently. The powders Rosendale gave me don't seem to be working. I shall have to see someone else in town.'

'Have you had the results of your tests yet?' I gazed at him anxiously. 'I'm so sorry if I annoyed you earlier. I didn't realise you were feeling unwell.'

I wondered if he had had more of those unpleasant fits and what had caused them if he had.

'I'm not ill,' he said and frowned as though he did not like to be questioned about his health. 'Just out of sorts. It's nothing really. I shouldn't take it out on you. Will you forgive me? I do love you very much, Julia. It's just that I don't want to lose what we have together.'

'Oh, Charles! Of course I forgive you. I love you and I know I'm just a silly girl, but I do want to grow up and be someone you can be really proud of.'

'I am very proud of you. You are everything I ever wanted in my life.'

Charles's look at that moment was so tender and loving that I forgot my slight feeling of unease. It would be foolish to let a small disagreement put doubts in my mind. Even my parents argued sometimes and I knew they were still very happy – still very much in love.

Yet I lay wakeful for some time after I went to bed that evening. I loved Charles and he loved me, but there was undoubtedly a vast divide between us in so many ways. I could not help feeling slightly anxious about the future, and I wished he would suggest a visit to his home so that I could meet his parents. He had said nothing definite of where we should live, but I imagined some of our time would be spent at his family home, and I longed to see it. Why had he not taken me there?

For the first time I wondered if perhaps I ought to have got to know Charles a little better before promising to marry him.

During the following week I gradually forgot my doubts in the rush to fit in all our shopping and dressmaker's appointments with our visits to the hospital. Charles was more attentive than ever and seemed as if he could not do enough to please me. He bought me small gifts – one of them a book of poems by Rupert Brooke, now so sadly dead – and went out of his way to ask questions about my hospital work.

He seemed to want to make up for having been annoyed with me and even took me to see Marie Lloyd singing her wonderful songs about the war. She was a comedienne, of course, but her songs touched my heart and I thought I saw beneath the laughter to her private sadness and heartbreak – despite her ever-growing popularity, according to the newspapers, her private life was far from happy.

So Charles went out of his way to spoil me, and assure me of his affection. We were so close in many ways, and he was able to talk to me more and more as time passed.

'I am beginning to remember things and people,' he told me one evening. He seemed excited, as though he had thrown off many of his own doubts. 'I saw someone in the street this morning, Julia, and I knew him immediately. We hadn't met since we were up at Oxford together, but I knew his face and his name. We were able to speak of things I had totally forgotten until that moment.'

'I am so pleased, Charles.'

61

In his excitement he looked younger and happier. The last of my doubts evaporated as I felt the love flow between us. There were bound to be differences between us. Marriage was an adventure to be shared. We would learn to understand and accept each other's faults as well as the good things – of which there were so many.

I began once again to look forward to the day when we would be married. We were due to part again for a while, because Charles needed to be in London and Mama wished to return home at the end of the month. However, Charles was to come down sometimes at the weekends, and my mother had relented over the date of the wedding, deciding that there was no longer any need for delay, and that it should be at the end of May. So I had not had to wait so very long after all.

I had received a letter from Lady Hamilton which I read with some misgivings, yet I need not have been apprehensive. It was couched in polite terms and welcomed me as a prospective member of her family. Mama and I had returned from London some weeks earlier and it was now the beginning of April. My mother had thought it odd we had heard nothing from Charles's mother before this and she had asked him if his parents would welcome the marriage. He had replied vaguely to this question, but now this letter had arrived and I felt much happier.

'She appears to have only just learned of the engagement,' Mama said when I gave her the letter to read. 'That seems a little odd . . .'

'I do not think Charles is on particularly good terms with Lady Hamilton,' I replied and wrinkled my brow. 'I do not know why exactly, but he said something once about not being able to like her.'

'Oh dear.. I hope for your sake that she is not a disagreeable woman,' Mama said and looked anxious. 'Has Charles spoken about where he intends to live when you are married?'

'His work is in London, and of course he has an apartment there, but I think he intends to live at Rondebush for at least part of the time.'

Mama nodded, her expression thoughtful. 'Now that Lady Hamilton has written I can send her an invitation to the wedding, but I think we should invite her to visit us here before the wedding. It will give you an opportunity to meet her in your own surroundings, Julia, which will be more comfortable for you.'

'Yes, Mama. I think that is a very good idea. If you will allow it, I shall include a short note in your letter to her.'

My mother gave me an approving look. 'You are growing up, Julia. I think you should make every effort to be on good terms with Lady Hamilton.'

I wrote my letter at once, saying how much I was looking forward to meeting Charles's mother. Then I wrote to tell Charles about Lady Hamilton's letter to me, and of my mother's intention to invite her for a visit.

I also replied to Brent Gregory's latest letter. His letters were always brief, usually just to say that he hoped I was well and asking me to continue writing. 'It is amazing how good it feels to get a letter from home,' he had written. 'You are the only one who writes to me, Julia, except for lawyers of course. I have made up my mind to stay in England after the war. Some interesting news about my grandfather has come to light. I am almost sure his brother did marry your mother's grandmother . . .'

I told Mama about Brent's discovery. She nodded but seemed uninterested in the information, and I sensed that it was not a surprise to her.

'Well, it hardly matters now, Julia. We are not likely to see much of him in the future, are we?'

'No, I don't suppose so,' I said. 'But don't you think it's rather nice that our family has a sort of connection to Brent's?'

'My grandmother's husband was not a very pleasant man,' Mama said and pulled a wry face. 'He caused his wife – and other people – a lot of grief. I see no reason to celebrate the connection.'

There was something in her face at that moment – a hint of grief or pain – which kept me from pressing her for more details of Mr Ruston.

'But even if Mr Ruston wasn't nice, it doesn't mean his brother was the same, does it? And it doesn't mean Brent and his family are unpleasant people.'

Mama sighed, then gave me an odd look. 'No, of course it doesn't, Julia. I suppose if you put it that way I was a little unfair to Brent. I knew there might be a connection but I did not wish to acknowledge it for various reasons. However, it was impolite of me, and if Brent calls here again I shall be more friendly towards him.'

'I don't suppose he will – at least until the war is over. He seems to be flying almost non-stop missions. They don't have anywhere near as many pilots as they need.'

'Well, we must pray he continues to be lucky,' Mama replied. 'When you write again you may tell him I would be pleased to have him stay with us when he comes back.'

'I shall not be here then . . .'

'You will be married very soon. As you know, I had first thought a longer engagement would be necessary but now I am content that you will be happy with Charles,' my mother replied. 'It is only a matter of a few weeks now – unless you have had second thoughts?'

'No, of course not, Mama. I love Charles.'

She smiled. 'Your wedding dress should be here soon, dearest. The dressmaker is coming down for two days to make sure there are no alterations necessary.'

'It is all so exciting,' I said. 'I can hardly wait.'

My mother received a letter from Lady Hamilton. She was grateful for the invitation to visit us, but her husband was too ill for her to think of leaving him at the moment.

'I have asked Charles to bring Julia to stay,' she had written to Mama. 'But he maintains that he is too busy. I hope very much that I shall meet your daughter soon after the wedding if not before.'

'I do not feel it right,' Mama told me. She seemed anxious, uneasy in her mind. 'I understand Charles has invited a distant cousin and a few friends, but I would have hoped Lady Hamilton would come. It makes it look as if she does not approve. I am beginning to wonder if I was right to agree to such an early wedding, Julia. You ought properly to have been introduced to Lady Hamilton before this.'

'She sent me a kind letter,' I reminded my mother. 'And you

cannot expect her to leave her husband if he is very ill. You would not leave Papa at such a time.'

She acknowledged the truth, saying, 'You are growing up so fast, Julia. Sometimes I wish all this had not happened so soon. I miss my little girl.'

I laughed and swooped on her, kissing her cheek. 'I shall always be your little girl, Mama – even when I am old and grey.'

My mother had always been protective of me – almost too much at times. Her eyes twinkled back at me. 'Yes. Very well, Julia. I know I have sometimes been a little overprotective of you, but I love you so very much. I almost lost you when you were a baby, and I suppose I've never quite forgotten that.'

'Was I ill, Mama?' I stared at her in surprise, for she had never spoken of this before. 'What was wrong with me?'

'I had a maid,' Mama told me, an odd faraway look in her eyes. 'She was devoted to me – obsessed. I was ill and you cried a great deal. She put laudanum in your bottle. You became so quiet that I thought you were dying. I dismissed her as soon as I discovered what she had done – or at least it was Kate, your paternal grandfather's second wife, who caught her out. If she had not confronted Marie over what she was doing I think you would have died in the end.'

'Oh, Mama,' I said. 'How upset and frightened you must have been. Why did she do it?'

'I believe she imagined she was helping me.'

'But she could have harmed me – or both of us!'

'Yes, that is what Philip always insists and it is true, for later she came back to Cornwall and she had lost all control. Yet if it had not been for Marie I might have been killed. Someone attacked me and she saved my life, losing her own in the struggle.'

'What do you mean?' I stared at her in surprise. 'Who tried to kill you?'

'He was the stationmaster at the little village near my grandmother's home, and he was . . . I believe he *was* evil. Philip came looking for me, but might have been too late had Marie not been there.'

'Then she did not really mean to hurt you. Though had it not been for Kate I might have died because of what she did, and that would have harmed you. She was a foolish woman, Mama. I think she meant to be your friend, even if she went too far sometimes.'

'Marie was obsessed,' Mama said looking thoughtful. 'Philip always said it. Kate on the other hand was a true friend to me then as always. I am glad she and Laurent are safe in Switzerland, though unfortunately she says it is too difficult for them to travel here for your wedding. Laurent is much older, of course, and has been ill.'

'I am so sorry. I do hope he will be better soon. You will give them my love when you write? I think Kate was brave to confront that maid of yours.'

'It was a long time ago and you came to no harm after all. Philip has often told me that I must not fuss too much.' She smiled at me lovingly. 'You must forgive me if I seem too careful, Julia, but all I want is your happiness.'

'I have always known I was loved,' I said. 'Why should I mind that you want me to be happy? Whatever you say or do has always been to that end.'

'You have such a sweet nature,' Mama said. 'Charles is very fortunate to have captured your affections.'

'I have been lucky too, Mama.'

'Yes . . .' She hesitated as though she wished to say more, but one of the maids came in to tell us that several packages had arrived for me. 'Thank you, Elsie. You may have them taken to Miss Julia's room.'

'It may be my wedding gown,' I said, a note of excitement in my voice.

'Or more wedding presents,' she replied with a smile. 'You must keep a list of everyone who has sent you something, darling. You will have to write so many thank-you letters by the time your wedding actually gets here.'

Five

B efore my own wedding there was all the fun and excitement of Marina's. My friend had managed to put her grief aside for the occasion and her parents did the same, though I knew some of the tears Mrs Carstairs shed as she watched Marina walk down the aisle were for her lost son.

I was Marina's chief bridesmaid. After the ceremony I went up to her room to help her tidy herself for the reception.

'You look beautiful,' I told her. 'Be happy, my dearest.'

'I already am,' she said and hugged me, a glimmer of tears in her eyes. 'I shall miss you, Julia, but we shall be living in London for the foreseeable future, which means that when you come up, we shall be bound to see each other.'

'Oh, I do hope so,' I replied. 'Though I am not really sure where we are going to live yet. Charles is very vague about that sort of thing.'

'You should ask him,' Marina said with a little frown. 'Paul always asks my opinion about important details like that.'

Marina's relationship with her new husband was very different from my own with Charles. Paul seemed anxious to do whatever she wanted. Charles was far more dominant. He was considerate and loving towards me, but he did rather expect me to fall in with his wishes.

I had not forgotten his annoyance when I'd defied him by visiting the hospital that first time, nor that strange incident in Mama's garden. He had talked so wildly then, and the violence in him had been unlike the man I knew and loved.

My wedding was to be a smaller affair than Marina's. Sadly, because she had been married only a few weeks earlier, she would still be on her honeymoon and unable to attend mine, though she sent me an affectionate letter and a very pretty silver candelabra.

Mama had invited all our most intimate friends and the small church would be packed on my side, which made it all the more odd that Charles had invited so few of his own family.

'I know only one or two people other than colleagues,' he had explained when he came down to visit the previous weekend. 'I dare say my mother has masses of relatives and acquaintances, but I see no point in inviting a pack of strangers.'

Charles's memory was still very patchy. He now recalled large chunks of his life at college and his time in the army, but still nothing of his home and family.

'I know only what Lady Hamilton told me when she visited me in hospital,' he said, 'and what I discovered for myself when I visited Rondebush for those two days before Christmas.'

He frowned as he spoke. I sensed something more but did not press for an explanation. I had made up my mind that I would never ask Charles for explanations. He would tell me all I needed to know in his own good time.

The last few days before our wedding were very special. Charles had seemed as if he wanted to show me how much he loved me, and I had received bouquets of fresh roses every day. He had also given me several gifts of jewellery. When I protested that he would spoil me, he laughed and shook his head.

'If Philip has not managed it before now, then I doubt I shall. Besides, one thing I do know about myself is that I happen to be quite wealthy. I was left a sizeable fortune by my maternal grandfather – quite apart from the Hamilton money.'

'But you don't have to spend it all on me, Charles!'

'What else should I do with it?' he asked and kissed me lingeringly on the mouth. 'You have given me so much to live for, Julia. Please do not deny me the chance to give a little back.'

There was nothing I could do but accept his gifts and look forward to our wedding. At Christmas I had thought the time would never pass, but now the days flew by and all of a sudden it was my special day.

I woke early and went for a walk in the garden. Mama's roses had already begun to bloom and I picked a perfect bud to give to Charles on our return from the church.

I felt a little nostalgic as I walked back to the house that morning. This had been my home for the whole of my life and now I was about to leave it. Charles was taking me to the sea for a few days before returning to his job in London.

'When the war is over I hope to take you to Paris,' he had told me. 'But for the moment I'm afraid all we can have is a few days in Torquay, Julia.'

'As long as we are together that's all I want.'

What did I care where we spent our first few days? Charles was all I needed. Just to know that I was loved by the man I adored was enough.

Mama was watching for me as I walked into the house.

'I had begun to wonder where you were,' she said. 'Are you all right, dearest? I was a little anxious because I did not know where you had gone.'

'Just for a walk to your garden. I wanted to pick a rose to give Charles later.'

Mama nodded, her eyes searching my face. 'You are happy, Julia? Even now, if you have any doubts . . . ?' She seemed anxious, almost as though she wished I were not about to be married. But she was my mother, and she had always worried about me, from the time I took my first steps. Perhaps, I thought now, because of what had happened when I was a baby.

'No, of course I don't.' I smiled at her confidently. 'I have known Charles for more than six months now, Mama. I love him and want to be his wife. You know he is a good man. Papa likes him.'

'I am foolish to worry,' she said. 'You know your own mind. It is just that . . .' She laughed and shook her head. 'I am always here for you, darling. If you need me you have only to ask for me and I shall come.'

'Yes, Mama. I know.'

We went into the house hand in hand, then I ran upstairs to bathe and change into my wedding gown, which was a very simple style in white silk, embroidered with beads at the hem. Mama came up to me just as I had finished dressing. She smiled, touching my cheek with her fingertips.

'You look beautiful, darling. I've brought you a little present. It is just a trinket that Gérard gave me once.' She handed me a box containing a tiny jade heart and smiled as I exclaimed with pleasure. 'I have always kept it, though it has no true value. I wanted you to have it today – tuck it somewhere in your bodice for luck, dearest.'

I thanked her and kissed her, and then I went downstairs to find Papa waiting for me in the hall. His expression was one of loving pride as he came to greet me.

'You look lovely,' he said, 'but then, you always do, Julia. I am very proud of you. I have always loved you, my dearest daughter. I know Charles is a good man. He will look after you. But if you should ever need us your family is here.'

He kissed my cheek, then I took his arm and we all left for the church. Papa and I in his automobile, Mama and my brothers a little ahead in her carriage.

A small crowd of well-wishers from the village had waited outside to see me arrive, and Mama's guests had filled both sides of the church so it did not look odd at all. I had asked the children of some of Mama's friends to be my attendants; six little girls in pink satin and two tiny boys in blue.

My brothers had preferred to sit with Mama rather than be pageboys, so that she should not be alone as Papa stood with me, Phil had declared. I felt serenely happy as I walked down the aisle on my father's arm to join Charles. Any doubts I'd ever had had fled long ago, particularly when Charles turned to look at me, his face tender with love.

Our few days in Torquay were perfect. It was warm by the sea and pleasant to stroll on the cliffs, but my happiness really came from being with the husband I loved.

Charles was a gentle, considerate but passionate lover. Few women can ever have been so tenderly initiated into the joys of the marriage bed. Despite my innocence, I had heard whispers from other young women of my acquaintance and Mama had made sure I understood what would happen. However, I had not been truly prepared for the pleasure Charles would show me in our bed.

I clung to him that first time and my cheeks were wet with tears. He wiped them away with his fingertips.

'Did I hurt you, Julia? Forgive me. I have wanted you so much.'

'It did hurt a little at first,' I admitted. 'But I am crying because I am happy.'

'My foolish love,' he murmured and gathered me to him.

My heart raced and I pressed myself closer, relishing the heat of his flesh against mine. Already I had begun to realise that I, too, had a passionate nature and I could feel my body responding to the throb of his manhood.

'We must wait a while,' Charles murmured softly, his breath tickling my ear. 'I do not want to be greedy. You will be sore if I make love to you again too soon.'

'If you are greedy then so am I,' I replied and wound my arms about his neck. 'I love you, Charles. I am so glad you married me.'

'How wrong I was to imagine you still a child,' he said ruefully. 'You are all woman, Julia. A lovely, passionate woman any man would adore.'

'I love you, Charles. Only you. Always.'

'You must, Julia,' he said as he began to possess my body once more. 'Never, never stop loving me. I couldn't bear to lose you, too.'

His words were lost as we kissed, swept on together to a far shore by the desire that consumed us both. This time Charles was almost fierce in his need to possess me and I cried out as the waves of pleasure broke over me, making me writhe beneath him, my nails raking his shoulder.

I was dissolving into him, into the pleasure of this wonderful new sensation. After the tumultuous throb of passion had at last been satiated, I lay drowsing in his arms, the salty taste of his sweat on my lips. It was only as I was drifting into sleep, too tired to rouse myself, that I wondered what he had meant.

He had said he could not bear to lose me too, which sounded as if he had already lost someone special. Yet why would he have said that? Even if there had been another love in his life he could not remember her.

He had told me during our very first walks that he had no ties

– no one special in his life. Yet his words had implied something else. Was there some secret locked in his past – a secret that might affect our lives together?

No, no, it was just a slip of the tongue. In the heat of passion he had spoken without truly thinking of what he said. I let the tiny doubt fade away as I slipped into a contented sleep, held close in my husband's arms. Charles adored and needed me. I could not doubt that.

It was dark when I woke. The bed beside me was empty . . . cold. Charles must have left me while I slept. I sat up, reaching for the lamp switch. As the electric light flooded the hotel bedroom, I saw Charles standing by the window. He was fully dressed and had been staring out at the night.

'Did I wake you, Julia? Forgive me. I was unable to sleep so I went for a walk. I quite often do that at night if I'm restless.'

'What's wrong, Charles? Is it one of your headaches?'

He hesitated, then made a negative gesture. 'No, they are not troubling me at the moment; they seem to come and go in spasms. It's just that I have dreams – unpleasant dreams. Then I prefer to get up rather than try to sleep.'

'Tell me about them, Charles,' I invited and patted the bed beside me. 'Are they about the war?'

'No, funnily enough, they aren't,' he said. 'They told me to expect that sort of thing but it hasn't troubled me much.' He came to the bed and sat down, reaching for my hand. 'In the hospital I did have one or two fits of the shakes, but it was seeing the other poor devils who had suffered so much more than I.

'What happened in your mother's garden was different. It has never happened since. But in the hospital I couldn't bear to see men in agony. Seeing them suffer was far worse than my own pain, Julia. These dreams are more recent, all jumbled up, strange. I imagine they must be scenes from my past life. I see the house and then a young boy running. I think it must be me. He is very frightened of something, Julia, but I don't know why.'

I held his hand to my cheek. 'My poor darling. Do you think you are reliving some incident that happened to you as a child?'

'Yes, I think I must be,' he replied and his voice was husky

72

with emotion. 'It is the same dream over and over again and sometimes when I wake up I am crying. I remember once . . .' He hesitated, clearly unsure and anxious.

'Don't stop, Charles. Tell me. It might help you to remember more.'

'I was begging someone to forgive me,' Charles said. 'I can't be sure, but I think I called out a name several times. I could not recall it afterwards, but it makes me think I must have hurt someone badly.'

'No, I can't believe that,' I said and smiled at him. 'I know you too well, Charles. You would never deliberately hurt someone.'

'That is why I adore you so much, Julia,' he said and now an air of amusement had replaced the sadness in his eyes. 'You are always so positive, so certain. You love me so therefore I must be perfect.' He stroked my cheek with his fingertips. 'What would you do if you ever discovered I was not quite as perfect as you imagined?'

'I should go on loving you.' I gave him my answer at once. Charles was my husband. I could not imagine that he would ever have done anything that would make me feel he was not worthy of loving. No matter what might lie in his forgotten past, it could be nothing he had done. I believed in him totally. 'Love isn't something you measure, Charles. It is there. That doesn't stop just because someone makes a foolish mistake. Besides, you are a good man. If you ever hurt me it will not be intentional.'

'No, I shall never hurt you,' he vowed. 'I would die first.'

'Don't talk of dying!' I cried, suddenly fearful. 'That would break my heart.'

'My beloved Julia,' Charles said and bent his head to kiss me. 'The day I met you was the best day of my life.'

'And of mine.'

How could I have asked Charles if he had ever loved another woman when he was so tender and loving towards me? A tiny, niggling doubt did linger somewhere deep in the recesses of my mind, but I did not allow it to surface. I was happy, Charles was happy most of the time, and I wanted it to stay that way for ever.

Our few days in Torquay were perfect. They would stay

enshrined in my memory for the rest of my life. I would need that memory, for things were about to change.

'We must go to Rondebush,' Charles said to me when we were changing for dinner on the last evening of our honeymoon. 'I've put it off for as long as I could, Julia, but I cannot do so any longer.'

'Why don't you want to take me there, Charles?' I gazed at him anxiously. 'Is there something wrong with me – something your family will not like?'

'Foolish one!' he chided. 'It was for your sake that I delayed. Please don't ask me questions now. I haven't told you every-thing I ought, Julia, but I wanted us to be married before I spoke. I wanted you to be sure of my love for you. You will need to be strong, my darling.'

'You know I am strong,' I said, putting my arms about him and shutting out the tiny fears that troubled me from time to time. 'You know I love and trust you.'

'But do you know how much I adore you?' He kissed the tip of my nose. 'No questions this evening. Let's enjoy every minute of our honeymoon, darling. Please?'

'Yes, of course, Charles.'

I could see that he was deeply troubled and I wished he would tell me what was upsetting him, but he was still trying to protect me. What could be so unpleasant at Rondebush?

Was his mother some kind of ogress? Her letter to me had seemed perfectly polite, and yet I knew Charles disliked her. I sensed he almost feared her in some strange way. His cryptic words and his haunted look had frightened me, but I made an effort to forget them for our last evening. He wanted it to be perfect and so did I.

It was as we were driving towards Rondebush, in Kent, that Charles told me what was on his mind. We had left Torquay just after breakfast and stopped for lunch at a charming old seventeenth-century inn. He had been rather quiet and thought-ful since leaving the inn, and when he suddenly pulled the car into a layby on a secluded stretch of country road and turned to me, I knew the moment had come.

'What is it, Charles?'

'Please don't hate me, Julia. You must promise not to stop loving me.'

'Charles! You are frightening me. Just tell me.'

'I was married once before,' he said and his knuckles turned white as he tightly gripped the steering wheel. 'I have no memory of her, Julia. My mother told me all I know about it. Apparently, I married against Mother's advice – Angela was rather ill-bred. I was very much in love, or so I am told, but my wife had several affairs and she drank rather too heavily. It seems that one afternoon she drank too much, then took one of the horses out. She fell while trying to jump a gate and broke her back.'

'She was killed – how terrible!' I stared at him in shock. 'That must have been awful for you, Charles. I'm so sorry.'

'Angela did not die immediately. She was paralysed from the neck down and lingered on for some months before she died in her sleep. I think from what I can gather that she must have suffered a great deal.'

'That was terrible for her – and you.'

'As I said, I have no memory of her at all. I could hardly believe it when my mother told me; it just didn't seem right.' His gaze narrowed, intent on my face. 'Aren't you angry, Julia? I haven't behaved well over this.'

'No, you haven't,' I said. I was too stunned to really feel anything just then apart from shock. 'I imagine I might feel upset once I've thought about it. You should have told me, Charles.'

'Yes, I know, but you said the past wasn't important, and it means nothing to me.'

'But it might if your memory returns.' If he remembered loving her, I thought miserably to myself.

'No! That's what I was afraid of,' Charles said. He reached out and took my hands, gripping them tightly. 'I love you, Julia. I shall always love you. Even if my memory of Angela does return it will not change that. She will not be a ghost between us, I promise you.'

'You cannot be sure of that.' I was remembering little things he had said, odd remarks that had not quite made sense at the

75

time, which were now perfectly clear to me. 'I wish you had told me sooner.'

His face was white, stricken. 'Would it have made you think twice about marrying me?'

'Charles! Of course not. I love you.' I leaned forward to touch my lips to his cheek. 'No, nothing has changed between us. I am just a little upset that you didn't tell me. It makes me feel you think I am too young and silly to understand.'

'No, I don't think that,' Charles said. 'I think you are lovely, wise and very loving. I can't believe that I've been lucky enough to find you. I am sure I don't deserve to have you.'

I put my fingers against his mouth, hushing him. 'That is nonsense,' I said. 'I am a very ordinary girl and you will have to be patient with me, but no more secrets, please? If something is worrying you, Charles, tell me. I want to share everything with you, not just the pleasant things.'

'Yes, I see that.' He looked and sounded contrite. 'Forgive me, please?'

'You promise not to hide things from me in future?' I pouted at him in a way that showed he was forgiven.

'Cross my heart!' Indulgent laughter was back in his eyes and he was once again the man I loved and admired. We were so fortunate to have found so much happiness – surely nothing could come between us?

'Oh, my dearest,' I cried and smiled. 'I do love you so much. I want us to be happy always – for as long as we both live.'

'Thank God for that,' he said fervently. 'I was afraid you would hate me for not telling you before we married.'

'Was that why you didn't want to go down to Rondebush before the wedding?'

Charles gave me a rueful look. 'It is a part of the reason why I delayed,' he admitted. 'Lady Hamilton might have mentioned it, but she is the main cause of my reluctance, Julia. It must sound terrible to someone who has a family like yours, but I really find her most disagreeable, and I am certain that she dislikes me.'

'Oh no!' I cried. 'Surely not? She is your mother after all.'

'Unfortunately, we neither of us seem to feel the bond. At least I have the excuse of not remembering her, Julia, but what

76

excuse does she have? Have I done something in the past to arouse her dislike?'

I could only gaze at him in silence. My instinct was to deny it instantly, but how could I? Yet I knew he needed the reassurance that this was all part of the recurring dream that haunted him.

'You should ask her,' I said. 'It may simply be her manner. Some people are incapable of showing their feelings. All I know for certain is what I feel inside. You could never do anything evil, Charles. You may in the past have been careless or made some error of judgement, but you are not a wicked man.'

'Bless you for your certainty, my darling.' His eyes had come alive with laughter. 'No wonder I wanted you with me before I went back to face the dragon in her lair.'

I giggled helplessly at his irreverent description of his mother. 'You are very naughty,' I told him with mock severity. 'I'll have you know that your mother sent me a very kind letter and a pretty diamond bracelet as a personal wedding gift.'

'Oh, I am certain she will approve of you,' Charles replied, flicking a strand of hair from my cheek. 'She told me I should marry a suitable girl and provide an heir for the family. She will love you, darling. It is just me she dislikes.'

I shook my head at him as he restarted the car. Lady Hamilton was clearly a formidable woman. Even before Charles's confession, I had been nervous of meeting her, but now I felt increasingly apprehensive as we continued our journey. Obviously Lady Hamilton had felt it her son's duty to marry again, but would she approve of his choice?

'Oh, Charles – this is beautiful!' I stood looking at the house. There were three wings, each with a deep sloping roof and twisted chimneys. Built of soft grey stone, it was much larger than my home; very old but well preserved with a mellowed charm that instantly appealed to me. 'You didn't tell me your home was going to be like this.'

'Yes, it is rather á lovely house,' Charles replied. 'I fell for it myself when I came down last year. I suppose that's why I thought we might live here one day – if you like it? I shall have to spend time in London until the end of the war, but I think that, despite some setbacks and bad news from the front, things are turning our way. I have hopes that the end may not be too far distant.'

'I do hope you are right, Charles.'

'Well, I feel the scales are tipping very much our way, Julia. But until then, we can spend weekends down here sometimes. And we might settle here afterwards, if you are happy. It depends very much on you, darling. I want you to feel comfortable. We can live elsewhere if you prefer.'

'The house is much bigger than I've been used to,' I admitted. 'I feel a little overawed at the moment, but it is lovely.'

'We'll see how we go . . .' I heard the change in his voice and saw a woman come out of the house. 'This is my mother . . .'

Turning to look at Lady Hamilton, I saw a tall, thin woman with grey hair, which was swept back off her face into a tight roll at the back of her head. Her nose was long and a little pinched at the ends, her pale lips set in a hard line. Eyes the colour of bitter chocolate were icy cold as she looked directly at her son.

'I was expecting you earlier, Charles. You might have telephoned to let me know you would be late.'

'Yes, I am sorry.' His tone was as cool and flat as hers. 'Mother – this is Julia.'

She turned towards me, her eyes studying me intently for several seconds. She must have approved of what she saw for her expression relaxed and she smiled, extending her hand to me.

'How pleasant to meet you at last, Julia. I was happy to receive your sweet letter and I am delighted to welcome you to your home. Please come in. You must be tired after your journey. Why do I not take you upstairs? You will want to rest before you change for dinner.' She glanced at her son once more. 'Your father asked if you would visit him as soon as you arrived, Charles.'

'Yes, of course.' His expression was strained, tense. 'You are all right, Julia?'

He was asking if I was ready to go with his mother. I smiled at him reassuringly. 'Yes, of course I am, darling. Please don't worry about me. I'm fine.'

'Of course you are,' Lady Hamilton said, giving me a brisk

nod. 'Come along, Julia. I hope I may call you that? And you must call me Mary. I want us to be comfortable together.'

Her welcome was, if not warm, at least friendly. Yet I had sensed her hostility towards Charles immediately. Until that first moment of meeting I had believed he might have imagined her dislike, but now I knew that was not so. She disliked her own son, but she was prepared to welcome his wife.

I did not have to search for the reason. Charles had given it to me earlier in the car, and as his mother led the way upstairs she began to talk about the portraits hanging on the wall and the family. I understood why she was prepared to welcome me. I was necessary. She wanted an heir for the future.

'There have been Hamiltons here for the past three hundred years,' she told me. 'Although part of the house was destroyed by fire in 1760. The then Lord Hamilton had it rebuilt in the style you see now, though there is part of the old wing left. We seldom use those rooms, of course. The Hamiltons have always been great collectors and many of the treasures you see here were brought from abroad in the eighteenth and nineteenth centuries. I will show you the important portraits another day, Julia. I should like you to understand and appreciate the history of the family – to know why it is so essential that Charles should have a son.'

'Yes, of course,' I replied. 'I do understand that it is important in a family like this. Besides, I want lots of children. I have two brothers myself.'

'What a sensible girl you are.' Lady Hamilton was clearly warming to me. 'I had wondered if Charles had made yet another mistake, but I see I had no need to worry. I believe we shall get on well together.'

'I sincerely hope so,' I replied. 'I am looking forward to getting to know Charles's family and to making friends with all your neighbours.'

'I shall invite a few of my close friends to meet you this weekend,' she said. 'Well, here are your rooms, Julia. You and Charles both have a bedroom of your own, which connect via the dressing room. There is also a sitting room and a bathroom, which was put in recently. I believe everything is satisfactory, but you must tell me if you require changes. I want you to feel comfortable. After all, this is your home now.'

'I am not sure that Charles has made up his mind about living here,' I said. 'We shall visit, of course, but for the moment he needs to be in London for his work.'

'I asked him not to take that post,' she said and her mouth curved sourly. 'There was no need, none at all. He could easily have pleaded ill health. Charles has surely paid his debt to society – if indeed there was one, which I doubt. His debt is to me, to this family.'

'He felt it his duty to do what he could,' I replied, wanting to defend my husband. 'We all have to do what is necessary while there is a war on. I have been hospital visiting – just writing letters and arranging flowers. It was very little but I enjoyed helping soldiers who had been wounded.'

'I do hope you are not one of those liberated young women – like that foolish Emily Davison, who threw herself in front of the King's horse at the Derby and was killed.'

'It was a very shocking thing, of course. I remember Mama reading about it in the paper a long time ago. Mama was interested because her friend once belonged to the Women's Suffrage movement. No, I would not dream of doing anything of the kind – or parading through the streets dressed as 'Belgium' demanding the right to serve as some women did during the first year of the war, but I do think it is right to help in some small way if we can.'

'I am surprised that Charles allowed it,' his mother said. 'He cannot bear to see anyone – or anything – suffer pain. I remember when a pet dog of his was injured. He went running to his father begging him to help the creature. I told the grooms to shoot it as soon as I saw it. It had been caught in a trap, you see. The injuries to its leg were horrific. The only thing to do was put it out of its misery.'

'How horrible,' I said. 'It must have been unpleasant for you – having to give the order to destroy a pet.'

'It is always sad to put a creature down, but one has to cope. I have always done what must be done. Lord Hamilton was always soft with Charles. Had I been given a free hand I should have been stricter. He needed discipline. It would have made a better man of him.'

'Charles is a very fine man,' I replied, lifting my head to challenge her. 'He saved lives during his time at the front. I should have thought you would be proud of him, Lady Hamilton.'

'I see my plain speaking has upset you, Julia. I am sorry. It was not meant to. Charles has his failings, as I dare say you will discover one day. Yet I should not expect you to see them. You are very much in love with him.' She gave me a thin smile. 'I shall leave you to explore your apartments yourself. I hope we shall be friends, but you will have to accustom yourself to my way of speaking or I shall hurt you. I have always called a spade a spade and I cannot change – even for you.'

'Yes, of course,' I said politely and opened the door into my rooms. 'Thank you for explaining about the family, it was very interesting. I shall hope to learn much more.'

'I shall see you at dinner.'

I nodded, smiled vaguely and went into what was obviously an attractive sitting room feeling as if I had been flattened by Lady Hamilton's harsh character. Charles's mother was certainly a lady of strong convictions!

The first room I entered was decorated with pale green silk wallpaper and furnished with two small sofas covered in cream brocade, occasional tables and cabinets at each end. These were stuffed with pieces of porcelain, most of them Derby figurines, but also some pretty tea bowls and a tiny round teapot in the Chinese style. Not for use, I assumed, merely part of the larger collection throughout the house.

Opposite the door I had entered was a pair of double doors, which led into an exceptionally pretty bedroom with hangings of pale rose and silver. A satinwood desk stood near the window, which looked out over the garden at the back of the house, which was now a mass of flaming colour in the rose beds. The quilted bedcovers were a deeper pink than the drapes, as was the padded top of the long stool at the foot of the bed. Little satinwood chests stood at either side of the room and there was a dainty dressing table of the same period and style.

To the right was a door, which led to a dressing room with

several huge wardrobes, and beyond that a bedroom done out in shades of crimson and gold. To the left of my bedroom was another door. I discovered the very modern bathroom with its Art Deco fittings and stylish tiles all in shades of a turquoise green. I thought the room might once have been a maid's waiting room, or perhaps another dressing room.

Some of my personal belongings had been sent down from my home, and I discovered fresh clothes already laid out for me on the bed. I was looking for an alternative to the dress that had apparently been chosen for me when Charles entered through the connecting door.

'Is everything all right?' he asked, seeming anxious. 'It wasn't too much of an ordeal, darling?'

'No, of course not,' I said and pulled a laughing face at him. 'I expect Lady Hamilton can be overbearing at times, but I am not afraid of her. Besides, she seems to rather approve of me at the moment. I am not sure how long it will last, but we must hope we can be on friendly terms.'

'Mother's opinion hardly matters,' Charles replied with a frown. 'You are my wife and you are perfect. All I am interested in is that she is not unpleasant to you. If that happened I should take you away from here at once.'

'No, she certainly was not unpleasant to me, although I did sense some tension between you and Lady Hamilton. What do you think it can be? Is it simply because she didn't want you to take that position in London?'

Charles shrugged. 'I really have no idea, Julia. She told me it was my duty to look after the estate now that my father is ill . . .'

'How is your father, Charles?'

'He seems better than when I came down at Christmas. His stroke has made it difficult for him to leave his room. He has to be carried everywhere, you see. However, his mind and speech are quite clear.' Charles smiled. 'I do like him, Julia. In fact I am rapidly becoming rather fond of the old boy. He is looking forward to meeting you. He was a little concerned because the stroke has affected one side of his face, and he thought his appearance might upset you. I told him it wouldn't – was I right?'

'Yes, of course you were, Charles. How soon can I meet him?'

'Not until after dinner. He has to be fed with a spoon by his man. Mother cannot bear to see him that way, so he takes his meals alone these days.'

'Oh, how sad,' I said. 'I am sorry, Charles. We must spend some time with him while we are here.'

'Yes. I am glad you feel that way.' Charles smiled at me. 'I was wrong about the hospital thing, and you were right, Julia. I wanted to protect you from the kind of thing I was forced to see when I was a patient, but that was foolish of me. I am glad that you insisted on going. I shan't stand in your way if you want to resume your visits while we are in town.'

'Thank you.' I went to kiss him. He held me close for a moment, then let me go with a sigh.

'We had better dress. Have you rung for a maid to help you yet?'

'No. I was just deciding what to wear. I can manage most of it myself if you will fasten me at the back.'

'Oh, you had better ring,' Charles said. 'It will be quicker. I have been warned not to keep Mother waiting.'

'Then I might as well wear the gown prepared,' I said. 'I don't suppose it matters this once.'

'No – choose something else.' Charles threw open one of the wardrobes and took out a simple yellow silk dress. 'I know it isn't part of your trousseau, but I've always liked you in this. Show your independence, Julia. Never allow my mother to dictate to you – now or in the future.'

'No, I shan't,' I promised and accepted the gown he had chosen. 'This is one of my favourites, too. But I do need help with it so I had better ring for the maid at once.'

I smiled at him and we separated to change our clothes. I wasn't sure I liked the arrangement of different bedrooms, though I knew most people conformed to the ritual – at least, people of the Hamiltons' class. My own parents shared a room, though there was a bed in Papa's dressing room in case either of them was ill. I doubted it had been used many times. I presumed that Charles would share my bed.

The maid who answered my summons was an older woman.

Her name was Alice and she was very respectful and discreet, offering no comment when I indicated that I would be wearing the yellow dress rather than the more formal one which had been laid out in readiness.

'Would you like me to dress your hair up, madam?'

'No thank you, Alice. Mrs Hamilton will wear it loose this evening,' Charles said, coming in at that moment. 'You may go – unless there is something more you need, Julia?'

'No, nothing. Thank you, Alice.'

Charles took a flat box from his pocket, opened it and showed me an unusual pendant. 'It is a yellow diamond,' he said as I exclaimed over its particular beauty. 'Quite rare I believe. Father gave it to me for you. I believe it was his mother's, but not a Hamilton heirloom. It is a personal gift from him.'

'It is lovely,' I said, 'and it will complement my dress so well. That is why you chose this one, of course. How clever of you, Charles.'

'He will be pleased to see you wearing his gift,' Charles replied. 'I was sure you would not mind?'

'Of course not. It is beautiful. I was going to wear the pearls you gave me, but this will look wonderful with my gown.'

Charles fastened the clasp for me. He touched my hair and smiled at me as I glanced at my reflection in the mirror.

'Adorable. You look just as you did the day we first met – fresh, innocent and as sweet as a rose. I am sure my father will love you, too.'

'I am so glad you have formed a good relationship with him,' I said. 'It will help you to feel better about your home – and the past.'

'Yes, I am beginning to feel as if I belong here, Julia. Things will be different now that I have you.'

We kissed briefly as a gong sounded downstairs summoning us to dinner. It would not do to keep everyone waiting on our first night.

Six

I liked Lord Hamilton immediately. He was a charmer and I could see that as a young man he must have looked very much as Charles did now. His stroke had disfigured one side of his face and sometimes he had difficulty in pronouncing a particular word, but his mind was sharp and clear and if you listened attentively it was easy to understand what he was saying.

'So you are Charles's beautiful bride,' he said. 'Come and sit beside me, Julia. Let me look at you.'

I went forward, impulsively bending to kiss his cheek. He took my hand in his as I sat beside him, a gleam in his eyes.

'I see that my son has found himself a warm-hearted girl. That's even more important than beauty, my dear. Without mutual respect and affection marriage can become a penal sentence. It is time Charles had someone to make him happy.'

'I shall try very hard to do that,' I said. 'But he already has you, sir. I think you care for him as much as he does for you.'

'We are friends, I think,' he replied with a glance at Charles, who had drifted across to the window and was gazing out. 'But I haven't always given him the support he needed in the past. I could have been a better father. I am very glad he has found you, Julia. He needs a family to settle him down. Not that he was ever wild – just restless after . . .' He paused and I imagined he had been speaking of the death of Charles's first wife. 'Well, well, we don't want to talk about that on your first evening. Tell me about yourself, my dear. Do you ride at all?'

'No, she doesn't,' Charles said and turned round to look at us. He had seemed not to be listening but obviously he had been. I saw an oddly haunted expression in his eyes at that moment and wondered what had caused it. 'Julia prefers to walk, don't you, darling?'

'Yes. I've never ridden. I am not sure why. It did not appeal to me somehow and Mama did not encourage it – though my brothers were both taught. I think I might like to drive a car though. Do you think I could learn, Charles?'

I knew that other women drove their own cars sometimes these days, but until now I had never really thought about trying myself.

He smiled at me and the haunted expression had gone. 'I see no reason why not, darling. It might be possible to get you something of your own for when we are down here. You won't need it in town, of course, but here it would be useful.'

'What else do you like?' Lord Hamilton asked. 'Do you enjoy reading? I used to read all the time, but now I find it too much of a strain for my eyes.'

'I could read to you sometimes if you would like that? I often used to read to Mama in the afternoons.'

'I should like it very much,' he said. 'Yes, you must come and read to me in the afternoons now and then. And now Charles is going to take you away and show you the house or perhaps a walk in the gardens. I always enjoyed a stroll at night, before I became tied to this infernal bed. I am tired now, my dear, but do visit me again tomorrow.'

'Yes, we should go and leave you to rest,' Charles said. 'Goodnight, Father.'

'You will think about what I asked earlier, Charles?'

'Yes, of course. But I have my life in London, Father – to give it up entirely and live here is not something I had considered.'

'Please do, Charles.'

Charles inclined his head but did not look as if the idea had appealed to him, nor did he give his father an answer.

'Goodnight, sir,' I said. 'I am so very pleased to have met you. I shall look forward to another talk tomorrow.'

He nodded, seeming suddenly weary. As we left the room, his manservant entered from the dressing room. He had obviously been waiting to settle his master for the night.

'That is Saunders,' Charles told me as we walked away from Lord Hamilton's apartments, which were similar in shape and style to our own. 'He is devoted to my father, always has been.'

'Do you remember him, Charles?'

'Yes.' Charles looked at me oddly. 'Yes, I remembered him almost at once. I think I must always have liked him. I seem to remember people I feel comfortable with. Do you think I have deliberately shut out what I don't want to remember, Julia? Rosendale said that the mind can play tricks on one sometimes – it is like a series of little storerooms. Some are kept locked because we don't want to know what's inside. People like me, that is, who are . . . emotionally damaged.'

'Did Mr Rosendale say you were emotionally damaged?'

'No. I think that was someone else.'

'Who?' I stared at him as he did not answer. 'Not your mother?'

He pulled a wry face, then nodded. 'She said something of the kind at the hospital. Before I really knew who I was or what had happened. Not to me – to one of the doctors. I only caught fragments of their conversation. I believe she said something about my having deliberately risked my life because I wanted to die . . . that it was an act of stupid recklessness and not out of a desire to save others.'

'Oh, Charles,' I cried. 'Surely she could not have meant that? You must have misheard. What you did was brave and unselfish. I cannot believe your mother could have said anything so cruel – it was wicked of her if she did!'

'Perhaps I was dreaming. I have never been quite certain what was said that day. It was a long time before I understood what people were saying to me. Everything was like a dream. Faces came and went and had no substance. I heard voices around me, but I could not distinguish if they were real or imaginary. Some of them said terrible things . . .' He shuddered and I knew he was disturbed about those voices in the mist. 'I must have imagined them.'

Charles had never spoken so openly of that time before. I was aware of changes in him. Perhaps it was because we had opened some of those locked storerooms of his mind when we

87

made love. Being as close as we had been then was sure to bring some kind of emotional change. Charles had lost a little of the tenseness I had sensed in him when he had returned after his first visit to his home. It was as if he had stopped fighting the past, as if he was prepared to let it come back to him at last.

We did go for a walk in the gardens before retiring. It was a warm evening and the perfume of night-scented shrubs was exquisite. The birds had ceased to sing; it was peaceful, almost silent in the falling darkness. I thought that this could be a perfect place to live.

Lady Hamilton and her companion were sitting over the tea tray in the drawing room when we looked in to say goodnight.

'Goodnight,' she said and the rather colourless Miss Henderson echoed her. 'I shall see you in the morning, Julia.'

Again there was no more than a curt nod for Charles.

'Goodnight, Mother,' he said courteously. 'Miss Henderson.'

'Goodnight, sir,' the companion replied.

'I shall ride over to see William Straw, the estate manager, tomorrow, Mother. I can sort out a few problems while we are here.'

She gave him a sour look. 'You must do as you see fit, of course. You know my feelings.'

Charles took my arm, almost pushing me from the room. His relaxed mood seemed to have been lost again. What was it that made Lady Hamilton so harsh towards her son? What had happened in the past to cause her dislike of him? Her hostility was so intense that it bordered on hatred.

No, that was a terrible idea. Of course she did not hate Charles. She was probably just annoyed that he had refused to do as she asked.

Clearly Lord Hamilton was too ill to oversee the estate himself. He had a manager and staff to do all that was necessary, but work was sometimes neglected if the master was not in full control. I could understand that Lady Hamilton might be angry with her son for not agreeing to come home and take over the reins – but hatred was something else. Hatred would imply that they had hurt one another beyond bearing.

What could Charles have done to arouse such feeling in his own mother?

I quickly put the thought out of my mind. I would not allow Lady Hamilton's attitude to poison my mind towards Charles. He was my husband. I loved and respected him. He could never hurt anyone. If anyone was to blame it must be his mother. Now I thought about it, I realised that Lord Hamilton had hinted that his own life had not been as happy as it might. And that was his wife's fault, of course. She was clearly a difficult woman.

'You are very thoughtful, Julia,' Charles said as we reached our apartment. 'Has something upset you?'

'No,' I replied and smiled at him. 'Perhaps I am a little tired. It has been an eventful day.'

'Yes – in several ways.' He reached for me as the door closed behind us, drawing me close to him. 'You are still glad you married me, Julia? All this – what I told you earlier, my mother – it hasn't made you wish otherwise?'

'No, of course not.' I reached up to kiss him. 'If anything I love you more after meeting your father. He is a lovely man, Charles. If you are like him when we are both old and grey I shall be quite content.'

'You will never be old and grey,' Charles replied, that indulgent look in his eyes. 'I adore you, my beautiful wife. Are you very tired? Shall I sleep in my own room tonight?'

'Only if you let me join you!'

Charles laughed. 'How lucky for me that Philip took pity on me,' he said. 'If we had never met, I'm not sure that I would still be alive. I had nothing to live for before I saw you. Now I have everything.'

'Help me undress,' I whispered, the desire coursing through me urgently. 'And never speak of having no reason to live, Charles. What would I do without you?'

'You would make a very attractive widow,' he said wickedly. 'But you are right, my darling. Why should I think of dying when I have you?'

Our loving reached new heights that night. If I had ever been in any doubt of his love that doubt was swept away by the tide of passion that engulfed us. I knew with an inner certainty that I was of paramount importance to my husband, especially here in this house. When we returned to London the world and his work would ease the intensity of that need, but it would always be there.

Charles was an intelligent, educated man. Outwardly, he seemed to be self-possessed and certain of his place in the scheme of things, but I had begun to see that deep inside Charles there was another man. A man who was a little unsure, a little frightened of what he might discover about himself and his past. That man needed to be loved. He needed me.

After our loving he lay clasped in my arms, his head against my breast as he slept. It was almost as if our roles had been reversed. I had seen myself as the one needing support – needing someone to lean on – but Charles was more vulnerable than I had ever imagined. Especially here in this house.

Charles had gone when I woke the next morning, but I found a note on his pillow beside me. It bore just four words: I love you, Charles.

I smiled as I kissed the name. My husband was proving more romantic than I had thought at the start. Marriage was, as I'd expected, a journey of discovery.

I rang my bell for a maid. Alice came in answer to my summons. I asked her to run a bath for me and then to lay out the blue striped linen gown I intended to wear that morning.

'I shall not need your help to dress, thank you, Alice.'

'As you wish, madam. If you change your mind you have only to ring.'

There was no need to summon her back. I had seldom needed the services of my mother's maid at home. Sometimes for a special occasion I had asked for a little help with my hair, but I preferred to dress myself if I could.

Once I was ready I went downstairs to the breakfast room. I discovered that Miss Henderson was there alone.

'Good morning, Mrs Hamilton,' she said. 'Shall I ring for fresh tea or would you prefer coffee?'

'Tea please,' I said, investigating the contents of the silver chaffing dishes on the gleaming Georgian sideboard. I helped myself to a little scrambled egg. 'Are you the first down, or am I the last?'

'Lady Hamilton was here long before me. She usually rides early each morning – then has breakfast. She is a marvel. I wonder at her energy sometimes. But there, I shouldn't chatter on.' A faint blush stained her cheeks. 'You will want to eat in peace. I'll go—'

'You haven't finished your toast. Please don't run away. There is no need. If you tell me things I ought to know I shan't need to ask.'

'Well, of course.' She looked flustered, but also pleased. 'If there is anything I can do to help you, you have only to say.'

'I should like to be shown the way to the library later.'

'I shall attend to that personally,' Lady Hamilton said entering from behind me at that moment. 'You will naturally want to see everything of importance, Julia. Normally I would leave it to Charles, but since he insists he remembers nothing that would not serve our purpose. This family has an interesting history. You will want to know about what happened to it in the past.'

'Yes, thank you. I should like to see over the house.'

She nodded her satisfaction, then looked at her companion. 'You may pour me a cup of tea, Emily. I shall sit with you both until Julia has finished her breakfast.'

'Yes, of course.' Miss Henderson looked uncomfortable. 'I only offered to be of help to Mrs Hamilton to save you trouble.'

Lady Hamilton did not deign to reply. She took two sips of her tea, then looked at me expectantly.

'I've had enough – if you are ready?' I said, sensing her impatience.

'I do not wish to rush you, Julia. However, there is a great deal to see.'

I stood up. 'Shall we go?'

'Good.' She gave me a nod of approval. 'We shall begin with the library since you expressed an interest.'

'I wanted to find a book to read to Lord Hamilton later.'

'Well, you will discover quite a variety. My husband was a keen reader in his youth.'

'Papa has many beautiful books. Some of them are rare,

but he also has the novels of Jane Austen and Mr Dickens, as well as Galsworthy's *A Man of Property* and Mr Kipling's *Jungle Book*.'

Lady Hamilton frowned. 'I do not approve of Mr Dickens, though I find Miss Austen's works quite acceptable. I have read neither of the others so cannot offer an opinion.'

She led me from the breakfast room through a small adjoining salon and then through what was clearly a music room into the library. It was a long, narrow room, a little dark and lined with open bookshelves. The books were all covered in leather in either a dull maroon or brown colour and most of them looked as if they had never ever been opened.

'These are mostly educational or historical books, some of it concerning the family,' my guide told me. 'My husband's personal books are in his study, which is through there. She pointed to a door at the far end. 'I seldom go into his study these days. Now, if you will follow me, I shall take you to the portrait gallery and the main reception rooms.'

I followed dutifully through a series of interconnecting salons and sitting rooms. It was a very large house, with the family rooms in the East wing, and the library and Lord Hamilton's study in the West wing, together with yet more salons.

The picture gallery was at the back of the house and ran the whole length of the central area. It was here that Lady Hamilton lingered as she began to recite the history of various members of her husband's family. There were poets, generals and government ministers amongst them, also a very beautiful woman who was rumoured to have been the mistress of King Charles II at one time.

'The connection did not last long,' Lady Hamilton said with a frown of disapproval. 'Somehow she lost the king's favour. Her husband sent her to live here alone and she fell down the stairs in the old wing and broke her neck – her ghost is said to haunt the place still. Not that I believe it, of course. Legend has it that she was carrying a child – a child that might not have been either her husband's or the king's. It was also rumoured that she was murdered – none of the tales can be proved, of course. Any papers that might have done so were lost in the fire.'

'Perhaps she was banished here because she had been unfaithful,' I said. 'It is a sad story.'

'Not at all,' Lady Hamilton replied briskly. 'She deserved to be punished. I do not approve of adultery – even with the king, though that had its uses, of course.'

'It was supposed to be quite an honour in those days, I believe?'

'In certain circumstances,' Lady Hamilton agreed. 'But she had not given her husband an heir. That is unforgivable in my opinion, and to attempt to foist a bastard on a family like ours! Fortunately, her husband soon married again – to a young and rather plain girl who gave him three sons and a daughter, all of whom were most certainly of his blood.'

Her attitude was perhaps a little judgmental, but I did not think she intended it to be. She was merely stating what she saw to be the facts, and I had begun to see that it was her habit to face things squarely and not dress them up in clean linen.

Lady Hamilton went on to tell me about several other gentlemen in the family who had distinguished themselves in the service of their country. Since she was clearly so proud of their exploits I wondered why she should dismiss what Charles had done so lightly.

'Is there a portrait of Charles's first wife?' I asked.

Lady Hamilton's gaze narrowed. 'Has Charles told you about her?'

'He has no memory of her other than what you told him yourself.'

She nodded, frowning for a moment. 'I believe there may be a photograph somewhere. Charles did not commission her portrait. I believed she scoffed at the idea. She thought it ridiculous to put so much emphasis on the family history. She was rather a vulgar woman, and I never understood what Charles saw in her.'

'Perhaps he was in love with her?'

'Perhaps . . .' Her mouth pursed sourly. 'He should have thought more about his family before allowing himself to be trapped into such an unsuitable match. She was never faithful to him – even before the wedding. I challenged her once and she laughed in my face, told me that I was a nosy old witch, and informed me she would do exactly as she wished. I disliked her very much, and I believe Charles came to feel the same shortly before her accident.'

There was something odd in her voice then, but when I looked at her she turned away and began to tell me about other members of the family.

'They had no children? Charles did not say but I thought he must have mentioned it if—'

'Oh, no,' she said. 'That would not have been at all satisfactory. Charles would never have been certain the child was his own. We were very fortunate that the accident occurred before she conceived a child.'

I felt chilled by the look in her eyes. She was so cold, so calculating. I wanted to leave her then, to run away and find somewhere I could hide from her eyes – the eyes of a reptile. I felt that she was a dangerous woman.

'But I see I have distressed you again,' she said and gave me a cool smile. 'I shall have to learn to think before I speak. If I sound cruel or heartless it is because I love this family. I want Charles to have everything he deserves. He is my son . . . my only son.'

I stared at her as I caught the subtle change in her voice. 'Did you have another son, Lady Hamilton?'

Her eyelids flickered for an instant and I thought I saw a flash of pain in her eyes. 'Mary, I told you to call me Mary,' she said. 'We shall not speak of my son today, Julia, though there are many things I might say to you one day. I want us to become friends. Tell me, do you think you will be happy living here?'

'I shall need to become accustomed to the house,' I replied. Why had she avoided the question? I knew she was keeping something from me, but what? 'I think it is a very beautiful place, and the collections of porcelain and silver are magnificent. Yes, I think I might love the house in time.'

'That is what I wanted to hear,' she said and smiled at me. 'Angela hated the place and tried to make Charles leave. She wanted to live in London or France, I believe, but Charles belongs here. It is important that he comes home after this foolish work of his is finished. His sons should be born in this house – they must learn to love it, too.'

I felt a little disturbed by her manner at that moment. My father would say she was obsessed with the house and family tradition and he disapproved of obsessions of any kind. I did not think he would approve of Lady Hamilton's almost fanatical interest in this house and her husband's family.

After my tour of the house, I took my writing case down to one of the pleasant sitting rooms in the family wing. When I mentioned how much I liked it, Lady Hamilton had told me I might use it for my own.

'It does have a nice view of the park,' she said. 'I never sit here, so it would be quite private, though you have your own apartments, of course.'

I had been used to sitting in a downstairs parlour with Mama and thought I would enjoy spending some time in the pretty little salon. It was equipped with an elegant French writing desk and had lots of little drawers inside. I made a brief examination, but discovered they were all quite empty except for a stick of sealing wax. I imagined the desk had not been used in years.

I laid my writing case on the leather surface, then decided to pen some letters. I wanted to write to Mama, and also begin to thank all my friends for their generous gifts. Most of our wedding presents were still at my parents' home, for I had not been sure where to send them. I thought now that one or two pieces would fit rather well into this room, and also there were some more personal things that I would like to have in the apartments upstairs. Most of the gifts would probably go to London with me for the time being. I believed that Charles would retain his apartment there for some months at least.

He was not yet completely certain that he wanted us to live here on a permanent basis. I thought it might be very pleasant – providing Lady Hamilton did not try to interfere in our lives too much.

I wrote my letter to Mama and sealed it in its envelope, then began on the list of people I wanted to thank. I had completed five letters when I noticed Charles approaching the house. He was dressed for riding and I thought he must have come from the stables. I left the rest of my correspondence on the desk, opened the long French widows out on to a small patio and went out to greet him.

The scents of lavender and roses were very strong here, and I noticed the old stone pots spilling over with fragrant herbs, around which bees worked feverishly. This was a sheltered corner, protected from the wind, and sunny. I thought I might like to sit here with a book on a warm afternoon.

'I saw you coming,' I said as Charles quickened his stride. 'I was writing letters in there and happened to see you.'

Charles slid his arm about my waist, looking down at me indulgently. 'I'm sorry I was away all morning. My business for Father took rather longer than I had expected. I'm afraid things have been neglected here for a while. Have you found something to amuse you this morning, my darling?'

'Yes, thank you, Charles. Lady Hamilton showed me over the house. You have some interesting ancestors. One of them was the mistress of a king.'

He laughed. 'Trust Mother to tell you that story. Please don't imagine you are likely to see that poor woman's ghost, my darling. I never have, although Angela swore she had once.' He looked at me in bewilderment. 'How did I know that, Julia? I cannot remember what she looked like, yet I come out with some ridiculous statement like that!'

I glanced up at him, realizing it had upset him. 'It doesn't matter, Charles. It's like when you told us you had learned to drive when you were at Oxford. I expect it's being here in this house. You are becoming more familiar with it and things are gradually coming back to you.'

'Yes, I suppose they are. The first time I came down it was all so strange and I just wanted to get away as soon as I could, but now it is all oddly familiar. I feel I have always lived here. I know where things are without being told.'

'That is good,' I said. 'You are beginning to let yourself remember, darling. You were afraid you might not like what was locked in your past and you held back because of those dreams and voices in the hospital. They became all jumbled up in your mind so that you were not sure what was real and what was imagined.'

'Yes, I think that is just what I felt,' he agreed. 'For some reason I was very unhappy here just before the war started. I know that for some reason, Julia, though I have no idea why.'

'Your wife had just died,' I said carefully. 'That must have hurt you, Charles. You were grieving for her when you went to war, and the horror of that time made you vulnerable to bad dreams and strange doubts.'

Charles smiled lovingly at me. 'How understanding you are, Julia. You make it all sound so simple. Your father told me you were wise beyond your years. He visited me many times at the hospital, you know. He often told me things about you as we talked. I think I was a little in love with you before we met that day.'

We walked into the little parlour together. I indicated the desk and my writing case.

'I have decided this will be my room for the mornings,' I told him. 'I shall come here to write letters and make lists.'

'What kind of lists?' His eyebrows arched. 'Mother will not expect you to meddle in her management of the household. Besides, you do not want all the bother of running this place – that will come to you one day in the future.'

'I did not mean that sort of list. But I daresay you will want to invite friends down here sometimes?'

'I suppose I might in time,' he agreed. 'We are bound to be asked out a great deal in London. We shall entertain there, but weekend guests are something we shall have to face in time.'

'Don't make it sound such an ordeal,' I said and laughed up at him. 'I enjoy having friends to visit. Mama's house was often full of her friends and mine.'

'Yes, of course. You must feel free to invite anyone you like, but make sure you don't clash with my mother. That would never do!' He pulled a wry face.

'No, I shan't do that,' I promised. 'I should naturally consult with her. We must all try to get on together. If we are to spend any amount of time here, that is.' I glanced at him inquiringly. 'Have you made any decision yet, Charles?'

'If you find you can live here . . .' He touched my cheek. 'We'll see how things go. We shall be in London for most of the time – at least until Christmas. By then, we shall both know whether or not we want to make our home here.'

A gong had sounded somewhere in the house, summoning us to lunch. Charles grimaced. 'I suppose we must obey. That is one thing I should very much like to change. I have always hated it – that sound.'

He had spoken of the gong as though it was well remembered from his childhood. Little by little, the memories were trickling into his mind. I was sure that one day the barrier would crumble and all those things he had forgotten would come flooding back.

A part of me wanted it to happen so that Charles could be a whole person again, but there was a tiny bit of me that feared what might be revealed.

After lunch, Charles took me driving round the estate. He had decided to teach me to drive, and after he had shown me various parts of the grounds he stopped the car so that we could exchange seats.

'It is perfectly safe here,' he told me. 'You can't do any damage to yourself or others. We are unlikely to meet anyone in this part of the estate at this hour.'

I had a few false starts, but Charles was patient and explained the various procedures slowly and clearly so that I began to understand what he meant, and after a few minutes I was able to control the pedals well enough for us to continue our drive. I kept to a very stately pace around the open roads circling the house and the park. There was nothing to worry me, no sign of anyone on foot or in another vehicle, and gradually I began to enjoy myself. It was rather exciting to be in control of Charles's car. He was very gentle with me, patient even when I did veer on to the grass verge a couple of times. By the end of my first lesson I was feeling confident.

'Once you have true control, we shall go as far as the village,' Charles said. 'You did well for your first try, Julia. And there is plenty of time. We'll go home now and have tea – not with Mother, though. We'll ring for Alice to serve it in your sitting room.'

'Will Lady Hamilton mind?'

'It hardly matters whether she minds or not. She cannot expect to rule our lives.'

I made no comment on his decision, though I felt instinctively that Lady Hamilton would not care for any break with tradition. However, Charles was right. If we were to live here we must have some privacy. We rang for a maid and Charles gave the order. The surprise on the maid's face was almost comical.

'Madam is taking tea in the drawing room, sir. She has a visitor with her.'

'Then she does not need us,' Charles said. 'In future – when Mrs Hamilton and I are staying here – we shall require Alice to serve us tea in here.'

'But . . . Yes, Captain Hamilton.'

The maid departed and thirty minutes later Alice arrived looking flustered with a tray containing tiny sandwiches and biscuits together with tea in a china pot.

'I'm sorry it took so long, sir, but tea was sent into the drawing room. All the fancy stuff is there. I hope this will do? The silver is being used.'

'This is perfectly adequate until our own silver arrives,' Charles replied. 'But I shall expect more variety and some cakes for Mrs Hamilton in future.'

'It is all right,' I said as Alice set the tray down and departed. 'I never eat much at tea. Otherwise I have no appetite for dinner.'

'That is your choice,' he replied and frowned. 'But if you wished to entertain a friend this would not do, Julia.'

'No, I imagine not,' I said. 'It isn't Alice's fault, darling. The staff obviously provided a lavish tea for Lady Hamilton, expecting we would join her.'

'Then they must learn differently. I have no intention of being a marionette on Mother's string, and nor must you, Julia. If you let her dominate you she will make you over in her image. I don't want that for you – for us. If we live here it will be on our own terms. She must understand that.'

Charles looked angry. It was clear to me that his feelings

towards his mother had not improved, and I wondered what lay between them. Something had caused this mutual antipathy and distrust – but what?

After tea, I went up to Lord Hamilton's apartment and knocked. His manservant opened the door, giving me a friendly smile.

'Ah, Mrs Hamilton. His lordship wondered if you might come. Please follow me, madam. He is quite bright this afternoon.'

'I am so glad he is feeling better.'

Charles's father was sitting in an armchair by an open window. Pillows were wedged round his head and back for support, and a blanket had been placed over his legs. He was clad in a rather dashing black and gold smoking jacket, cleanly shaven, white hair slicked down with a pomade that smelled a little like cedarwood. He smiled as he saw me and held out his hand.

'Welcome, my dear. I was hoping you might find time to spare me a few minutes.'

'I was hoping for half an hour before I change – if that will not be too much for you, sir?'

'It would be delightful,' he said. 'I have few visitors these days; all are gratefully received, but none more so than you, Julia.'

'I have brought a book of poems,' I said and showed him the slim volume. 'Or Mr Kipling's *Jungle Book*. Papa gave it to me, but I was not sure what you would like?'

'Either would be equally acceptable,' he replied with a gentle smile. 'But why do you not just talk to me, my dear? I am very interested in hearing about how you met Charles. He has told me very little – except that you are lovely and good, which I can see for myself.'

'Papa sent him to us last year. He was ready to leave hospital, but not . . .' I hesitated, blushing as I realised what I had almost said.

'But not ready to come home?' Lord Hamilton nodded. 'I am surprised he came at all, Julia. When he left to join the army he vowed he would never return.'

'He does not remember that,' I said. 'I am sure he has no

100

recollection of saying that. Was it a quarrel – between Charles and his mother?'

Lord Hamilton sighed and looked sad. 'So I understand. I was not present when it took place. I had been out on estate business. When I returned to the house Charles was about to leave. He told me he would never return to this house while his mother lived. I asked him why, but he refused to tell me.'

'They must have had a terrible argument. Has Lady Hamilton never spoken to you about it, sir?'

'She said only that Charles had made his bed and must lie on it. I wrote to Charles several times asking him to reconsider, but he would not. He told me I would always be welcome if I cared to visit him, but flatly refused to come here.'

'Have you mentioned this to Charles?'

'No, I have not. At first I imagined he must have made it up with his mother when she went to the hospital, but now I fear that is not the case. Charles simply does not remember the quarrel.' Lord Hamilton looked at me anxiously. 'Has he mentioned anything to you, my dear?'

'No. He really has no memory of it. He is aware of the hostility she feels, and I fear he cannot like her. I believe she may have said something that upset him when he was ill.'

'Charles and his mother have not liked one another for years. Something happened when he was twelve—' Lord Hamilton broke off as the door opened and Charles put his head round the door asking if he might come in. 'Ah, there you are, my boy. I was just telling Julia how good it is to have you both here.'

'Am I interrupting?' Charles asked. 'I came to tell Julia she ought to start getting ready. Apparently Mother has invited guests to meet us this evening. You must ring for Alice and get her to help you put your hair up, darling. Lady Watson and her husband are among the guests. You will want to look your best.'

He did not need to tell me that! I felt irritated, as though he was afraid I would let him down in front of important guests, but no, that was unfair. Charles was merely thinking of me – of how I might feel if I wore only a simple dress.

'Yes. Thank you for warning me.' I leaned forward to kiss

Lord Hamilton's cheek. 'I have enjoyed our chat, sir. I shall come again tomorrow.'

'I shall look forward to it, and why don't you call me Henry?'

'Why don't I?' I replied and gave him a wicked look. 'As long as no one hears me!'

He was chuckling as I went out, leaving father and son together.

Our chat had given me much to think about as I went to my own room. It was no surprise to learn that Charles and his mother had quarrelled. I had sensed that from the first moment I saw them together. But what was their quarrel about, and what had happened when Charles was twelve years old?

Whatever it was, it was clearly the cause of his dream – the recurring nightmare that had disturbed his sleep when we were on our honeymoon.

There was obviously a mystery to be solved. I thought that if I knew the cause of Charles's nightmare I might somehow be able to help him overcome it. Something very dramatic must have taken place, something that had caused a rift between a young boy and his mother.

Seven

I chose a very fashionable gown of dark green silk that evening. It was a part of my trousseau and more sophisticated than I had worn before my marriage. The material was cut so that it wrapped itself in deep swathes about my body, showing off my figure in a way that none of my other gowns did, and the neckline was cut low over my shoulders with a ruffle to give it modesty.

Charles looked at me for several minutes in silence when he came into my room, then gave a reluctant nod of approval.

'Yes, I do like it, Julia. It makes you look older, of course, but I suppose I must accept your wish to be fashionably dressed.'

'I can change if you hate it, Charles. Neither Mama nor I was quite certain about it, but the shop said it was the very latest thing and copied from a French design.'

'It is a beautiful gown,' Charles said, 'and you look wonderful in it – I am simply a very foolish and slightly jealous husband, who wants to keep you all for himself.'

'Oh, Charles!' I laughed. 'I am all yours and I always shall be.'

'I know it.' He smiled and kissed me. 'You won't let me down, Julia. No one would ever think it.'

I gazed up at him. 'I want to look and be everything you want me to be, Charles. I really don't mind changing if you dislike this gown.'

'I think it is wonderful,' he said. 'I am very proud of you.'

He offered his arm. I slipped mine through his, reassured. There was no reason for Charles to be jealous. I was completely his.

We went down to the drawing room. Lady Hamilton was

103

already there, awaiting her guests. She threw Charles a look of disgust.

'We shall not discuss it now,' she said. 'But I shall not put up with further discourtesy, Charles. You were expected for tea. I had guests and you made me look a fool.'

'I am sorry you feel that way,' Charles replied in a cool tone. 'But we must have some privacy. Otherwise, we must find a house of our own.'

'Another threat? I haven't forgotten the last.' She glared at him, but before more could be said the butler announced that Lord and Lady Watson had arrived.

'Oh, are we the first? How awful of us!' Lady Watson said in what I felt was a slightly theatrical way. Charles, it is wonderful to see you again. My dear Lady Hamilton!' She kissed her cheek, then turned her critical blue eyes on me. 'Julia – may I call you that? What a perfectly divine gown. One would almost think it came from Paris.'

Her tone made the compliment sound like an insult, at least to my ears. I decided then that I did not find her at all pleasant. I would of course be polite to her since Charles had requested it, but she would never be a friend.

'Thank you,' I replied. 'Your own gown is very pretty.'

'So it should be – cost a fortune,' her husband said with a harsh laugh. 'Delightful to see you again, Mrs Hamilton. You look very attractive if I may say so. Nothing like the bloom of youth. No money buys it, m'dear.'

Lady Watson glared at her husband, then turned her back on him as she drew Charles into conversation. I sensed that she was not on the best of terms with her own husband, and that she was very interested in mine. I felt a flicker of jealousy as he responded gallantly to her flirtatious manner, but then the other guests began to arrive and I was caught up in a flurry of introductions.

'Mr and Mrs Howard Bryce Jones. Mrs Henry Forbes and Miss Forbes. Major and Mrs Richard Thorton. Mrs Matthew Scott and Miss Scott. Mr Paul Langan. Captain Edward Dickson. Mr and Mrs John Forsythe and Miss Forsythe . . .'

My face ached from smiling by the time all the introductions were made. I had imagined a small intimate gathering, but before dinner was announced twenty-one guests were ushered in, filling the large room with the noise of their laughter and chatter.

It was impossible for me to remember everyone, or to make judgements about them. I just smiled and answered their questions as best I could. Glancing at Charles, I saw that he was almost as bewildered and uncomfortable as I was.

At dinner, I was placed between Mr Bryce Jones and Mr Paul Langan. The former was a rather florid-faced gentleman who owned a large house in the village and, I soon learned, a flourishing factory making stock for the railways.

'We don't talk about it much,' he confided to me as he tucked his napkin into the neck of his shirt. 'Not done in polite company, but it's where the money comes from. My wife is from a good, old family, of course. We shouldn't be invited here otherwise. Lady Hamilton wouldn't tolerate me on my own, even for the money.' He winked at me. 'Not quite up to scratch – any more than Angela was. Her folk were new money and vulgar with it.'

'Did you know Charles's first wife?'

'Introduced them. Worst thing I ever did. She led him a right dance, but he's done much better this time. Lucky fellow! I wouldn't mind being in his shoes right now.'

I blushed at the look in his eyes and did not know how to answer.

'Take no notice,' Mr Langan whispered close to my ear. 'No manners and no sense, but he is right about Charles being lucky.'

I glanced at him. He was undoubtedly a gentleman born and bred, some years older than Charles and attractive with his slicked down fair hair and curiously dark blue eyes.

'I think *I* am lucky, Mr Langan.'

'In love with him?' He nodded. 'He is quite the war hero now, of course. Angela found him a bit of a dull dog. Is it true he has no memory of the past?'

I was offended by his remarks and thought his question carried a hidden meaning, though I had no idea why it should. What was I implying? Most people must be wondering what

Charles remembered and what he didn't, but this particular person seemed slightly apprehensive.

'Charles is gradually remembering things – and people. Particularly people he likes.'

'Probably not me, then.' He pulled a face. 'We haven't always been friends.'

There was at that moment something about him that I disliked. I made no reply to his comment, and the next moment Mr Bryce Jones reclaimed my attention. I turned to him gratefully. His comments were at times a little embarrassing, but beneath that bluff manner I detected a well-meaning man.

I liked his wife, Sarah, too. Later in the evening, she came to sit beside me on a small gilt sofa.

'I hope Howard didn't embarrass you too much? He is a dear man, Mrs Hamilton, but apt to speak before thinking at times.'

'Yes, but I rather liked him,' I admitted. 'Once I realised that he was actually a very kind person.'

'Yes, how odd you should see that immediately – he is, underneath.' She laughed, clearly pleased that I had been honest with her. 'I do see Howard's faults, but I love him despite, or perhaps because of them.'

'Yes, I should imagine he could be quite endearing if one knew him well.'

'Oh, I am going to like you,' she said, giving me an approving nod. 'You must come and have lunch with me soon. Howard is always out until the evenings.'

'I should not mind if he were at home. I should love to come.'

'Yes, I *do* like you, Julia. We shall be friends.'

'Yes,' I replied. 'I believe we shall, Sarah.'

Sarah and her husband were the only two of Lady Hamilton's guests that evening that I really took to immediately, though some of the other ladies were disposed to be friendly. I would be happy to meet them occasionally at a social occasion, but Sarah was the one with whom I could truly be comfortable.

I told this to Charles when we were alone later that evening.

'You will try to like Lady Watson? For my sake?'

106

'I shall be polite to her, Charles. Of course I shall. And I do like her husband.'

'Well, I suppose that is something,' he admitted. 'It is simply that I have been discussing a business venture with Watson. However, it may not come to anything.'

'I shall not do or say anything that might spoil your business plans, Charles.'

'No, of course not.' He put his arms about me and kissed me. 'If you don't mind, Julia, I shall sleep in my own room this evening. I have a headache coming on and I might disturb you.'

'No, of course I don't mind – if you think it best.' I did mind but I could not make a fuss if he was feeling unwell. 'You must take one of your powders, Charles. I hope it won't be too bad.'

'It is threatening to be quite unpleasant,' he said and touched my cheek. 'Goodnight, darling. I'll make it up to you another time.'

I watched as he walked through the connecting door, and my heart felt as if it were being squeezed hard. Somehow, as that door closed behind Charles, I felt that he was shutting me out.

I found it almost impossible to sleep, though I did try for a while, but after some restless tossing and turning, I sat up and switched on the lamp beside my bed. At home I had often found that reading helped to relax my mind, and I picked up a book of favourite poems. I had just begun to lose myself in the beauty of the prose when I heard the first scream.

I sat up, startled and unsure of where the sound had originated, but then when it was repeated again even more loudly, I realised that it had come from Charles's bedroom. Throwing off the covers, I jumped out of bed, wrenched open the door to the dressing room and ran straight through to Charles's bedroom.

He had somehow thrown off all the covers and was lying half across the bed, his arms and legs thrashing wildly as if he were struggling with someone. I hesitated, watching for a moment as he made odd movements, and then it came to me that he appeared to be swimming or attempting to swim in a strange, clumsy movement like a child learning to swim.

'I'll get you, Billy.' I heard the cry of sheer desperation break from him. 'Don't go under . . . don't drown . . . I'm coming, Billy.' Then there was a loud moaning sound followed by sobbing. 'Don't die . . . don't die. I'm so sorry, Billy . . . so sorry.'

He was sobbing bitterly; loud, noisy sobs like a child in despair. I walked carefully towards the bed. Charles was clearly lost in one of his dreams again, and remembering the incident in Mama's garden I did not want to startle him.

'Charles dearest,' I said softly and reached out to stroke his head. 'Don't cry, my darling. You tried to save Billy. It wasn't your fault . . . you did your best but you couldn't reach him.'

Charles's eyes flicked open and he stared at me, though I wasn't sure he could see me. 'Billy was my little brother,' he said quite distinctly and I had the impression that he was telling me something that had only just returned to his memory. 'He fell in the millpond and went under the wheel. I tried to get him out but I couldn't swim well – Mother had always forbidden us to go near water. She blamed me . . . she blamed me for letting him die.'

No wonder he had had such a terrible dream! The memory must have been there in his subconscious all this time, but it had only now returned to haunt him – now that he was back in the house where the tragedy had occurred all those years ago.

'It wasn't your fault,' I said. 'It wasn't your fault, darling.'

'No,' he said, and suddenly his eyes were clear and focusing on me. He was awake now and understood what he was saying. 'I did try to save him, Julia. Truly I did.'

'Yes, I know. I saw you having the dream. You were trying to swim but you couldn't manage it very well. I've seen young lads at home swimming in much the same way at the edge of the river.'

'The millpond was deep,' Charles said, and his eyes were dark with remembered grief as he sat up and looked at me. 'I couldn't get to him before the wheel dragged him down. When the men pulled him out his face was—' He shuddered

108

uncontrollably. 'It was awful, Julia. I was twelve and his death lived with me for years. She blamed me, you see. Billy was always her favourite, and she hated me for living when he died.'

I sat on the edge of the bed and gathered him close to me, holding him as he wept out his grief and pain. Now the dream that had haunted him made sense and I understood – I knew what Lord Hamilton had been going to tell me when Charles had disturbed us the previous evening. Charles had been seeing things in his dream – things that he could not remember properly, but now it was all back in place, and it was bound to be painful.

I put my lips to his hair and kissed him. 'It was a long time ago, my darling,' I whispered softly. 'You couldn't help him, but it wasn't your fault. It wasn't fair to blame you.'

After a moment the weeping stopped and he looked up at me. 'Forgive me,' he said. 'I don't know why it hurts so much. It was years ago. I should be long over it now.'

'I doubt that anyone ever gets over something like that completely,' I said. 'It has all been brought back to you because of the war.'

'It was something she said when I was in the hospital,' Charles said and now his tone was one of anger. 'She sat by my bed and told me I was a murderer – that I had killed my brother and should have died in the trenches. She had prayed I would.'

'Oh, Charles . . .' I said, feeling sick inside. 'How could she have said such a thing to you?'

'She hated me,' he replied. 'She hated me for years.'

'Do you remember everything now, Charles?'

'I'm not sure,' he said and frowned. 'I can remember Billy very well, and that day is as clear as clear can be, but I still can't remember being married or what happened just before I left Rondebush.'

'Your father told me you had quarrelled with your mother.'

'Yes, I thought I might have. Her attitude towards me has been so hostile the whole time – did he tell you what the quarrel was about, Julia?'

'He doesn't know. Lady Hamilton has never told him, and

you wouldn't. You should speak to her, Charles – have it out into the open. It is clear that you haven't liked each other for a long time, and we know why . . . she wrongly blames you for something you didn't do. But you ought to discuss the reasons for your quarrel and see if you can sort things out, that's if you want to live here?'

I thought that the memories of his brother's death might have changed his mind. It must be painful to live in a place where such a terrible tragedy has happened, and to know that his mother still blamed him for having allowed his brother to drown.

'Yes, I think I do . . .' He gave me an odd look. 'I think I must have conquered that old grief long ago, Julia. My experiences in the war, my illness . . . and Mother's accusations all brought it back to me. I loved Billy and it still hurts, but it wouldn't stop me wanting to live here. Unless there is something more.' He shook his head. 'I have a fear that there is, Julia. I have had it for some while now. I don't know what it is, but I think it must have something to do with Angela.'

'Can you not remember anything?'

'No – not about this. It's there . . . behind the curtain. I can sense it, feel it, but I must still be blocking it out.' He looked at me and I saw fear in his eyes. 'What did I do, Julia? What did I do that frightens me so much?'

'Why do you think you must have done something?' I asked him, but his eyes were looking past me, into the distance. 'Perhaps it was something done to you that caused you pain.' I put my hand up to his brow, stroking a lock of hair back from his brow. 'Has your headache gone now, Charles?'

'Headache?' He stared at me as though puzzled. 'Yes, I did have one when I came to bed, didn't I? It has gone now. Perhaps the dream released it.'

'I'll leave you to sleep,' I said, preparing to go. 'You will begin to feel better now that the mystery of the dream is solved, Charles.'

'Don't leave me,' he said. 'Get into bed with me, darling. I want to hold you.'

I slipped in beside him, snuggling up to his body and

110

letting the love flow between us. Charles had been haunted by his brother's death. It was the cause of those dark dreams that had disturbed his sleep. I believed that he would soon remember everything that had eluded him, and then he would be completely cured. There would be no more headaches to plague him, nothing to spoil our happiness.

I had known that Charles could never do anything evil. It was hardly surprising that he should have wondered about this when his mother had said such cruel things to him as he lay in the hospital bed. She had called him a murderer and in his confused state he had believed her. Now that he had remembered the truth he knew that her accusation was false – an unjust grievance harboured by a mother who had lost a beloved son.

I could understand Lady Hamilton's sorrow at losing her younger son, but she had inflicted terrible pain on Charles by her insistence that he was to blame for what had clearly been an accident.

I was angry with her, but I doubted that anything would ever change her attitude. Charles had lived with her hatred for a long time and must continue to do so. All I could do was to show him that my love for him was as strong as ever.

The next morning Charles took me for another driving lesson. I felt much more comfortable behind the steering wheel this time and Charles said I was making good progress.

'I shall look for a small car for you, Julia. We shall be going back to London tomorrow, of course, but when we come down again you shall have your own car.'

'You are always so good to me, Charles.'

'Nonsense! I want you to be independent if I am not always around. And I should prefer it if you did not let Mother persuade you to ride.'

'I have no intention of taking it up,' I replied. 'I have never particularly liked being near horses. It is foolish of me, but something I have not been able to overcome.'

'Do not try,' Charles said. 'There is no need. You can walk about the grounds if you wish to exercise as you did at home, and you will have your own car if you want to go into the village.'

He was making it clear I was not to go riding, though he had not tried to forbid me. Of course Angela had died because of a riding accident so it was perfectly understandable that Charles would not want me to risk such an accident. Fortunately, riding horses was something that did not appeal to me.

We had lunch with Lady Hamilton and Miss Henderson. It was a subdued affair. No one spoke more than a few words until it was almost over, then Charles turned to his mother.

'May we talk privately?'

'As you wish,' she replied. 'I suppose we may as well get it over and done with.'

A hushed silence fell as they left the room together. Miss Henderson shot a terrified look at me when I spoke to her a moment later, asking if she could tell me whether there was a Post Office in the village.

'Yes, there is a little shop with a counter for dealing with letters and parcels. If you have letters to send I could take them in for you this afternoon if you wish. I have an errand at the Vicarage – though perhaps I ought to tell you that letters are usually left in the hall for collection.'

'Yes, we did that at home,' I replied, 'though I sometimes walked to the village with them. I enjoy long walks.'

'I could take your letters this afternoon – if you wish?'

'There are six on my desk. I will fetch them for you – where shall you be?'

'I have to see Cook, then I shall be ready to leave. If you place your letters on the silver salver on the table in the hall I shall see them on my way out.'

'Thank you. I should like them to go today if possible.'

We parted and I went to my sitting room. My writing case was just as it had been, but when I took out the envelopes for the five thank-you notes I had the oddest feeling that someone had looked through my correspondence. A letter had been removed from its envelope and not replaced properly. It was not something I could prove, but I knew it was not as I had left it. The letter was the most recent I had received from Brent Gregory before my marriage.

Who would want to read my private correspondence? Perhaps one of the maids had come in to clean? Yet at home I had been able to leave my writing case open and I had never had cause to suspect the contents had been touched.

I recalled Miss Henderson's frightened glance when I mentioned wanting to post my letters. Was she the sort of person who would spy on others? She could not have a very happy life at the beck and call of her employer.

There was nothing in Brent's letter to concern me. I had often shown my letters to Mama, and Papa if he was interested. I had nothing to hide, and yet it was unpleasant to feel that someone would do such a thing. I decided not to mention it to Charles. He was already annoyed by his mother's desire to regulate our lives. It was not worth making a fuss over.

I sealed the five letters, took those and the letter to Mama and left them in the hall. Then I went upstairs to visit my father-in-law. He greeted me as warmly as he had the previous day. We talked for a while and I told him that Charles now remembered his brother's tragic accident.

'I have been anxious about that,' he admitted. 'It was many years before he recovered fully from the trauma. His mother blamed him unfairly. I did my best to shield him from her anger, but Charles was always a sensitive child. He feels things so deeply, Julia. I was always too busy to give him the attention he needed, so I agreed that he should go to boarding school. I wondered if he might feel we were punishing him, but it seemed to do him good – settled him down. He stood up to his mother more when he came back – became a bit of a rebel.'

'It was a terrible tragedy for you all.'

'Yes. Billy was a loveable lad, but always into mischief. It was his own fault he fell into the millpond. I told Mary that, but she could not forgive Charles for letting it happen. Billy was her favourite, you see.'

'Yes, Charles told me that.'

Lord Hamilton sighed. 'It was a long time ago. Very sad, but one has to live with these things.' He smiled at me. 'Would you read to me for a little while, my dear?'

'Yes, of course.'

I read some poetry and Lord Hamilton listened with his head back against the pillows. After a while I realised that he had fallen asleep and I crept out so as not to disturb him. He was a dear, kind man and very fragile. It made me sad to see him so frail. Charles would miss him when the end came, and so should I.

My letters had gone from the salver when I came back downstairs. I thought I might enjoy a little walk in the grounds, and wondered where Charles was and whether he might like to go with me. As I hesitated in the hall, unsure of where to find him, Lady Hamilton came out of what I knew to be her private parlour.

'If you are looking for Charles he left a few minutes ago.'

'Did he say where he was going?'

'Some estate business, I imagine.' She looked angry. 'Since he insists you are both leaving tomorrow I asked him to see to it this afternoon. I really cannot be expected to do everything myself.'

I wondered about the private talk between Charles and his mother, but although I was curious about what they had needed to discuss so urgently, I dared not ask Mary. Perhaps Charles would tell me later, but if he did not choose to then I would not ask. It was only too obvious that there was tension between them, and I felt it best not to interfere in what I did not understand. The very fact that Mary did not wish to talk about it, showed that it was something that had annoyed her.

'No, of course not. I shall go for a walk alone then.'

'Yes. Charles must learn to accept his responsibilities. No matter what has gone before. He owes it to his father and the estate – if not to me.'

'I am sure he will do what he can to help.'

She nodded, hesitating as though she wished to say more, then, 'Charles informs me you have no wish to ride – is that correct?'

'I have never cared for the idea of it.'

'As you wish. I would have taught you not to fear the horses, but you must do as you please. I want you to be happy here, Julia. Whatever the situation between Charles and I – whatever he believes – I hope you will not think me your enemy. I did not like or approve of Angela. She was not a suitable wife for Charles, but you are very different.'

114

'Thank you. I have no wish to quarrel with you, Mary, but I must do what Charles wants.'

'Yes.' She looked thoughtful. 'As a child he was weak, but I see a difference in him now. Yes, I do see that you must do as he wishes. All I ask is that you remember I am not a threat to you, Julia. The future of this family lies with you. And I have nothing left, but the hope of a grandson.'

She turned away, leaving me to stare after her. I was chilled by her words – so bitter and so regretful – and I felt pity for her. She had nursed her resentment against Charles for so many years, and it had brought her a bitter harvest.

I went for a long walk in the gardens, which were very beautiful, though rather too formal for my own taste. I thought that if I were ever to make this place my true home I should like to create a garden of my own. A place where roses would bloom in winter.

Lady Hamilton's assertion that she was not my enemy was reassuring. Her hostility towards Charles did not include me. I thought she was sincere in wanting to be on good terms with me, though it was unlikely we should ever be friends. Yet when I returned to the house and found that Charles was not back, I was tempted to have tea with her. It seemed foolish that we should both sit in lonely state in our own rooms when we might be together, but Charles had made such a point of having tea in my parlour. It would seem as if I was betraying him if I went behind his back the moment he was away.

So I drank my tea alone, then went upstairs to rest before changing for dinner. Charles came to me as Alice was fastening my gown. I had chosen one of his favourites and he smiled as he saw it.

'Yes, you are always lovely in that, Julia. I am sorry I was gone all afternoon. Have you missed me?'

'Yes, of course. But you must have had a great deal to do, Charles.' Alice had gone as I turned to him. 'Did you ask your mother about the quarrel?'

'Apparently it was because I had decided to join up,' he said and frowned. 'She thought I should not have volunteered, that I owed a duty to the estate.'

115

'But your father was not ill then.'

'No. Mother was afraid I would be killed. She is – as you must have realised – obsessed by the history of this family.'

'Yes, I know. She has told me more than once that she expects an heir from me.'

'She has no right!'

'It doesn't bother me, Charles. I want to have your children – several of them if I can.'

'Bless you, darling. You have made this visit so easy for me. I couldn't have contemplated a return without you.'

'You are glad you came – in spite of everything?'

'Yes. Billy's death was an accident. This last quarrel with Mother was obviously over nothing at all. She has apologised for her behaviour at the hospital. Apparently, she did not realise I could hear her, and was merely letting out the anger and bitterness that had festered inside her for a long time. Of course she did not wish for my death – I am necessary to her hopes for the future.'

'Oh, Charles, please do not be so bitter – there is no point.'

'No, I suppose not. Mother wants us to live here. I have said we may – when I am released from duty.'

'I am so pleased you have made up your quarrel, Charles. Perhaps now you can put it all behind you.'

'Lord, yes,' Charles said with a rueful laugh. 'I am feeling much better, Julia. I thought I must have done something terrible to make Mother so angry. She never forgave me for what happened to Billy, of course, but I thought there must be more. Billy died so long ago.'

'Yes, darling, I know, and you did your best to save him. You must always remember that.'

'I prefer not to think about it at all,' Charles said. 'We have so much to look forward to, Julia. I have accepted that the past is over. We can forget it and move on – can't we?'

'Of course we can,' I agreed at once.

I was a little surprised that Charles seemed to dismiss his brother's death almost lightly. He had been devastated when he first remembered exactly what had occurred, but now it was as if it had happened to someone else.

When I thought about it, though, I realised that Charles had had to get over his grief and guilt long ago. I was probably more upset because I had known nothing about it until the previous night.

Charles wanted to put the past behind him. He had at least begun to repair the breach with his mother, and there was no reason why I should feel uneasy – yet I did.

Eight

We returned to London the next day. I had visited Charles's apartment only once before, and I had seen only the large and rather elegant sitting room. There was an equally impressive dining room, three bedrooms, one of which was no more than a box room, a bathroom and kitchen.

'It was quite adequate for my needs,' Charles apologised when we were beginning to realise that I should need more space for my considerable wardrobe. 'But I see it will not do now.'

'We can manage for a while,' I said. 'I can use the hanging space in the spare room, darling.'

'No leave it for now,' he replied. 'I shall arrange for Mrs Watts to move my clothes there. I may sleep in the spare bed sometimes – when one of us is feeling unwell.'

Mrs Watts was Charles's cleaning woman. She came every morning to tidy the place and cook his breakfast. Charles had usually dined out in the evenings before our marriage, but Mrs Watts was now prepared to come in and cook for us at night when it was required.

'I can prepare a cold luncheon for you before I go home, Mrs Hamilton,' she offered when we spoke of the new arrangements. 'But I must have a few hours off in the afternoons to see to my husband.'

Since Mr Watts was an invalid I could only agree. I had always been used to living in a house where everything was done for me and the idea of having to fend for myself for a few hours was both novel and daunting. Mama had encouraged me to visit the kitchens at home, and to take an interest in the management of a house, but that was very different to actually doing something for myself. I had never been expected to actually make myself a cup of tea, and I realised to my shame that I was not quite sure how to do it.

'I should have thought sooner,' Charles said as we dressed that evening. He was taking me to a hotel to dine. 'I suppose I shall have to find someone else, but this place is hardly big enough for a housekeeper to live in.'

'We can manage as we are for a while, Charles. I might even try cooking a meal for us sometimes.'

'You most certainly will not!' He frowned. 'Mrs Watts will come in until we can arrange something. It would probably be best to rent a decent house until we move down to the country permanently.'

'I shall be happy here for a while,' I replied and kissed him. 'After all, we shall go down to Rondebush at the weekends whenever you can manage it, darling.'

'If you really don't mind? This is convenient for me. I hadn't bothered about finding somewhere just yet as I wasn't sure where we would settle. Had you disliked Rondebush I should probably have bought a house in town. I may do so even now.'

'Oh no, Charles,' I said. 'I would prefer to live in the country. Your apartment will do for the time being. Later on we may decide to rent or buy when we come up on visits. There is no hurry to decide.'

'Well, if you think you can manage just for a while. I'll see if anything suitable is available. If not, you could always stay at Rondebush for a few days. I could travel back and forth. It would be easy enough for me on the train.'

'I want to be with you,' I protested.

'And I want you here.' Charles kissed me. 'This is entirely my fault. I shall do something about it, Julia.'

I did not mind the prospect of living at the apartment for a few months. I should only be alone in the afternoons, and as I pointed out to Charles later, I could go shopping or visit friends.

'If I visit the hospital twice a week, and see Marina now and then, the time will fly by.'

'If things go well for us in France I may be released from my post before the end of the year.' Charles smiled

119

at me. 'We can put up with a little inconvenience until then, I suppose.'

'Yes, of course we can.'

Charles did fuss over little things sometimes! I had led an indulged and sheltered life until now, but I was sure that with some help from Mrs Watts I could manage.

It was a little strange that first morning Charles left me to go to his office. I kissed him goodbye, then went to find Mrs Watts who was about to carry a tray of dirty dishes into the kitchen.

'May I do something to help?' I inquired.

'Goodness gracious me, no!' she exclaimed. 'Captain Hamilton would never stand for that, and I would like to keep this job if I can. I need to work and the hours suit me.'

'I see no reason why you shouldn't.' I wrinkled my brow. 'I feel a little foolish at having to ask, but what does my husband do about laundry? And what should I do about my own? I have always had maids to see to that sort of thing, you see.'

'The captain has the laundry sent out, madam. I see to that, but some of your things need special care. I know a young woman, Sally Trotter, who could do with the work. Shall I ask her to call?'

'Is she used to handling silk do you think?'

'She was maid to a titled lady until she married. They wouldn't keep her on then, but I am sure she would be just what you need, Mrs Hamilton. She could come in when I go and do any little jobs you needed, that way you wouldn't be left to fend for yourself – especially if you have visitors for tea.'

'That sounds like an excellent idea. Will you ask her to come and see me tomorrow, please?'

'I shall be glad to. It will be good for Sally, and a help to you, madam.'

'Thank you.' I smiled at her. 'I think I shall go shopping this morning. I need very little to eat in the middle of the day, Mrs Watts. Perhaps some bread and butter and cold meats.'

'Yes, Mrs Hamilton. I'll see that everything is left ready.'

I allowed her to get on with her work while I put on my hat and coat. I thought it would be amusing to go shopping alone. It would be for the first time in my life and I was beginning to see that I had far more freedom to please myself than ever before.

I picked up my purse, remembering to slip the key Charles had given me inside it. There were some small personal items I needed, and I wanted to buy flowers for the apartment. It was very elegant and well furnished in the modern style, but slightly cold and impersonal. I intended to make it seem more of a home.

Over the next few days I made various changes to the apartment. I ordered fresh flowers to be delivered daily, bought some rather special embroidered chairbacks and soft cushions from a large and exclusive department store, and asked Mrs Watts and Sally to move small items of furniture around to give the rooms a more cosy appeal.

'You have transformed this place,' Charles remarked on the Thursday evening when he came home. 'I never realised how impersonal it was, but then, I hardly noticed it most of the time. It was just a place to sleep.'

'It was ideal for an unmarried man,' I teased. 'But not very comfortable. Marina came to visit me this afternoon. She said they have a huge house and the staff does everything. She envied me having so much freedom to do as I liked.'

'So you are quite happy here, Julia?' Charles gave me that indulgent look. 'Is Mrs Trotter useful to you?'

'Sally is exactly the person I needed,' I replied. 'She takes over from Mrs Watts and helps me in all sorts of ways.'

'Then I need not look for a house just yet?'

'Not for the moment. Besides, we shall be spending the weekends in the country – shan't we?'

'Yes, quite often, but unfortunately I cannot get there this weekend. There is an important meeting I must attend on Saturday. It means I shall be out the whole day.'

'Oh, Charles! I was looking forward to being at Rondebush with you.'

'You could go down on the train, Julia. Mother would have a car waiting at the station if you let her know.'

I shook my head. 'Marina asked us to lunch. I said we would

121

be away, but I can telephone her. She won't mind me going alone. It was meant to be informal.'

'Do that then,' Charles said. 'This doesn't happen often, darling. It is a nuisance, but it can't be helped.'

'I don't mind for once,' I replied. 'I might go to the hospital tomorrow, Charles. If you don't mind?'

'No, of course not. I told you I was wrong to question your judgement, Julia. I suppose I wanted you to remain innocent, but that was bound to change. Go if you wish, but don't tire yourself. You have been busy these past few days.'

'Oh, Charles,' I cried and laughed. 'I've done a little shopping and arranged flowers. Sally and Mrs Watts do everything else. I've had such fun. It's much better than having everything done for me.'

Charles nodded. He might have said more, but Mrs Watts came to tell us she was ready to serve dinner.

'I am glad you're happy,' was all he said as we went through to the dining room.

I bought flowers, magazines and a large tin of biscuits from an exclusive shop before I hired a taxi to take me to the hospital. I had telephoned earlier and been told that my visit would be welcomed.

'I hope to come every week now that I am living in London,' I told Matron. 'If you will permit me?'

'Of course Mrs Hamilton. I doubt if you will know any of the patients. We've had many new ones since you were here earlier in the year, but I am sure they will be pleased to see you.'

'How very kind of you to say so.'

'It was my patients who gave me their opinions of you, Mrs Hamilton. We shall be glad of any time you can spare us.'

I needed no one to show me the way that afternoon. A few visitors were already there talking to the young men sitting in the large, sunny common room, which overlooked a lawn and rose beds. There were long windows that opened out on to a veranda for those who could venture outside on a pleasant day.

I glanced around the room, looking for someone who might welcome a visitor. Three of the men were in wheelchairs and already had visitors. I looked further and saw a young man sitting alone by the window. He was staring out at the gardens and seemed to be ignoring everything going on around him.

'Hello,' I said as I went up to him. 'I am Mrs Julia Hamilton. Is there anything I can do for you? Would you like a magazine, or perhaps a cup of tea and a biscuit?'

'Go to hell!' he said, turning icy blue eyes on me. 'I'm sick to death of being pitied by rich bitches like you. Go and talk to someone else if you must – better still just go.'

For a moment I felt as if someone had poured cold water over me. I had been warned on my first visit that some of the men might be rude, but I hadn't experienced it until now.

'I am very sorry if I disturbed you,' I apologised. 'If you're sure I can't help you . . . ?'

'Get lost!' He turned back to the window and resumed his fixed staring.

'Ignore him,' a pleasant voice said behind me. 'Come and talk to me. I can't see you, but you sound pretty.'

I looked round and saw a young man sitting in an armchair. His head was swathed in bandages, which also covered his eyes, and his left sleeve was empty. I deposited my magazines on an empty table and went to join the man who had spoken, and who was wearing a jacket with the insignia of the RFC.

'Have you got roses?' he asked. 'I can smell roses.'

'Yes – aren't they lovely?' I held the bouquet close to his nose so that he could smell their perfume more deeply. 'I adore roses, don't you?'

'I am Flying Officer Mike Rowlands,' he replied. 'Before the war I used to grow roses. I thought I knew them all, but I'm not sure of this one.'

'I believe it is a new variety, bred for its perfume and colour. It is a gorgeous dark red and the petals have a velvety feel to them. Touch them and see.'

'Ah yes, they feel as good as they smell.'

'I will put them in water and bring them back to stand near you,' I said. 'Would you like a cup of tea? I brought some rather gorgeous biscuits from Fortnum and Mason.'

'That would be nice.' He caught my hand as I was about to leave. 'I didn't catch your name just now.'

123

'Julia Hamilton.'

'Julia . . . Are you as pretty as your name?'

'I'm not sure.'

'She's beautiful,' a voice said from behind me. 'Hello, Julia. Marina told me you were in town . . .'

I turned with a start of surprise as I recognized the voice. It was Brent Gregory! My eyes went over him swiftly, searching for the wound I knew he must have.

'A mere scratch,' he told me as I saw the scar on his neck and chin. I was given leave and I'm here to visit a friend, that's all. Hi, Mike! I see you still know how to chat up the best girls – this one is married, though.'

'Brent . . .' My throat went tight as I caught the note of reproach in his voice. 'I am very glad to see you.'

'Trust you to barge in,' Mike Rowlands said. 'Go away, Brent. I saw her first.' He laughed cheerfully. 'At least, I smelled her roses.'

'She smells like a rose herself,' Brent said. 'I'll keep you company while Mrs Hamilton does her flowers.'

Once again I caught that slightly angry tone in his voice. He couldn't be angry because I was married? I had written and told him about Charles at the beginning.

I felt guilty and confused as I went away to put my flowers in water. A volunteer was bringing a tea trolley round. I gave her the biscuits and she promised to see that everyone got to taste them. When I took the flowers back both Brent and his friend were eating theirs.

'Where did you get these?' Brent asked.

'Fortnum and Mason's.'

'I'll have to go shopping there – take some goodies back for the lads.'

'Are you going back?'

'Of course. It isn't over yet.'

'Charles says it soon will be, now that we've begun the Allied counter-attack.'

'He may be right, but soon isn't now.' Brent shrugged. 'We'll see what happens.'

'My mother said she would like to see you. I think she wants to talk to you about your grandfather and Mr Max Ruston.'

Brent nodded. 'She wrote to me after I telephoned and asked to speak to you a few days ago.'

'But you must have realised I wouldn't be there?' He shook his head. 'I wrote to you, Brent. I told you everything.'

'If you did I never got the letters.'

Now I could see the anger in his eyes. Was he implying that he hadn't known I was married until he telephoned? Surely he must have done? And yet I recalled now that I had wondered if some of my letters had gone astray . . . if that particular letter had never reached him I could understand his anger now.

'I wrote when I became engaged and when I married.' I tried to excuse myself, because his eyes were so cold, so accusing that it hurt.

'So Mrs Allington told me in her letter.'

'I'm sorry, Brent.'

'So am I, Julia.'

Mike Rowlands turned his head towards me. 'Is Brent giving you trouble, Mrs Hamilton? Shall I call a nurse and have him thrown out? Go away, Brent. She came to see me and you're distressing her.'

'Yes, I can see I'm in the way. See you later, Mike.'

I watched as Brent walked away. He was obviously angry, but he had no right to be. I had never promised him anything, except that I would write, and I had kept that promise.

'You must be the girl Brent used to talk about,' Mike said suddenly. 'He was always looking for your letters. You should have told him you were getting married.'

'I did, of course I did, but the letter must have gone astray. Besides, we were never more than friends.' And yet at one time I had thought it might become something else in time and I could not blame Brent for thinking it, too.

'That wasn't the impression he gave me. Brent believed you were just too young when you met – that you would learn to love him. He is in love with you, Julia. He wanted to marry you after the war.'

He was making me feel guilty. Perhaps I had allowed Brent to hope for something more than friendship. Perhaps I had thought it myself until I fell in love with Charles.

'Look, I need to talk to Brent. Will you excuse me please?'

'Of course. Come again if you have time.'

'Yes, I shall – next week.'

I walked hastily after Brent, catching up with him at the front door of the main wing.

'Brent! Please wait a moment.'

He turned and looked at me. At first I thought he was still angry, but then he gave me a rueful grin.

'I'm a damned fool, aren't I? You told me at the start. You warned me not to expect anything more than friendship, but I didn't listen. I'm sorry I lost my temper just now.'

But I had told him that one day our friendship might become more. It had not been a promise, just a silly girl enjoying her first flirtation, but it had meant more to Brent than I could ever have suspected.

'I'm very sorry you didn't get those letters.'

'I knew there was someone else,' he admitted. 'You mentioned Charles often, but I kept thinking it might not work out. It was a shock when your mother told me you were married last month – actually, your last letter is probably waiting for me back at camp.'

'I never wanted to hurt you, Brent. I am sorry you were hurt by what I did.'

'You kept your word, even after you found you were in love with Charles. I have nothing to reproach you with, Julia. I am the fool for thinking I could make you love me. Love isn't like that.'

'No, it isn't, Brent. I do like you, but I fell in love with Charles. Please forgive me?'

'Of course.' He smiled oddly. 'It was still nice knowing you, Julia. You are even prettier now than you were. Marriage must suit you.'

'Yes, I think it does.' I offered my hand and he took it, just holding it for a moment. 'Are we still friends?'

'If you want to be?'

'I see no reason why not.'

'Will you still write to me?'

'Yes – if you want me to?' He nodded and I took a card from my purse. 'That is my address in the country. I'll write my town address on the back. I should write there for a while. When we move to Rondebush I'll tell you.'

'I can always get in touch through your mother. She did give me your telephone number in her letter, but I thought you might not want to hear from me. I've written to Mrs Allington to tell her I am returning to France in the morning, but I shall go to see her when I come back. I've decided to settle either here or in Ireland after the war.'

'You won't go back to America?'

'No. I am selling my property here, and I shall buy something suitable for breeding horses I can race.'

'You could do that in America, couldn't you?'

'England is the home of racing – all the history and the romance of it is here,' Brent said. 'My father would expect me to go into banking if I went home. I was undecided, but now I've made up my mind.'

'Then we may meet sometimes in the future,' I said.

'Yes. Perhaps – one day.' He smiled again, that natural, engaging grin that was so attractive and infectious. 'I'm like the proverbial bad penny. I could turn up anywhere. Take care of yourself, Julia.'

'You too, Brent.'

I stood and watched as he went back inside the hospital. Obviously he was going to say goodbye to his friend.

I asked the hospital porter to get me a taxi, and gave him a shilling when he obliged.

I thought about Brent as I was being driven home. Would I have fallen in love with him if Papa had not sent Charles to the house? How different my life might have been if I had.

For one moment I felt regret, as if I had lost something rather special. As I realised what I was thinking I felt horrified. Whatever was I doing? I could not – did not – regret my marriage. I was very happy as Charles's wife.

The memory of Charles showing annoyance that morning flashed into my mind. Why had I conjured up that picture? He had not been irritated with me. One of his favourite shirts had been returned from the laundry with a button missing. It had made him cross.

'I can sew it on, Charles. It won't take more than a moment.'

'It should have been attended to by Mrs Watts – it is a part of her job to take account of things like that, Julia.'

'She has more than enough to do now there are two of us living here. In future I shall check myself. I hadn't realised it might happen, but now I shall look at your things when they are returned from the laundry.'

He had changed into another shirt without comment, but I had sensed he was still displeased. Charles did not often become angry, but he was inclined to fuss over small details.

It was his one fault in my eyes. Papa had never allowed little domestic issues to bother him. Had his shirt been missing a button he would simply have laid it down on the bed for Mama to find. I had thought Charles was just like Papa when I married him, but I had discovered there were several differences.

Papa was not as moody as Charles could be at times, but then he was not plagued by terrible headaches. Charles was increasingly prone to them and he had slept alone the previous night. Perhaps it was the aftermath of his headache that had made him fuss over a missing button.

'You saw Brent at the hospital?' Marina was instantly apologetic. 'I should have mentioned that I had seen him, but I thought he would have returned to France.'

'He was leaving the next day.'

She nodded. 'Was it very awkward for you, Julia?'

'A little at first. He didn't know I had married until recently.'

'Yes – we spoke of you.' She frowned. 'He seemed genuinely upset. I think he is fond of you, Julia.'

'Yes, I know. He was angry with me, but then he apologised. We are still friends. I shall continue to write to him.'

'Does Charles mind you having correspondence with another man?'

'I told him I had a friend in the RFC. He has never mentioned it. I cannot see why he should mind. There has never been more than friendship between us.'

Yet even as I spoke I was remembering the way Charles had reacted when he saw me in the green dress. He had spoken of being a jealous husband, but surely he had merely been teasing me?

Perhaps I would make a point of telling him I had seen Brent. It might be best to let him read Brent's letters, so that he could see for himself there was no need for jealousy.

I intended to mention the chance meeting that evening, but when Charles came home from his meeting he was pale and withdrawn.

'Forgive me if I don't have dinner with you, Julia. I have another of my stupid headaches. I shall go straight to bed.'

'Oh, Charles. I am so sorry.' I looked at him anxiously. 'Do you think you should see another doctor?'

'I have already made an appointment.' He smiled wearily. Please don't worry, darling. I just need some different pills, that's all.'

I kissed him and said no more, but I was anxious. I had thought that he would feel better now he had remembered so much of his past, but it seemed his headaches were becoming more frequent.

It was the middle of the following week before I was able to visit the hospital again. I put my flowers in water, distributed magazines and placed a basket of fruit on the table, and then looked round for the young man I had spent some time with the day Brent visited.

'If you're looking for Mike you won't find him.'

I turned to see that I was being addressed by the man who had been rude to me on my last visit. His expression was still hostile, his tone harsh as if daring me to react.

'Oh, hello,' I said. 'Are you feeling better today?'

'Better than Mike anyway. He died last night.'

I felt as if he had punched me in the stomach and swayed as a wave of dizziness went over me.

'Hey! Don't faint on me,' he said. 'I didn't think it would upset you that much.' He grabbed my arm and practically forced me to sit down. 'Are you all right – or shall I call a nurse?'

I took a deep breath to steady myself, then looked up. 'I'm all right now. It was just a bit of a shock. He seemed so cheerful when I was here before. I thought he must be over the worst.'

'It seems there might have been a bit of shrapnel in his brain

129

– that's what was causing the problem with his eyes. It moved suddenly and that was curtains.'

'How tragic,' I said. 'I had no idea he might be close to death.'

'I doubt if anyone else knew either. It was just one of those things. Like putting a pistol with one bullet to your head and spinning the chamber before you press the trigger. Mike could have lived years as he was, but his luck ran out.'

'Yes, I see. I'm so sorry. Was he a friend of yours?'

'Just another ship passing in the night. I'm Keith Hallis by the way. I'm sorry I was rude last week. I just got tired of well-meaning wealthy women asking me what they could do for me and smiling before they pass on and forget I exist.'

'I shan't forget Mike.'

'No,' he said, giving me a direct stare. 'I don't think you will.'

I didn't tell Charles about my visit to the hospital that evening, because I thought it might upset him. He was feeling better and talked to me about his day as we were dressing for dinner. We had been invited to the house of one of his colleagues at the War Office and Charles thought we ought to consider giving a dinner party ourselves the following week.

'You should invite eight couples, Julia,' he said. 'Marina and her husband and any other friends you know are in town. You can make up the rest from my list of people I need to repay for their hospitality.'

'Yes, I should enjoy that,' I agreed. 'But won't eighteen people be too many for Mrs Watts to manage?'

He laughed and arched his brows. 'You didn't imagine I would ask Mrs Watts to cook and serve for our guests? No, darling, that would never do. I always use a professional catering service from one of the best hotels in London. You will find all the information in the top drawer of my desk. There is a selection of menus, all numbered to show when they were last used. You just give the service the next number in line, tell them the day, time and how many people in all, and they do the rest. It's all very simple.'

'Oh . . . can't I choose what we have for dinner?'

'It would only confuse them, Julia. No, just stick to the menus I've used in the past. I believe we're on number three at the moment. Please don't try to do anything different. I assure you my system works very well.'

'If that is what you want, Charles.'

There was no point in making a fuss, but I was disappointed at having so little to do. It all seemed so impersonal. I would have liked to make my first dinner party a little special, but at least I could arrange the flowers and see the table was set with the silver we had been given as wedding gifts.

'We shall be going down to Rondebush this Saturday,' Charles said and came to kiss my cheek. 'Cheer up, darling, or I shall think you are beginning to wish you hadn't married me.'

'Charles! Don't say such things. They are hurtful.'

'I'm sorry,' he replied. 'I don't mean to hurt you. I just need to keep reassuring myself that you are happy.'

'I love you, Charles. Of course I'm glad I married you.'

'Then that's all right, isn't it?'

He gave me such an odd look at that moment. I wondered what could be going on in his mind. Why should he have begun to doubt me? Surely he could not be jealous? There was no reason, no reason at all.

My mother telephoned me the next morning. We had written to each other but not spoken since I was down at Rondebush just after my honeymoon.

'I'm sorry I haven't telephoned,' she said, 'but your father took me away for a few days. How are you, Julia?'

'Very well, Mama – and you? Papa and the boys?'

'They are fine, though Phil did something silly the other day, which is another reason why I haven't had time to telephone you. He absconded from his school and tried to sign up for the RFC. Fortunately, the recruiting officers realised he was far too young. They got the name of his school out of him and informed the headmaster. We had to go down and talk to him.'

'Oh dear,' I said. 'Is Phil in trouble?'

'He has been given a lecture and three hours detention, but that is so much better than what might have happened . . .' She hesitated, then, 'I gave Brent Gregory your telephone number last week. He said he wanted to contact you before he left for France. I hope that was all right? I wondered if I ought to have refused afterwards.'

'No, it was perfectly all right, Mama. Brent is a friend. Besides, I've seen him myself since then.'

'Well, I thought I ought to tell you. Anyway, we're coming up to town next week. You and Charles must dine with us one evening.'

'Yes, we should love to see you, and we're having our first dinner party. You and Papa must come to that.'

'How thrilling for you, Julia. You'll have such fun planning it all. Well, I mustn't keep you. I am sure you have lots to do.'

'It was lovely to talk to you,' I said. 'I am so glad you are coming up next week. I've missed you.'

'Is everything all right, Julia?'

'Yes, of course. I must run. I'll see you soon – love to Papa.'

I was frowning as I replaced the receiver. Everything *was* all right, wasn't it? I was very happy with Charles. He was gentle, considerate and loving. Why shouldn't I be happy?

There was no reason I could point to, and yet something wasn't quite right. My life wasn't what I had expected it to be, but then, what had I expected?

I hadn't thought beyond my wedding day. I suppose I had imagined our lives would be similar to my parents', with me gradually learning to run our home. Sometimes I felt that I had no part to play other than as a possible mother for Charles's children.

At Rondebush Lady Hamilton was firmly in charge, which was only right and natural as it was her home. Here in London, Charles had everything he needed sent in.

I had found the prospect of so much freedom exciting at first, but now time was beginning to weigh heavily on my hands. Just what was I supposed to do with the rest of my life?

Nine

Charles had a surprise for me when we went down to Rondebush that weekend. He had arranged for a rather attractive little open-topped car to be delivered and it was waiting for us when we arrived.

'You will soon be able to take this out for a spin on your own, darling,' he said when I exclaimed in delight. 'Mine is too big for you to handle easily, but this is just right.'

'It is wonderful, Charles!' I said and kissed him. 'The best present I've ever had.'

'I am glad you are pleased, darling. I want to make you happy. You've given me so much.'

I felt ashamed of my disloyal thoughts. It was wrong of me to have had them when Charles was so good to me. In London his work had taken him away from me and I had felt a little lonely and bored, but here he was able to spend more time with me.

We went for long walks together as we had when Charles was my father's guest, and he took me driving as far as the village in my new car. I saw Sarah Bryce Jones crossing the village green, and waved and honked the horn as we passed. She laughed and waved back.

'Really, Julia,' Charles said. 'There was no need to make such a fuss just because you saw someone you know. You are supposed to keep your eyes on the road.'

'But there was no one else coming,' I said. 'It was just a bit of fun, Charles.'

He gave me a disapproving look, and I thought he was rather like his mother at that moment. Did he know he resembled her in so many ways? In looks he was his father's image as he must have been as a young man, but his manner was becoming more and more similar to Lady Hamilton's.

Charles *had* changed in the past few weeks. Before our wedding he had been less critical, more inclined to laugh than he was now. I thought about it, trying to remember when the change had begun.

Was it before he had the dream? Or after the talk with his mother? I couldn't be sure, but I was aware of him watching me now . . . as if he were waiting for me to do something. But what?

'You must come again soon,' Lord Hamilton said when I bent to kiss his cheek after spending half an hour talking to him. 'You make me feel so much better, Julia. I look forward to your visits.'

'Charles had a meeting last weekend,' I said. 'But I should like to come as often as we can. I enjoy being down here.'

'This is your home now, Julia, and I hope you and I are friends. You can always come to me if you want to escape from that husband of yours.' His eyes twinkled naughtily. 'Mary approves of you, my dear. We both want you to think of this as a place you feel happy in. You mustn't think of yourself as simply a guest. If you would like to change anything you must tell us.'

'There is something . . .'

'Yes?' He smiled as I hesitated. 'What would please you, my dear?'

'I should like a garden of my own. Somewhere I could plan the planting and make it special.'

'What a wonderful idea. Yes, you must have your garden, Julia. I shall speak to Mary and something will be arranged for when you come down again.'

'Oh, you are a dear man,' I said. 'If you continue to spoil me like this I shall not want to return to London at all.'

'We should like nothing better than to have you here,' he replied. 'But I think Charles might object. If we are patient for a little longer, Julia, the war may soon be over, and then you can both come home to live.'

'It all went splendidly, darling,' Mama said to me as she was preparing to leave after our dinner party. 'You must come to me tomorrow for lunch and we shall spend the afternoon talking.'

'Oh, yes, that would be lovely,' I agreed. 'So you thought it was all right then – the dinner? Charles always uses that particular service and he thought it would be easier than trying to plan something individual.'

'Much easier for you,' Mama agreed. 'You could never have coped in this tiny apartment, Julia. Charles was very thoughtful. When you are living at Rondebush things will be different. You will be able to talk things over with Lady Hamilton and ask her advice. No, I think Charles was very sensible to stick to what he knows works, and you arranged some beautiful flowers.'

'Yes, they were rather lovely,' I agreed. 'Lord Hamilton is going to arrange for me to have my own garden at Rondebush. You must come and stay when I begin to design it and tell me what you think.'

'I should love that, my darling,' she said and hugged me. 'Now promise you will spend the day with me tomorrow? Philip has meetings all day . . . something to do with the war, of course. It really does seem from what Charles was saying this evening that the Allies are planning to make a final push. I shall be so glad when all our poor boys can come home and this dreadful fighting is over.'

'Yes, Mama – so shall I.'

After our lunch the next day, I told Mama about Mike Rowlands and what had happened to him.

'It was so sad,' I said. 'I had no idea anything was likely to happen. He was very cheerful when we were talking, and I thought he must be well on the way to recovery.'

'It was a terrible shock for you,' she said. 'Are you sure you should continue to visit, Julia? You are looking a little peaky.'

'I want to go as often as I can, Mama. I know I can't do very much, but the patients like to see me. They get visitors most days, of course, but some of the ladies are not very tactful I'm afraid.'

'And very few are as pretty as you,' Mama said with a

laugh. 'I am not surprised you are popular, my darling, but you mustn't overdo things.'

'I am perfectly well.' I blushed and then laughed. 'I might have known you would see something. I haven't been certain myself, but I was a little sick this morning, and I have been thinking that perhaps I might be – well, you know.'

'You mean you think you might be with child?' Mama got up and came over to kiss my cheek. I rose and we embraced. 'That is wonderful news, darling. What does Charles say?'

'He doesn't know yet,' I admitted. 'I thought it was a little soon so I didn't tell him, just in case I am wrong. I shall visit a doctor this week and then tell him if he says there is cause for hope.'

'Yes, that is much the best,' Mama agreed. 'I am glad you confided in me, darling. I can give you the name of a very good doctor who specializes in attending women in childbirth. He is very much sought after and it would be prudent to book his services well in advance.'

'Oh, Mama!' I cried. 'We don't even know if I am carrying a child yet.'

'I think it very likely,' Mama replied. 'I fell for you very early in my relationship with your father.' She hesitated, a faint blush in her cheeks. 'I think it is time I told you something, Julia . . . something I have long wanted to tell you.'

'Yes, Mama?' I looked at her curiously. 'She was embarrassed, even nervous. 'Please tell me what is bothering you.'

'I have not told you the whole truth about your own father, Julia. He was Gérard de Arnay as you know, but he was never my husband. We planned to marry, but Gérard's father forbade the marriage for reasons that he thought valid at the time. Later he discovered his fears were unfounded, but by then it was too late. We had been forced to part and Gérard was killed in a riding accident, brought on by his despair. I did not discover I was with child until later.'

'Mama . . .' I stared at her, feeling shocked. I had never for one moment suspected anything like this. 'Why did Grandfather not want you to marry?'

'It is a very long and involved story,' Mama said. 'Laurent thought – he thought he might be my father. Adele Heron, who as you know was my own mother, never married. She allowed Laurent to believe that I might be his child in the hope that he would do something for me in a financial way. She had only what he gave her and what she managed to earn as a seamstress in Paris. Although she came from a good family, she was forced to run away from her home . . . because she was carrying a child.' Mama looked at me oddly. 'I have not told you the story because it is a little shocking. I wanted to wait until you were married, so that you could understand how a man and a woman might – for the sake of love – do something that would seem wrong in the eyes of the world.'

'Yes, of course,' I said. 'I think I can understand how easy it would be in certain circumstances to do things that might be considered a sin. When one loves one is capable of doing anything.'

'Yes, I thought you would understand now,' she said. 'I am not, and have never been, ashamed of my love for Gérard. We loved one another very much and should have married, although I doubt we would have been as happy as I have been with Philip. Gérard was inclined to be restless and moody. I do not know if he would have found enough in me to content him for the whole of our lives. I think in time he might have looked elsewhere, even if he still loved me.'

'Yes, I can understand that, too,' I said. 'I believe there are different kinds of love, Mama.'

She nodded, and touched my cheek. 'Such a wise child always. Now I must tell you the rest of my story and you will understand why I did not want you to like Brent Gregory too much.'

'Brent – what has this to do with him, Mama?'

'Nothing . . . I have realised that since then,' she admitted. 'But what I must tell you is that I was the child of my own grandmother's second husband. Max Ruston raped Adele Heron – his wife's only daughter. Adele could not face telling her own mother the truth and so she ran away. Laurent and she had already been lovers, and she saw that it might be easier to let him think he was the father of her child rather than explain something she was deeply ashamed of, though of course it was not her fault.

'Later she saw it might be to her advantage to let him continue to believe it. You must understand that Adele was treated badly by both her mother and stepfather – though her mother regretted the breach for years. Anne Ruston did her best to make up the quarrel, but my mother could not forgive her for the cruel things she had said to her. I was the one who did that on her behalf years later.'

'Oh, Mama,' I said in hushed tones. I felt chilled, sickened by the story of rape and brutality that had unfolded in Mama's pretty little drawing room. 'That is a terrible thing to have happened to your mother – how she must have suffered. You must have been shocked and hurt when you discovered the truth.'

'It was worse than it might have been, because it meant that I could have married Gérard after all. Laurent liked me but he could not allow us to marry suspecting what he did, of course. It was simply a tragic sequence of events that none of us could have foreseen.'

'It was very sad,' I said. 'I am so sorry for what happened to you – and to Adele, Mama. But I am very glad you have told me the truth now.'

'I wanted to tell you long ago,' Mama said. 'It is right that you should know everything, Julia. I hope you will forgive me for not telling you sooner?'

'Perhaps I should not have understood then,' I said. 'It was best that you waited until I was married.'

'Philip urged me to tell you,' she said. 'I was a little nervous – I thought you might think me shameless?'

'Oh, Mama!' I laughed at her. 'It simply makes me love you – and darling Papa – even more.'

She smiled at me through a hint of tears. 'Perhaps now you understand why I have always been so concerned for your own happiness. I wanted to be sure that you would not suffer as I did – and Adele before me.' She looked thoughtful. 'I suppose that is why I discouraged your friendship with Brent that time. I simply couldn't bear to be reminded of that family at all. It was most unfair of me, Julia, and I am truly sorry.'

'Well, now you can stop worrying, dearest,' I replied. 'It

was just friendship after all, and now I am happily married, and hopefully I am carrying my husband's child.'

'Yes, my darling,' she said and hugged me. 'And I think we both know the truth about that . . .'

The following week I made an appointment to see the doctor Mama had recommended, but was unable to see him until the Friday afternoon. By this time I had been sick on several mornings in a row and I was fairly certain in my own mind that I was indeed with child.

Mr Meacham confirmed it after his preliminary examination. He smiled at me as I came out after dressing behind the screen.

'I think you can safely tell your husband the good news, Mrs Hamilton. It is quite early of course, but you are presenting all the signs and I would judge you to be into your second month.

'Oh . . .' I blushed. 'We haven't been married much more than a month. 'It must have happened almost at once – on our honeymoon.'

'It does happen that way for some young women,' he said. 'Are you concerned at the idea of having a child so soon after your marriage?'

'I'm not sure. It might have been nice to wait a little longer, but I do want children, so perhaps it doesn't matter. As long as Charles doesn't mind.'

'Well, it was his responsibility to take care of that side of things,' he said and frowned. 'If you have any difficulty ask him to come and see me Mrs Hamilton.'

'Oh, I am sure there won't be,' I said quickly. 'Charles wants children. It is just that he might be surprised it is so soon – as I was.'

'These things happen,' the doctor replied. 'Now, I don't want you to imagine you are an invalid because you happen to be carrying a child, Mrs Hamilton. You must keep going for those walks and do everything you would do normally. You are a perfectly healthy young woman, and having a child is a natural part of a woman's life. Just keep coming to me for regular consultations and we shall have no trouble at all.'

'Thank you – you are very kind. My mother said you would be.'

'Yes, I remember her. She wasn't one of my patients, of course, but she came with a young friend once. A very sensible lady, your mother. She helped calm a rather nervous young mother.'

'Mama always has a calming influence.'

He shook hands with me. 'Now remember what I've told you, and send your husband to see me. I like to have a word with the father before the birth.'

I promised that I would ask Charles to call and see him one day, then left the consulting rooms. It was a lovely afternoon and I walked through the park before looking for a taxi to take me home, enjoying the sunshine and the fresh air. I knew now that I much preferred living in the country, though it was nice to spend a few days in town from time to time.

I definitely wanted to bring my children up at Rondebush. Besides, the apartment would not be suitable. We should need a nanny for the baby and a nursery . . . the baby!

It was still a very new idea for me. I had known I wanted children, and I thought that once I had become accustomed to the idea I should be very excited. The baby would be born at Rondebush, of course. Mr Meacham had already promised to send a nurse three weeks before the birth was due, and to attend me himself.

'I shall make all the necessary arrangements, Mrs Hamilton,' he had told me, making notes in his diary. 'We shall know within a day or so when the child is due, and I shall be there – though my nurse is perfectly capable of taking charge alone should I be delayed.'

Yes, I thought, I would be very excited, once I was sure that Charles was pleased.

I intended to tell him as soon as he came in that evening, but when I returned to the apartment Sally had taken a telephone message to say that Charles would be late home.

I was asleep when he came home, and at breakfast he told me that he had not wanted to disturb me so had slept in his own room.

'It was business last night – an impromptu invitation to

140

dinner with Lord Watson, Julia. Had you been at home I might have arranged to meet you and we could have gone together.'

'I'm sorry I wasn't here, Charles.'

He did not ask where I had been and I did not tell him. He seemed a little withdrawn and I thought he might be feeling unwell. Perhaps when we were down at Rondebush he would be in a more receptive frame of mind. I would wait until then to give him my news.

We travelled by train and Lady Hamilton sent a car to the station. She welcomed us, kissing me and asking Charles how he was feeling.

'You both look tired,' she said. 'I have always thought town living unhealthy. You should ask for time off, Charles. You have been working too hard.'

'Yes, perhaps you are right, Mother.' He glanced at me as if seeing me for the first time that day. 'You do look pale, Julia.'

'I am perfectly well, thank you, and very pleased to be here.'

Lady Hamilton nodded. 'Well, I shan't scold you, Julia. Would you like to rest before tea?'

'I think I should like to have tea and then rest before dinner.'

'Very well.' She hesitated, glancing at Charles and then at me. 'Would you care to join me for once?'

'Why not?' Charles said. 'Yes, I think we shall – just for today.'

'Do you want to . . .' Lady Hamilton began, then looked at me hard before starting towards me. 'Julia? What is wrong? You're not well.'

I had quite suddenly begun to feel a little odd. I caught at her arm as the room began to spin at an alarming rate.

'I do feel a little faint.'

'Charles! Help your wife!'

Charles caught me as I half swooned. He swept me up in his arms and carried me to the sofa in the drawing room, laying me down gently. Then he knelt by my side, holding my hand and looking at me anxiously.

'Why didn't you tell me you were feeling ill, Julia?'

The dizziness had passed as swiftly as it had come. I sat up, resisting his arms urging me to remain lying down.

'It is all right, Charles. Mr Meacham told me not to worry if I felt faint now and then.'

'Who the hell is Mr Meacham?' he demanded, looking angry.

'A doctor, who specializes in childbirth,' Lady Hamilton said, and glancing up I saw a look of satisfaction in her eyes. 'Charles, do stop fussing! Julia is obviously with child. It was merely a little faintness.'

'Is this true?' Charles looked stunned. 'How long have you known, Julia?'

'Since yesterday afternoon. I was with the doctor when you telephoned, Charles. I wasn't sure until then, and I didn't want to say anything to you until I was certain.'

'Why didn't you tell me this morning?'

'I wanted to wait for the right moment.'

'Of course you did, Julia.' Lady Hamilton was smiling at me. 'For goodness sake, Charles! Is this an inquisition? You should be telling Julia how delighted you are, not scolding her.'

'Of course I am delighted. Julia knows that, don't you, darling?' He bent and kissed my cheek, then stood up. 'I was so frightened. For a moment I thought you were really ill.'

'No, I am very well,' I assured him. 'Mr Meacham says I am a very healthy young woman. He says I should take plenty of exercise and everything will be fine.'

'You must rest and take care of yourself,' Charles said with a frown. 'Are you sure this doctor knows what he is talking about?'

'He is the best there is,' Lady Hamilton replied for me. 'Stop asking so many questions, Charles. Julia is a sensible girl. She will not be doing anything foolish or taking any risks with your child.'

'No, of course I shan't,' I said. 'Please believe me, Charles. The faintness was just a passing thing. I am better now and I should like some tea please.'

'Of course you would,' Lady Hamilton said. 'I shall ring for it at once. It is up to us to spoil you now, Julia. I am thrilled by your wonderful news, and Lord Hamilton will be very pleased. He has a surprise for you, but I shall leave it for Henry to tell you himself.'

Charles gave me his hand as I stood up. His look was anxious, tender, full of concern for me.

'Forgive me if I was less than kind to you this morning, darling. I was a little tired myself. You do know that I love you?'

'Yes, of course, Charles. I knew you were tired this morning – that's why I didn't want to bother you with my news.'

'I should have noticed you were not well. Are you sure you feel better, Julia?'

'Yes, much better, Charles. It was nothing at all.'

He nodded and the subject was dropped while we had our tea, but I was aware of him watching me constantly. What could be worrying him now?

I visited Lord Hamilton for a few minutes before I went to change for dinner. He was very pleased to hear my news, though he merely took my hand and kissed it.

'You must take great care of yourself, my dear, but I know you will. Now, I have a little gift for you. Hold out your hand.'

I did as he asked and he placed a large black key on my palm. I looked at it curiously.

'What is the key for?'

'It fits a gate into the walled garden, which has been neglected for years, Julia. I have had the ground cleared for you, and Tom Banks awaits your instructions. You have only to tell him what you want him to do and he will devote his time to your garden.'

'A walled garden!' I looked at him in delight. 'How wonderful! Oh, I shall enjoy designing my own garden – it will be so exciting. Thank you so much for giving it to me.'

'Compared with the gift you have just given me it is nothing, my dear. Your child will bring new life to this family. We are sadly in need of it, Julia. This has been a lonely, empty house for far too long. It needs the laughter of children to fill it.'

'Yes. I want my children to be brought up here, Henry.'

'You must come down as much as you can. Persuade Charles to take more time for enjoying life. It goes too fast, Julia. You must not let him waste it.'

'We certainly cannot raise children in Charles's apartment,' I said and laughed. 'We shall need a nursery and a nanny – and lots of space.'

'Come to us soon, Julia,' he urged. 'I am not sure I shall see my grandchild, but I want to know he or she will be born in this house.'

'I promise you I shall have the baby here. I have already made arrangements for a nurse to move in before the birth.'

He smiled at me. 'If I should die before then I shall be happy to know the family lives on through you, Julia. Whether your child is a boy or a girl matters very little. Life goes on and with it there is hope. That is all I ask.'

'Charles and I will have several children,' I promised him. 'One day this house will be filled with the sound of their laughter.'

'How lovely you are,' he said. 'It was a good day for all of us when Charles brought you home to us. I thank God for it, my dear.'

'I am just a very ordinary, normal girl.'

'But that is exactly what was needed,' he said and smiled at me teasingly. 'Though I wouldn't call you *ordinary*, Julia.'

'But you are prejudiced in my favour,' I said and gave him a naughty look. 'And now I am going to leave you to sleep while I change for dinner.'

Charles came to me when I had finished dressing. His eyes went over me, searching for something, then he reached out and drew me into his arms, kissing me tenderly.

'You do know how much I love and need you?'

'Yes, Charles. I love you, too.'

'Are you pleased about the baby?'

'Yes, of course – as long as you don't mind?'

'I am thrilled by the news,' he said. 'It is very soon – when do you expect the baby to be born, Julia?'

'Mr Meacham says I must be into the second month, which means I must have fallen almost at once. I know it is very

144

early, but Mama said it was the same for her when I was conceived.'

He nodded, his eyes very dark and intense as he looked at me. 'It is sooner than I expected, but I am pleased, darling. A child will help to bind us together – do you not think so?'

'We are already bound together,' I said. 'I adore you, Charles. You must never doubt it.'

He nodded, but there was an odd haunted expression in his eyes. 'Forgive me. I try not to let myself doubt, but . . .' He shook his head. 'No, that is not fair to you, Julia. You would not betray me as she did.'

'Do you mean your first wife?'

'Yes. There were other men . . . but there are many forms of betrayal, Julia.'

'What do you mean?'

'It doesn't matter.' We heard the dinner gong sounding in the hall below and Charles swore softly. 'That wretched thing! I must speak to Mother about it.'

Charles had that look on his face again, the one I was learning to dread. I knew that he was annoyed by the summons to dinner, and that he would not answer any questions from me now, but I was determined that he should.

I wanted to know what he meant by 'many forms of betrayal'. I suspected that he had remembered his wife, that he knew exactly what had happened at the time of her accident and her death. I thought that he had known for a while now, but he had not told me.

Why had he not talked to me about it? He had told me everything else he had remembered – why not tell me this?

Charles asked me if I would like to take a stroll in the gardens after dinner. It was a warm July evening and the air smelled softly of roses and stocks. Somewhere in the gardens we could hear the melodious song of a nightingale – a rare and precious sound.

'How lovely,' I said. 'It is so beautiful here, Charles. Such a wonderful place to bring up children. I think I have fallen in love with your home.'

'I have always loved it . . .' He hesitated, then seemed to come to a decision. 'Angela hated it from the moment I brought her here. She disliked the house, mother and the whole idea of living here.'

I felt a tingle at the base of my spine as I realised what he was telling me. 'Have you remembered everything now, Charles?'

'Most of it, I think. There may always be gaps apparently, but yes, I can remember most things now.'

'Is it very painful for you to think of her, Charles?'

He stopped and looked down at me. 'Good grief! You don't think I am still in love with her?'

'You did love her – didn't you?'

'As a young and naïve idiot, yes,' he said, a harsh note in his voice. 'But that love died long before her accident. You mustn't imagine I'm still grieving for her, Julia.'

'I thought perhaps . . .' I faltered and then looked up at him. 'You have seemed withdrawn sometimes lately, Charles.'

'It's these damned headaches,' he said. 'When I leave you to sleep alone I do it for your sake, Julia. Sometimes I am very restless. I did not want to disturb you.'

'Can nothing be done to help the pain?'

'I have decided to have further tests,' he said. 'Rosendale was sure they would go in time, but they have become more frequent. However, I am sure there is nothing to worry about.' He smiled at me. 'I am more concerned about you, Julia. Perhaps you ought to stay on here when I return to town – just for a while? Mother is right, you do look pale. It might do you good to rest for a few days.'

'I would rather be with you, Charles.'

'I expect to be busy next week. You will be on your own most of the time and I shall be down again at the weekend.'

'Could I come back with you the following week?'

'Of course. I'm not telling you you must stay here, darling. I just thought you might enjoy a few days in the country. I know there isn't a great deal of amusement for you at the apartment.'

'Well, perhaps I shall stay for a few days then. It will please your father to have me here, and I can make a start on designing my garden.'

146

'Good. I'm glad you've made up your mind. I should have been anxious for you alone at the apartment. You will be much better here, Julia. Just take care not to overdo things.'

'Of course, Charles. I really am perfectly well.'

'I know that,' he said and touched my cheek. 'But I couldn't bear anything to happen to you, darling. I was not in love with Angela when she had that . . . accident. But it upset me terribly to see what it did to her. She didn't deserve that . . . whatever she had done.'

'No one does, Charles. If she was unfaithful to you that was wrong and unkind of her, but you couldn't have wanted her to be hurt like that.'

'She was such a confident horsewoman,' he said. 'She always wore breeches and rode astride like a man. I shall never forgive Mother for what she said to Angela that day.'

'What do you mean?'

There was a strange look in his eyes, a mixture of anger and reluctance as though the words were forced out of him despite himself.

'She forbade Angela to ride the new stallion she had just purchased. It was a wild-eyed, bad-tempered beast that was bought purely for breeding purposes, and a devil to master.'

'Then perhaps Angela should have listened to your mother's advice.'

'It was the worst thing she could have done – forbidding her to take the damned thing out. Telling Angela she must not do something was like waving a red rag to a bull. I sometimes think Mother did it deliberately – that she hoped Angela would fall.'

'Charles! No, surely not?' I was shocked. 'What are you saying? You cannot possibly mean that?'

'Oh, but I do,' he said and there was a strange, hoarse note in his voice. 'You see, Angela had just told me something that morning. She was having a child, and she was not certain the child was mine.'

The ice was creeping over my body. I stood there in that peaceful garden as the full horror of what Charles had just told me dawned in my mind.

'You are saying that your mother knew about the child –

147

that she deliberately goaded Angela into taking out the stallion because she wanted her to lose the baby?'

'You think I have imagined the whole thing? That it is a product of a tortured mind?' Charles nodded. 'I believed I must have done, Julia – when it first began to come back to me in dreams and stray thoughts that seemed to pop into my mind like maggots. I shut them out, not wanting to believe something so horrible. I could hardly bear to think of it. I thought I must be going mad.'

'Oh, Charles. My poor darling,' I cried. 'Is this what you've been worrying over for the past few weeks? I knew there was something.'

'I still feel I must have imagined it,' he said. 'But I spoke to one of the grooms. He told me the stallion was also injured in the fall. Mother had it shot immediately.'

'Have you spoken to her about your fears?'

'We quarrelled over it at the time. I accused her of murder, Julia. There was a terrible row. I believed she had done it out of spite – to punish me because of Billy – but later I realised it must have been for the sake of the family. Because she was obsessed by the need for a true heir.'

'It is horrible, Charles. I cannot believe that of your mother. Surely no one would do something like that deliberately?'

'She denies it, of course,' he said, still frowning. 'But there was a witness. Someone told me Mother forbade Angela to ride the stallion.'

'Who was that, Charles?'

'Anne Watson.'

'How did she know?'

'She was here when the argument took place. Apparently, Angela went off in a huff and immediately ordered the grooms to saddle the stallion.'

'When did Lady Watson tell you this?'

'A few days after the accident. She was a frequent visitor at the time. She and Angela were friends of a sort, and she continued to visit after it happened. Anne Watson was one of the few people Angela would speak to after she came back from the hospital. She could hardly move, you see, just a few of her fingers and her head and neck.'

'The baby was lost, I suppose?'

'Yes. Angela lost everything that day. It was pitiful to see her, Julia. I cannot bear to think of her lying there . . . No, I shall not think of it.' He reached out, drawing me close. 'Do you understand now why I dislike Mother, and why I have asked you to be careful?'

'Yes, I can understand your feelings for your mother, and your fears for me, Charles, but surely you don't believe your mother would harm me? I am carrying the child she so desperately wants – perhaps even the heir you need.'

'Yet she hates me because of what happened to Billy,' Charles said. 'I do believe you are safe here, Julia, or I would not leave you alone even for a moment – but be careful never to trust my mother too much. Promise me?'

'Yes, darling. I shall be careful. I promise.'

I lay thinking about what Charles had told me as he slept with his head against my breast. He had made love to me so tenderly, reassuring me of his desire to make me happy over and over again.

Could Lady Hamilton have deliberately driven her son's wife into riding that stallion in the hope that she would fall and lose the child she was carrying?'

It had been very foolish of Angela to ride at all once she was aware that she was with child – unless she too had wanted to miscarry? She had told Charles she was not sure it was his child, had she hoped she might lose it for reasons of her own?

To me the idea was so terrifying that it made me want to protect my unborn child. How could any woman want to destroy her own baby?

Surely Charles was wrong? He had been told something by a third person, and it was not always wise to believe such tales. Lady Hamilton could not have set out to destroy the child her son's wife carried – that would be murder.

The accident had led to terrible consequences. Angela had lost her life because of it – not immediately, but after months of suffering. I was not surprised that Charles had tried to shut out the memory. I found it very difficult to accept, and I wondered how I should face Lady Hamilton the next day.

Before I slept, I realised that I must ignore what Charles had told me. I must cling to my belief that there was some other explanation for what had happened. Otherwise, I should find it impossible to stay in this house.

Charles took me driving as far as the village again. He was very pleased with my progress and promised to continue with my lessons the next weekend.

'You will take care of yourself, darling?' he said before he left later that afternoon. 'You can change your mind and come with me, if you like?'

'No, I shall stay for a few days,' I replied. 'If we are going to live here one day I must get used to being here without you.'

'I am still undecided,' Charles said. 'Perhaps we should find a house of our own?'

'Stop worrying, Charles. Whatever happened between your mother and Angela – and we don't really know for certain – will not happen to me. I don't ride. Besides, your mother likes me.'

'Yes, I know.' He kissed me. 'Father will love having you here, but if you're unhappy come back to London.'

'Yes, of course.'

We kissed again and then I watched as his car drove away.

It felt a little odd as I walked back into the house. I noticed how empty it seemed and I felt suddenly lonely. For a few minutes I wished I had gone to London with Charles, but then I remembered why I had agreed to stay here for a few days.

I had been feeling unwell. It would do me good to walk in the gardens and I wanted to begin creating my own garden. I was about to go upstairs when Lady Hamilton called to me.

'Ah, there you are, Julia. Would you like to have tea with me?'

'Thank you, but I have some letters to write,' I replied. 'I shall see you this evening, Mary.'

Her gaze narrowed as she looked at me. 'Have I done something to offend you?'

'No, of course not.'

I was tempted to ask her what had happened that day with Angela, but I decided it was best to let it pass.

'I shall rest on my bed and write my letters there,' I replied. 'Perhaps you would ask Alice to bring me something in my room?'

'Yes, certainly I will do that for you, Julia. You must take care of yourself. I shall make no demands on you, but I hope we shall be friends?'

'Yes, of course. Please excuse me, Mary. I am a little tired.'

I felt guilty at avoiding her. Charles could not be sure she had meant Angela to ride that horse. Besides, she would do nothing to harm me. I was carrying Charles's child.

Ten

I spent the next morning with Lord Hamilton's head gardener, discussing various possibilities for my special garden. It had high brick walls, and there were the remains of old pathways, also a stone sundial and a moss-covered bench.

'His lordship told me to clear the old planting, Mrs Hamilton, but I thought you might like to retain some of the statuary that was here?'

'Yes, perhaps. For the moment I want to think about the basic design. Now that I have talked to you, I shall draw some plans – then we'll begin the planting.'

'What about the paths, Mrs Hamilton? Shall I have the men take them up?'

'Yes, I think they must come out. I am beginning to get an idea of the form I want the garden to take. I would like to recreate what must have been here once – a medieval garden with herbs and old roses.'

'That would be very interesting, madam. I might be able to find some ideas for you amongst my records of how the estate looked years ago.'

'Yes, please do. We'll talk about it again tomorrow.'

After our talk, I went for a walk in the park, then returned to the house for lunch with Lady Hamilton and Miss Henderson. Lady Hamilton had been riding that morning, and she told me about one of her mares that was about to give birth.'

'It is a pity that you do not like horses, Julia,' she said. 'It is an interest we might have shared, although of course it would not be wise for you to ride at the moment.'

'I do not exactly dislike them,' I replied. 'But I prefer to walk, and now I am learning to drive. I wondered if I might have the services of your chauffeur one day?'

'Yes, of course. You have only to ask for whatever you want. I arrange the menus once a week with Cook, but should you prefer something different we can change. It is something I am quite willing to hand over to you when you are living here permanently, Julia.'

'I should be happy to help – once I have become accustomed to your routine. Perhaps we could discuss them before you see Cook? I could then benefit from your advice.'

She gave me an approving nod. 'You are such a sensible girl, Julia. So different from Angela – or Anne Makepeace. She is Lady Watson now, of course, but there was a time when I thought Charles was interested in her. Before his first marriage. It would have been a more suitable match, though not ideal.'

'You did not like Angela?'

'No, not at all. She was both vulgar and sly. I am sorry that she suffered so much before the end, but it was entirely her own fault.'

'She took out an unsuitable horse, I understand?'

Lady Hamilton's eyes narrowed. 'I hope Charles does not still believe I somehow engineered Angela's accident. I can assure you I had no such thought. I merely told her that in my opinion the horse was a rogue and said that I would be selling it. The grooms could not control the beast. After Angela was thrown and trampled I had it shot. It too was injured and I thought it a waste of time to save such an unstable animal. My only regret is that I ever bought it.'

'You did not forbid Angela to ride it?'

'To have done so would have been to provoke her into doing just that. I disliked her, but I am not an evil woman. Charles should simply have divorced her. She was not murdered, Julia – at least, not by me.'

'What do you mean – not by you?'

'She had been arguing with Charles earlier that day. Her mood of defiance may have been as a response to whatever he had been saying to her. I believe she had told him she wanted either an abortion or a divorce or – better still – both.'

Charles had not told me that!

'Do you think he would have given her a divorce?'

153

'In time I dare say. My son is inclined to jealousy. If you have not yet learned that, Julia, you will eventually.' Something like pain flickered in her eyes. 'He was jealous of his brother because Billy was my favourite. They were arguing before Billy slipped and fell into the millpond. Charles went in after him, but not immediately. I have often wondered if a part of him wanted his brother to die.'

'That is a wicked thing to say!' I stared at her in disgust. 'He had terrible dreams about it, and was so distressed when he remembered what had happened.'

'But why did he forget, Julia? Why did he want to get himself killed in the war? That is what I ask myself.'

'What are you implying?' I stood up, feeling angry with her. 'I shall not listen to this a moment longer.'

'Please sit down, Julia. I apologise if I have upset you. I was merely thinking aloud.'

'Excuse me,' I said. 'I have some letters to write.'

'Ah yes, you are a devoted correspondent. A word of warning, Julia. In this house there are curious eyes.' She glanced at Miss Henderson, who had blushed scarlet. 'You would be well advised to keep your writing case locked.'

'Thank you for your advice. I shall certainly do so in future.'

I walked from the room feeling angry. So I had been correct in thinking that Miss Henderson had read Brent's letter. Had she then gone running to her employer with the news that I was writing to an officer in the RFC?

Was that why Lady Hamilton had warned me that Charles was a jealous man?

I rested on my bed for an hour, then went to see Lord Hamilton. He was as pleased to see me as always, and we discussed my plans for a medieval garden.

After I left him to sleep, I went to my own sitting room and began to draw sketches of how I thought I would like my garden to look. I wanted a tree that would grow to large proportions in the middle of the garden, and I would have a wooden bench built around its girth so that I could sit beneath the shelter of its branches. I also wanted masses of roses, lilies and other scented flowers, and a bed of herbs. I thought I might have a small pool with a fountain playing into it. I was engrossed in my work when I became aware that someone had entered the room. Looking up, I saw Miss Henderson standing there watching me.

'Yes – did you want something?'

'You think I read your letters,' she said defensively. 'But it wasn't me. It was Captain Hamilton.' Her cheeks went bright red. 'I came to bring you a message from Lady Hamilton and saw him.'

I felt chilled. Was she lying? Surely Charles would not read my letters – yet I sensed that she was speaking the truth.

'I see. Thank you for telling me.'

Suddenly, she started to cry. 'I've been given notice. Lady Hamilton has asked me to leave at the end of the month.'

'Why? I don't understand. What have you done that displeased her?' Her face had gone red and blotchy. She was never an attractive person at the best of times, but now looked pitiful. 'I am very sorry you've lost your place here.'

She took out a handkerchief and blew her nose. 'I don't know what I've done. I've always tried to please Lady Hamilton. She simply said I was to have a year's wages and leave at the end of the month.'

'Did you tell her about Captain Hamilton reading the letter?'

She blew her nose again. 'Yes, but I've always told her everything. It was what she wanted. I told her about the quarrel . . . between Captain Hamilton and his first wife. And about the row with Lady Watson . . .'

'Did Angela quarrel with Lady Watson that day?'

'Yes, but I didn't hear why. They were shouting at each other – calling each other awful names – but I was not there when the argument began. As soon as Mrs Hamilton saw me she stalked off, and that was when it happened – her accident.' She faltered and bit her bottom lip, then, 'I wanted to tell you – Lady Hamilton said more than she admitted at lunch. She didn't forbid Mrs Hamilton to ride that horse, but she did say it would be foolish.'

Which was almost the same.

'Why are you telling me this – because you have been dismissed?'

Her cheeks went bright red. 'Well, she deserves it. I've nowhere to go and it is unfair to dismiss me.'

'So you thought you would pay her back?' My sympathy for her had gone. 'I think you should go to your own room, Miss Henderson. Being spiteful about your employer isn't going to get you your job back.'

She gave a sob of despair and ran from the room. I felt pity for her, and yet her behaviour could only arouse my disgust, and I could not be sorry she was leaving.

Miss Henderson did not appear at the dinner table that evening. Lady Hamilton said that she was lying down with a headache.

'I have dispensed with her services,' she told me frankly. 'I really do not know why I have kept her on so long. I would do better to employ a younger woman; someone who could act as a secretary for us both. Besides, now that you are here I shall have someone to talk to.'

'I am going back with Charles next week,' I reminded her.

'But you will both be living here soon. I shall not need a companion any longer. The house is bound to be full of visitors once you begin to make friends.'

She seemed to have forgotten our disagreement earlier, and I realised that I must do the same. I had always known that she blamed Charles for his brother's accident, and now I knew that he blamed her for what had happened to Angela. Neither of them was likely to change their opinion of the other lightly. For all our sakes it would simply be best to avoid speaking of either incident in future.

It was a long time before I could sleep that night. Why had Charles read my letter? I did not like to believe Miss Henderson, but I supposed that I must. It was rather unpleasant. Had Charles asked to read a letter that I had just received I would have agreed willingly, but to do so behind my back implied distrust.

Charles was constantly seeking reassurance that I was happy. I could understand his feelings to a degree, because of the way

Angela had behaved. I thought she must have been a very careless, cruel person. To tell your husband that you could not be certain whether the child you carried was his or another man's was a wicked thing to do. It must have hurt Charles a great deal. Even after the child was lost, he must have still wondered if the baby she had carried had been his.

I thought about his dark moods of late, and I felt chilled as I wondered if he had suspected I was meeting someone behind his back. He had been angry that I was not home when he telephoned to try to make a dinner arrangement, and he had acted oddly when he first discovered I was with child.

But he must know that I had come to him as a virgin on our wedding night. He must! He could not suspect me of betraying him as Angela had.

No, I would not let Lady Hamilton – or her companion – poison my mind against him. I had only Miss Henderson's word that it was Charles who had read my letter; she could have lied about it to cover her own guilt.

Charles had explained his moodiness. The headaches were troubling him more and more. I was anxious about the cause of those headaches. Was it only the stress and trauma Charles had experienced during the war as Mr Rosendale had thought – or was there something else?

The thoughts went round and round in my head, tormenting me, but in the end I slept. My dreams were uneasy, though in the morning I could not remember what had disturbed my rest.

The next morning I telephoned Sarah Bryce Jones and asked if I could visit her.

'Come for lunch today,' she invited. 'I would love to see you, Julia.'

Sarah's home was a large, modern house just at the edge of Eynsford, which was an old village which still boasted the remains of a Norman castle and had a beautiful church. Close to the ford in the river, a road formed a junction with Sparepenny Lane – said to be a route once much used to avoid paying tolls on the turnpike – and the toll cottage with its watchful keeper.

Sarah welcomed me to her home, taking me through to a sunny, comfortable parlour.

'I have been hoping you would come to visit me,' she said. 'I heard you were at Rondebush for a few days.'

'Who told you?'

'Lady Watson. She was riding through the village yesterday and paused to say hello. We are not exactly friends, but Howard has some business with her husband and we dine with each other every so often.'

'Yes, it is much the same with us.'

'She used to visit almost daily at Rondebush when Angela was alive. Not quite as much now I think?'

'I have not seen her since the evening you were there.'

Sarah nodded. 'How are you, Julia? You look a little tired.'

'I did not sleep well last night, but I am not ill. I am expecting my first child. I must have fallen on my honeymoon'

'Ah yes, it sometimes happens that way. We have two sons, but I took some time to conceive.'

'Are your children at home?'

'No – they both go to boarding school now. I should like a daughter. I could keep her at home longer – until she grew up and married. So far I haven't managed it, but we keep trying.'

She laughed and I did, too. I was already feeling much better. After all the revelations of the past few days I had begun to feel as if there were a dark cloud hanging over me, but Sarah's chatter had blown it away.

I was so glad I had come to visit her. Sarah was a very normal, generous woman and I was pleased to have such a friend living close by. When I left her that afternoon, she kissed me and said I was to come to her whenever I wished.

'Please do not think you have to be invited. I shall always be delighted to see you.'

'You must come to tea with me,' I said. 'Lunch would be more formal, but we can have tea in my parlour.'

'When shall I come?'

'Would tomorrow be too soon?'

'No, of course not. I shall come tomorrow, Julia.'

I kissed her again, and then I left. Lady Hamilton had sent her car to fetch me, and I did not wish to keep the chauffeur waiting. It would be much easier to visit friends when I was able to drive myself.

Lady Hamilton was waiting for me when I returned.

'Will you have tea with me, Julia?'

'Yes. Tomorrow Sarah is coming, but today I shall have tea with you.'

'Mrs Bryce Jones?' She nodded. 'She is a pleasant woman. Her husband is vulgar, of course, but she cannot help that. Yes, she will be a good friend for you, Julia. Lady Watson was here earlier. She says Charles has invited them for dinner this weekend – we shall have to discuss the menu. And we must invite a few others. It is too bad of Charles not to let me know he wanted to entertain this weekend. But it is always the same.'

'Perhaps he intends to telephone this evening.'

'Yes, perhaps. Lady Watson called in the hope of seeing you, Julia.'

'I am sorry to have missed her, but I shall see her this weekend.'

'She asked how you were. I told her your news. I hope you do not mind?'

'I would have preferred not to say anything to Lady Watson just yet, but I suppose it does not matter. Everyone will know soon.' I hesitated, then, 'May I ask Sarah and her husband this weekend?'

'Of course. You may ask anyone you wish, Julia. As I've told you before, this is your home now.'

Charles did telephone that evening. He seemed cheerful as he told me he had invited a colleague and his wife to stay for the weekend.

'You sound better, Charles?'

'I have been feeling better this week. And the mood here is optimistic, Julia. I really believe that things are going to turn our way soon. The war may be over within a few months'

'I do hope you are right, Charles.'

'What have you been doing, darling?'

159

I told him about my visit to Sarah and that I was enjoying myself and getting on with my garden designs.

'I think I shall ask Mama's advice before I decide finally,' I told him. 'I shall write to her and send her some sketches.'

There was a slight pause, then, 'I have several letters here for you, Julia. I'll bring them down at the weekend. One of them is from France.'

'Oh, that will be from Brent Gregory,' I said. 'I mentioned him to you a few times in my letters, Charles. He was a close friend of Marina's brother – you remember? He took me driving one day when you first came to stay with us.'

'Yes, I remember. I wasn't aware you were still writing to him.'

'He has no one else to correspond with,' I replied. 'We are just friends, Charles. You are very welcome to read his letter. I have nothing to hide.'

'No, of course not. I wasn't implying . . . I did read one of his letters to you, Julia. I was looking for an envelope in your writing case and was tempted. I shouldn't have done it, of course. I hope you don't mind?'

'You are always welcome to read any of my letters. I have many friends, Charles, but I love you.'

'I know,' he said huskily. 'I am missing you.'

'I miss you. Have you been to the doctor yet?'

'I had some more tests. I expect it was a waste of time. The pain comes and goes. I shall have to learn to live with it. I probably make too much fuss. You know how I am, Julia. I fret if a button goes missing!'

'You are my husband and I love you.'

'Bless you, my darling. I shall see you this weekend.'

I was frowning as I replaced the receiver. What could be the cause of Charles's headaches, and were they the reason for the moods that seemed to come on him at times?

When I turned, I saw Lady Hamilton looking at me. How long had she been standing there?

'Was that Charles?'

'Yes. He is bringing a colleague and his wife down for the weekend.'

'How like him not to have told me when he was here, but

160

that is always Charles's way.' She gave an odd laugh. 'Do not frown so, Julia. You must have begun to realise that Charles is very like me. I suppose that is why we disagree so often. We are both strong-willed, stubborn, selfish and jealous. Billy was more like his father; a gentle, sweet boy. Perhaps that is why I loved him more. However, you must not imagine that I bear Charles any ill will. I may have been harsh in my grief when his brother died, and I still believe that the accident was in part Charles's fault, but my recent anger towards him was because of his own attitude towards me.'

'Because he blamed you for what happened to Angela?'

'That – and other things. I thought him weak to let her walk all over him and I told him so, but I have begun to change my mind. I see there are inner strengths in Charles I had not suspected. I think that perhaps the war was good for him in a way.'

'Could you not tell Charles how you feel? If you could heal the breach between you it might make all the difference.'

'Make this a happy house?' She smiled her thin smile. 'You may not believe this, Julia, but I should like that. Whatever Charles and I may have done to each other in the past, I feel it is time to forget. We should be on good terms – for all our sakes.'

'Talk to Charles this weekend,' I urged. 'Tell him that Lady Watson exaggerated what you said to Angela. Tell him that you merely warned her of the danger.'

'You have decided to believe me, then?' For a moment her eyes were suspiciously bright. 'Thank you, Julia.'

'If you had deliberately forbidden Angela to ride the stallion, knowing her disposition, that would have been an act of murder. I simply cannot believe you would do that, Mary. You have it in you to be harsh, but you are honest.'

'Sometimes people find me too honest,' she admitted wryly. 'I see that you have wisdom beyond your years, Julia. We were fortunate that you fell in love with Charles. Now, would you like to do the flowers for the weekend? I find it an awful chore, but I believe you are rather good at it?'

'It is something I enjoy.'

'Then I shall leave them to you,' she said. 'And we shall discuss the menus for the weekend.'

Life was much fuller for me at Rondebush than it had been at the London apartment. I spent hours discussing the planting for my garden with the gardener, Tom, and I had begun to make small changes to our private rooms in the house.

Visiting my parlour at my invitation, Lady Hamilton told me how much she liked what I had done, cushions and personal items bringing more colour and interest to what had been a rather neglected room. I had picked some sprigs of lavender from the bushes outside on the patio and she crumbled one of the flowers between her fingers, then sniffed at the perfume on her hands.

'I love the smell of fresh lavender.'

'You wear lavender water all the time,' I replied. 'It is refreshing and light.'

'Your perfume is more subtle,' she said, returning the compliment. 'But still light and flowery. I dislike heavy perfumes.'

'Yes, so do I. I always find they give me a headache.'

'I wonder what they are covering up.'

We laughed together. Since our talk we had begun to feel at ease together. We were not exactly friends, but we might be one day.

Charles came down on the Friday evening, bringing Sir Frederick Harris and Lady Harris with him. Sir Frederick was also attached to the War Office, and his wife was a rather plump, friendly woman. She chattered away non-stop all evening, but there was nothing to dislike about her, and when I discovered her interest in gardens, I was able to show her my designs.

Charles was very loving towards me that night when we were alone.

'I am glad you like Lady Harris,' he said, his arms about me as we lay side by side in bed. 'I think her husband and I will be doing business in the future.'

'What about your business arrangement with Lord Watson?'

162

'I believe I shall drop that, Julia. It has turned out rather less interesting than I thought.'

'So I shan't have to see too much of Lady Watson?'

'No.' He laughed ruefully. 'I believe we shall be seeing less of the Watsons in future.'

'I shan't mind that.' I raised myself on one elbow to look at him. 'Is something the matter?'

'Oh – nothing,' he said. He smiled at me and pulled me down to him once more. 'You seem quite content, darling?'

'Yes, I am. I have enjoyed being here, Charles – except that I've missed you.'

His lips moved against my hair, his arms holding me close. 'You will come back with me this time, Julia? The apartment seemed empty without you.'

'Of course I shall.'

I felt warmed by his request. For a while it had seemed that he was withdrawing from me, but now he was my loving husband once more.

It was our first party at Rondebush. Lady Hamilton had insisted on giving up her place at the head of the table to me.

'This is your party, Julia. Yours and Charles's. It is only right that you should be the hostess this evening.'

'But this is your home, Mary.'

'And yours. Please do not make a fuss, Julia. It is time I stepped aside and allowed you and Charles to play larger roles in running this house as well as the estate.'

I had felt a little doubtful about playing the hostess at Mary's table, but the guests did not appear to notice anything strange and it was quite a merry party.

After dinner, Mary and I took the other ladies into the drawing room while the gentlemen stayed behind to talk business, drink their port and smoke. I spent some time talking to Lady Harris and Sarah, then excused myself for a few minutes.

Mary was pouring tea when I left, Lady Watson was at the window, Sarah and Lady Harris sat together on the sofa. Two other ladies excused themselves at the same time.

I spent a few minutes in my room tidying myself and visiting

163

the bathroom, then went out into the upper hall, which led to the main stairway. The lights were on in the hall below, but for some reason the landing was in darkness.

Charles had sometimes complained that the new electric lighting at Rondebush was unreliable, and there was usually an oil lamp burning on the landing just in case the supply failed. This evening the oil lamp was not lit. However, the light from the lower hall was sufficient to show me the way to the top of the stairs.

I paused there for a moment, then, hearing a slight sound behind me, I was about to swing round just as something struck me in the back. The next moment I had pitched forward and was tumbling down the stairs, striking my head against the heavily carved banister rail on the way down.

'Julia! Oh, my God! Julia!' The sound of Charles's desperate voice was the first thing I heard as I returned to consciousness.

'If she is badly hurt . . .'

'She has banged her head,' Mary said sharply. 'Please do not make a scene, Charles. She is coming round . . .'

'Julia.' Charles was on his knees beside me, his face white with shock and fear. 'What happened, my darling? Did you turn dizzy?'

'Are you in pain?' Mary asked. 'Can you see me? Who am I?'

'I fell . . .' My head hurt where I had banged it and I was feeling sick and shaken. Something warned me to be careful. What had happened just before I fell? I could not quite remember. 'Mary – what happened? Did I faint?'

I tried to sit up. Charles put his arm around me, supporting my head. I leaned against his shoulder gratefully.

'I feel terrible,' I said. 'Will you help me, Charles? I need to lie down.'

I could see several anxious faces staring at me – one that I thought seemed more slyly amused than anxious. Why did *she* dislike me? Lady Harris, Sarah, and several of the gentlemen made murmurs of concern as Charles carefully lifted me in his arms.

'I'll carry you upstairs, darling,' he said. 'We've already sent for the doctor. Don't worry, Julia. I'm sure everything will be all right. As long as you weren't too badly hurt nothing else matters.'

'My baby?' I stared at him as my mind began to function once more. 'Will the baby be harmed?'

Charles did not answer immediately. Instead, he gathered me up in his arms and carried me upstairs. Then he deposited me gently on the bed and sat beside me, taking my hand in his.

'I was terrified when I heard you scream, Julia. What happened, my darling? Was it another fainting spell?'

'No, Charles . . .' I stared at him in horror as I remembered what I had felt moments before my fall. 'I think . . . I felt someone push me in the back.'

'Oh, my God!' Charles was ashen. 'Did you see – do you know who did this, Julia?'

I shook my head. 'The light was off on the landing. I could see where I was going, but when I looked round . . . it was too dark to see more than a vague shape. I cannot be sure, but I think it was a woman.'

'Then it was a deliberate attempt to harm you!' Charles looked angry. 'Mother!'

'Oh no, Charles. She was with our guests. She wouldn't have left them while I was out of the room – that would have been rude.'

'Then who – who else would do such a thing?'

'I don't know.' I frowned. 'There was something else, but I am not sure. Something is niggling me at the back of my mind.'

'What do you think you saw or heard?'

'I don't know, Charles.' I shook my head as the tears gathered in my eyes. 'The baby—'

'You mustn't upset yourself,' Charles said. 'Perhaps nothing will happen. The bang to your head broke your fall. It stopped you tumbling all the way to the bottom.' He bent to kiss my forehead. 'My poor little love. I am so sorry this happened to you.'

'It wasn't your fault.'

'No. I was on the point of bringing the others through to

165

the drawing room when you screamed. But someone pushed you – if you are sure it wasn't just a dizzy spell?'

'No, I wasn't faint. And I did feel something strike me in the back, Charles. I have not imagined it.' I frowned as I thought of something. 'Miss Henderson went to her room after dinner complaining of a headache. I think she blames me for her dismissal. Do you think she might have done it?'

'She sounds the most likely candidate to me,' he said and looked angry. 'I cannot think any of our guests would do such a senseless thing. Well, she leaves this house tomorrow!'

'It may not have been her, but she does resent me.'

'Then I shall make sure she is never in a position to harm you again. Do not look so upset, Julia. I shall not tolerate her another day. You might have been killed in that fall.'

He looked so upset that I smiled and squeezed his hand. 'Well, I have a nasty headache, but nothing else hurts – so perhaps we were fortunate.'

A knock at the door prevented Charles from replying, and the next moment a man of perhaps fifty years entered. He was stout, greying at the temples and looked like a kind-hearted man.

'Doctor James!' Charles stood up. 'Thank you for coming so promptly. My wife had a fall and she is with child.'

'So Lady Hamilton informed me. Has there been any bleeding – any abdominal pain?'

'No,' I said. 'No pain. I do not think I am bleeding.'

'I shall examine you. If you will be so good as to leave us for a few minutes, Captain Hamilton?'

'Oh – Yes, of course. I'll be in my room, Julia.'

After a brief examination, Doctor James confirmed that he could find no broken bones and there was no sign of bleeding or any damage to my head, other than a bruise and a tender spot.

'We cannot be certain that a miscarriage will not occur,' he told me afterwards. 'Some ladies are prone to them at the early stages. However, I believe that you have escaped serious harm to yourself and your child. I would recommend that you rest in bed for at least two days. If nothing happens by then you may safely assume that it will not. But you must be very careful not to repeat the fall. Stay away from stairs if you are feeling faint, Mrs Hamilton.'

'Yes, I shall. Thank you for coming out to see me at this hour.'

'Call me at any time if you need me,' he said and smiled. 'I shall tell Captain Hamilton he can come back now.'

Charles came to sit with me after a whispered conversation with the doctor.

'He has given me something to help you sleep,' Charles said. 'It will ease your poor head, Julia.' He smiled and bent to kiss the tender spot on my forehead. 'It seems that we may have been lucky this time.'

'I was so frightened,' I confessed. 'I don't want to lose the baby.'

'We can always have another child,' he said and pressed my hand to his lips. 'But I could not bear to lose you, Julia. Without you, I should have no reason to live.'

'Oh, Charles,' I scolded. 'Please don't say such things. I do not want to lose you either.'

'But you are young and full of life,' he said. 'You could learn to be happy again. I am so selfish, Julia. I could not have faced these past months without you.'

'I think I should like to try and sleep now.'

'Yes, of course. I shall leave you to rest. Would you like one of the powders Doctor James left for you?'

'No, thank you. I think I should just like to lie here in the dark and rest.'

Charles kissed me gently on the mouth. 'Sleep peacefully, Julia. I must go down and reassure everyone that you are all right. I shall not disturb you when I come up, but I shall be next door if you need me.'

'Yes, Charles. I know.'

When he had gone, I closed my eyes and let myself drift into a kind of half-sleep. Someone had tried to push me. I had not imagined it. Was it Miss Henderson?

I had noticed something before my fall, but what was it? For the moment it eluded me.

Eleven

'How are you this morning?' Mary looked anxious. She had brought some magazines and a book of poetry. 'I thought you might want something to read?'

'Yes, thank you. You could pass me my writing case, if you would.' I was sitting propped up against a pile of pillows Alice had arranged for me earlier.

'More letters, Julia?' Mary smiled indulgently.

'I have several friends, and Mama will be anxious for news. Charles telephoned her this morning, but she will want to hear from me just to be sure I am not hurt.'

'Charles told me you thought someone pushed you. It was not Miss Henderson. Charles insisted she leave the house at once, but I told him he must give her a day or so to make her arrangements. I questioned her about this myself. She denied it, and I should have known if she was lying.'

'I am sure something did hit me in the back.'

'We discovered a large Chinese vase had toppled over at the head of the stairs. Do you think you might have knocked against it in the dark? It is rather heavy and could have caused you to lose your balance if it had fallen on you.'

'I do not recall knocking against the vase. I felt something in the small of my back, and I have remembered something else, Mary. I smelled something just before I was pushed – a heavy perfume.'

'Perfume? Then it was a woman.' She frowned. 'There were three of our guests absent when you fell . . . unless one of the servants—'

'Why should one of them try to harm me?'

'I cannot think why anyone should want to do such a thing, Julia. I believe that somehow the vase must have toppled over and knocked you forward. I think you must accept that it was an accident.'

Why was she trying to make me believe my fall had been caused by a vase? I was sure it could not have been. Just as I was sure Mary herself could not have been responsible.

It was possible that Miss Henderson had pushed me, and that Mary was covering up for her. Yet why should she?

I did not know why Charles's mother was lying to me, but somehow I knew that she was. What I could not guess was why . . .

'Well, I shall leave you to rest,' Mary said. 'I must apologise for what happened, Julia. It should not have done, and I promise you that I will do my best to see that no further accidents happen to you in this house.'

After she had gone, I read for a while and wrote some letters – one of them a reply to Brent's letter, and then I slept. When I woke again Alice had brought me a tray with a light lunch of soup and toast. She handed me a small sealed envelope.

'This was under the sitting room door, madam. I do not know when it was put there. I cannot remember seeing it when I brought your breakfast tray.'

'Thank you, Alice. I'm afraid I've made a lot of extra work for you.'

'Oh, I don't mind that, madam. I'm just sorry you had a nasty fall. And so is the rest of the staff. What we can't understand is why all the lights were out on the landing. They were all on a few minutes earlier, madam.'

'Yes, I know, Alice. I thought something must have gone wrong with the supply.'

'Someone had switched them off,' Alice said. 'I can't think why. They are always left on, as you know, madam.'

'I know that is usually the case,' I said. It was an unfortunate mistake.'

She gave me an odd look before she went out

I ate my lunch before opening the envelope. A single sentence was written on the sheet of paper inside.

Meet me in the library at three if you want to know the truth.

There was no signature, no indication of who had written the note, and yet I was sure it had come from Miss Henderson. She knew Charles was blaming her, and she wanted to tell me her side of the story.

I had been advised to stay in bed for a couple of days, but apart from some tenderness at my temple I was feeling perfectly well. However, if I told Mary or Charles, I knew they would insist that I stayed in bed while they went in my stead and demanded an explanation. Someone *had* pushed me, and if I wanted to discover the truth for myself I must go to the library at three.

Charles spent half an hour with me after lunch, then said he had business to do for his father on the estate.

'Forgive me for leaving you now, Julia, but I shall stay with you here for the whole of this next week. I have telephoned my secretary and cancelled all my meetings for the next few days.'

'You shouldn't have done that, darling.'

'I have no intention of leaving until you are well enough to come with me.' He looked at me anxiously. 'You will be all right here. I shall not be gone long.'

'Don't fuss, Charles. I am perfectly well.'

After Charles had gone I dressed in a simple grey skirt and a white blouse, leaving my hair loosely tied back with a ribbon. My head still felt a little sore but I experienced no dizziness as I left my rooms and made my way to the library just before three o'clock.

The house seemed quiet and empty, and I thought our weekend guests must have departed earlier. My accident would have spoiled the weekend for them.

Miss Henderson was sitting at the table in front of the window at the far end of the library, her chair set so that it was slightly turned away from me. The windows were wide open, and the sun was streaming in at this hour of the afternoon. Miss Henderson seemed intent on what she was doing, one arm resting on the table in front of her, the other hanging by her side. The way she was sitting seemed a little peculiar, but it was only as I drew nearer that I realised there was something very wrong with her.

170

'Miss Henderson?' I walked slowly towards her chair, my heart beginning to race wildly. Surely she couldn't be . . . ? Her eyes were open when I looked at her, staring at me but not seeing me, her face set in a contortion of surprise. She would never see anything again, because she was dead. 'Oh no! No . . .'

What had happened here? I could feel the scream building inside me, but I forced it back. This was terrible, shocking, but I must not give way to hysteria. I must think calmly about the situation. All kinds of ideas and possibilities came to mind, my imagination running wildly as I tried to assess what had happened to her.

I could see that Miss Henderson had been drinking what looked like a glass of sherry. In front of her was a sheet of notepaper on which had been scrawled the letter *M*. Nothing more . . . just the letter and then a blot across the page as though her hand had slipped.

Had she been writing her confession before taking her own life? From the expression of surprise and horror on her face I thought she must have died sooner than she had expected. Her lips had a strange purplish colour – had she taken some form of poison in her drink? Perhaps she had expected the effects of the poison to be less swift, giving her time to write her message. Yet why had she asked me to meet her if she intended to take her own life?

I picked up the sheet of paper and studied it, then compared it to the one I had placed in the pocket of my skirt. It was all too much to take in. I had come expecting to have my questions answered, and discovered a tragedy.

'You poor, poor woman,' I said, then crossed to the fireplace to pull the bell-rope and summon a servant before sitting down rather hard in a wing chair by the hearth. I had suddenly begun to feel rather sick and unwell.

My summons brought one of the parlour maids. She screamed as I indicated Miss Henderson and ran out of the room shouting for help. Within minutes the butler, three more maids and then Lord Hamilton's manservant arrived. He took one look at Miss Henderson's face before coming to me.

'You should be in your room, madam. Will you allow me to assist you?'

'I can manage, thank you. You must inform Lady Hamilton, and the doctor should be called.'

'You may safely leave everything to us, madam. Please do not stay here and distress yourself further.'

'What on earth was all the screaming about?' Lady Hamilton asked as she came in. 'Julia! You should be . . . good grief! What has that foolish woman done now?'

'I received a note telling me to come here at three. I will show it to you, Mary.'

'I was saying that Mrs Hamilton ought to leave this to us, my lady.' His lordship's man gave her a meaningful look.

'Yes, Saunders, I shall take Julia upstairs. I rely on you to do what is necessary.' She looked at me, her expression one of concern as I rose. 'I imagine this was meant to upset you, Julia. Please allow me to look after you. I really am most distressed by this whole affair.'

'It is very distressing,' I replied. 'Yes, I should be glad if you would give me your arm. I do feel a little shaky.'

'Of course. Please lean on me, Julia. This is most unpleasant for us all, but particularly for you. It is a pity you did not tell me you had been given a note.'

'It was not signed,' I said as we walked from the room. 'May we go to your sitting room, Mary? I would prefer to have tea rather than go upstairs. I think we should talk.'

'If that is your preference.' Her eyes narrowed in thought. 'What is on your mind, Julia?'

'In private, I think.'

She nodded, saying nothing more until we were alone in her parlour. She indicated that I should sit in the most comfortable chair and took a seat opposite.

'What is worrying you, Julia?'

I handed her the note Alice had given me, and also the single sheet of paper I had discovered in the library.

'The note was pushed under my door, the piece of paper was on the table by Miss Henderson. I decided not to leave it there.'

172

She glanced at them both, then at me. 'Why have you given them to me?'

'The handwriting is not the same. I know there is not much to go on, but the M in my note is very different to this one – do you not think so? Even if she was under some distress when she penned it . . .' I faltered as Mary looked at me hard and then at the letters again. 'I think it is not the same and that may be why only the one letter was written, because the second person knew they could not copy her hand.'

'What are you implying, Julia?'

What was I implying? My mind was still reeling from the shock of finding Miss Henderson, and perhaps my instincts were at fault, but something was telling me that the companion had not meant to die like that. But the alternative was unthinkable . . . wasn't it? Surely I was letting my imagination run away with me! I tried to think sensibly, to put my thoughts into clear precise words that were not hysterical.

'I am not sure. I think Miss Henderson sent the note because she wanted to tell me something, but I do not believe she wrote the second, though it was meant to look that way.'

'You think someone else . . . then you believe it was murder and not suicide.'

'I think it might have been.' I gave a sob of distress. It was not until she put my suspicions into words that I fully realised where my imagination had been leading me, and the true horror of it. 'Oh, no, not murder! What am I saying? How could it have been? She must have taken her own life – mustn't she? She must have been trying to leave me a message.'

'In which case *she* was trying to say I had pushed you down the stairs in an attempt to kill you – that is the significance of the letter M, isn't it, Julia?'

As an alternative that was even more distressing!

'But I know you didn't push me, Mary. You would never have left our guests alone while I was absent – even if you had wanted to harm me, which we both know you don't.'

Mary smiled oddly. 'Thank you, Julia. I am touched by your faith in me. No, I did not push you nor do I want to harm you. If Miss Henderson did not take her own life, then we do have a rather unpleasant person in our midst. Someone who wants

173

you to lose your child and have the blame fall on me.' She nodded. 'Yes, I see the thinking behind this awful tragedy. It is very hard to believe, Julia. I can only think that Charles was right to blame Miss Henderson for your fall, and that she took her own life rather than face her own conscience.'

'But what about the handwriting?'

'Perhaps . . . under duress?'

'Yes, perhaps.'

Once again, I had the feeling that Mary was hiding something from me. I was about to ask her what she was afraid to tell me when Charles came striding in. Mary slipped both the notes I had given her into the pocket of her gown.

'Is it true that *that* woman has committed suicide, and that Julia found her?'

'I felt better and came down to look for a book,' I said quickly. 'It is a terrible tragedy, Charles. Poor Miss Henderson must have been in such turmoil. She had been dismissed and she was being blamed for my accident.'

'But you thought you were pushed.' His gaze narrowed.

'I was confused, Charles. I may have missed my footing in the dark.'

'I should like to know why there were no lights on the landing.' He looked angry.

'I was not really harmed,' I said. 'Just shaken and bruised. We should all be more concerned about poor Miss Henderson.'

'Miss Henderson be damned!' he said harshly. 'She pushed you, Julia. She was jealous because she thought you had taken her place with Mother. So she pushed you, and then took poison because she could not face what she had done.'

'Yes, I agree with Charles,' Mary said. 'I shall speak to the police myself and explain.'

'The police?' Charles said, looking startled. 'Is it necessary to involve them, Mother?'

'Yes, I should imagine the doctor will inform them of an unnatural death,' she replied. 'But it should be a mere formality. We were fortunate when Angela died of course. Doctor James had been expecting it. Otherwise we might have had a tiresome investigation then.'

'That was different,' Charles said. 'Angela's death was a

174

happy release. She was in pain – both physical and mental.'

'Yes, of course. I would never deny that – yet it was rather sudden.'

'What are you implying?' Charles stared at her hard.

'I am only saying that there was no need for an inquiry into Angela's death,' Lady Hamilton replied. 'Unfortunately, that will not be the case this time. It is all very unpleasant.'

Mother and son glared at each other. I could sense the tension and distrust between them.

'Could I possibly have a cup of tea?' I asked as the angry silence deepened. 'I really do feel in need of one.'

'Yes, of course,' Mary said. 'I shall ring at once.'

Mary was right about the police being involved. They spent several hours at the house, going through Miss Henderson's things and taking statements from all of us. However, at the end they seemed satisfied that Miss Henderson had taken her own life and, after an interview with Charles, went away. An inquest would be held, but it should be simply a formality.

Mary told me later that she had burned the notes I had given her.

'We do not want this family to be a source of gossip and speculation, do we, Julia?'

'No,' I said. 'It is best forgotten. Nothing can bring her back.'

'I was sure you would understand,' she said.

'Is there something you need to tell me, Mary?'

'No, Julia.' She smiled at me. 'At the moment there is nothing – nothing at all.'

Charles and I returned to London a few days later. He was still uneasy over what had happened and did not want me to go down to Rondebush without him again.

'I could have lost you, Julia,' he said. 'And I need you. I need you with me, darling.'

'I want to be with you,' I told him. 'And I feel so much better now. I would much rather that we were together.'

'Life can turn sour so quickly,' Charles said. 'Happiness is a fleeting thing, Julia. I want to take all I can while it is there – am I very selfish, darling, asking so much of you?'

'If you are then I am selfish, too, Charles.'

He smiled and kissed me. 'One day you will understand. Promise you will forgive me, Julia – if you discover how selfish I have been?'

'What do you mean, Charles?'

His eyes seemed to me to be full of sadness then, but he merely shook his head and began to talk of taking me to the theatre that evening.

It was one of Charles's moods. I had begun to accept them. They came more often these days, but were not meant to hurt me. Charles loved me, and whatever haunted him was something separate from our love of each other.

Mama came up to town the next week. She had been a little anxious for my sake, and wanted to reassure herself that I was not hurt or upset over my accident.

'Philip told me not to worry,' she said, her eyes going over me anxiously as we kissed. 'As usual, I see that he was right. You are blooming, Julia.'

'I feel so much better,' I replied. 'The morning sickness has passed and so has the dizziness. Mr Meacham says I am doing very well.'

'Then I can stop worrying.'

'I am very glad you came, Mama. You can help me choose the things I need for the baby. What colour should I have in the nursery?'

'Stick to pale lemon and white,' she advised. 'If you pick blue you are sure to have a girl.'

'I suppose everyone is praying for a boy so that we have an heir, but I would not mind a little girl.'

'Well, someone will get their way,' Mama said and we laughed. It did not really matter as it would be loved whatever and I could always have more children. 'I still have your christening gown. Would you like to have that, Julia?'

'Yes, please. I am beginning to feel excited now, Mama.'

'It is a very exciting time for you, darling. I am so glad you are happy.'

Mama and I spent the next few days shopping for the things I would need when my baby arrived. We bought everything from an exclusive store and arranged for it all to be sent down to Rondebush.

Mary wrote to me when it arrived. She was thinking of getting someone in to refurbish the nursery carpet and curtains and asked me what I would like.

I telephoned her straight away.

'I have decided to have everything in pale lemon or white, Mary.'

'Yes, I thought that might be the case when I saw what you had chosen so far.' She hesitated, then, 'When are you coming down again?'

'I'm not sure. Charles is extremely busy at the moment. Some days I hardly see him. He wants me to stay in London with him for the moment.'

'Yes, of course. However, if you are anxious about what happened, I am sure there will be no more incidents, Julia.'

'We can't be sure, Mary.'

'Oh, but—' She sounded a little odd. 'We shall both be watchful now, Julia.'

'I will try to persuade Charles to come down soon, but at the moment he has no time, and he won't hear of my going down alone.'

'I suppose he blames me for what happened?'

'No, of course not. I've told him it was not your fault.'

'I wish I knew for sure.' She sighed. 'Then you would like me to see to the nursery carpet for you? It was my little gift to you, but I thought I ought to ask first.'

'I should be very grateful, thank you. I am sending the first designs for my garden. I shall look forward to seeing it when we come down. Please give my love to Lord Hamilton.'

'Henry is a little better at the moment. I think he is determined to see his grandchild.'

'You will see me before then,' I promised.

'I do hope so, Julia,' she said and rang off.

I spoke to Charles about a visit to Rondebush that evening.

'I am not ready to go down yet,' he said. 'I have too much on my mind, Julia. And I would prefer it if you did not visit alone. If you feel that you need a few days in the country go and stay with your parents.'

'I would rather be here with you, Charles. When we go away it will be together.'

He nodded but his expression was serious. 'I am not always good company for you these days, Julia. You won't want to be in town in a few months' time. You should think of going to your mother then – just until I can get away.'

The tide of war had definitely begun to turn in the Allies' favour. It could only be a matter of months before the war was finally over.

'I am perfectly happy here for the moment,' I said. 'When I begin to feel uncomfortable I shall go to visit Mama for a while, but the baby will be born at Rondebush, Charles. I promised your father.'

'I should be free to come with you by then,' Charles said and smiled. 'Forget about going there until then, Julia. I am not prepared to risk another accident. Next time we might not be so lucky.'

It was impossible to persuade him. I wrote a regretful letter to Mary, but I knew she would not be fooled. Charles simply did not trust her.

It was at the end of September that Charles decided I should visit my mother.

'You have been looking tired,' he said when I protested that I wanted to stay with him. 'I shall take you down, Julia, and stay for a few days before I return to London. This dreadful influenza is affecting so many people. I think you would be safer with your parents in the country.'

'If you really want me to go?' I looked at him anxiously. He said that I looked tired when he had dark shadows beneath his eyes! He was sleeping in his own room more and more these days. 'But you will promise to take care of yourself, Charles?'

'Yes, of course. I am feeling much better, darling. I haven't had a really bad headache for two weeks.'

'Yet you don't look well.' I smiled and kissed him. 'I think you work too hard, Charles.'

'Nonsense – I just don't sleep as well as I might. And I would rest easier if I knew you were safe.'

'Well, if that is what you want? Mama has found several things I might like to have for the baby.'

'You will enjoy yourself there,' he said. 'By Christmas I hope to be released from my post here. Then we can go down to Rondebush together.'

'That would be lovely,' I said. 'I shall telephone and let Mama know we are coming this weekend.'

'Yes, you do that,' Charles said. He touched my cheek. 'We have been happy together these past months, haven't we, darling? In another few weeks it will be almost a year since we met – the best year of my life.'

'Yes, of course we've been happy,' I cried and caught his hand to kiss it. 'We shall always be happy. We have so much to look forward to, Charles.'

'Yes.' He smiled a little sadly. 'Of course we have.'

My parents welcomed us with their usual warmth. Although it was now October, the weather was fine and pleasant, enabling Charles and I to walk often during the few days he stayed with me. The night before he left, Charles made love to me with such tenderness that I wept in his arms. He kissed my tears away.

'Do not weep, Julia. I want you to be happy – always. Remember that, my darling. I love you and what I want most in the world is for you to be happy.'

'Let me come back with you, Charles?' I did not know why but something in his manner was frightening me.

'Not this time, darling. I have things to do, and I want to think of you here.' He smiled at me. 'I often think of you as I first saw you, Julia – with a rose in your hand. You seemed like a rose yourself. A rose in winter.'

'I love you, Charles. I love you so very much.'

'And I have loved you, my darling.'

'What do you mean – have you stopped loving me?'

'No, of course not. I was merely trying to tell you that I have loved you from the moment I saw you.'

I was reluctant to part from Charles the next morning, but he insisted he must leave and I must stay.

'I have something important to do, Julia.'

'Tell me – please?'

'I shall tell you next weekend when I come down.' He kissed me again. 'I hope and believe I shall have good news for you then.'

I knew better than to ask what he was planning. Had he decided to buy us a house of our own after all? I knew Charles was reluctant to return to Rondebush. He was angry because of what had happened there, and he blamed his mother.

'*That* woman pushed you down the stairs and then committed suicide in the library, knowing that you would hear about it – she probably hoped you would find her, being well aware that you like to go there. She was evil and vindictive, Julia – and Mother defended her.'

'Your mother did not believe Miss Henderson was guilty, Charles – at least, not at the beginning.'

'The whole thing was her fault,' he said. 'She dismissed the woman – a woman she had employed for years – and then look what happened. My mother is a careless, thoughtless woman, Julia. I must warn you again never to trust her too much.'

I had not argued with Charles then, and I did not argue now when he refused to allow me to return to London with him.

I was to regret that.

I had been for a walk as far as Mama's garden. There were several plants from which I wished to have cuttings, and I spent an hour or more with Papa's head gardener, discussing how best to transport them safely. As I returned to the house that afternoon, I saw a rather smart sports car drawn up outside and I felt a start of surprise. Surely that was Brent's car!

I quickened my pace, feeling pleased at the prospect of seeing him so unexpectedly. He was sitting with Mama in the parlour and the tea tray had just been brought in.

'Ah there you are, Julia. I was just telling Brent that you were staying with us.'

Brent had stood up as I entered. He came towards me with a smile, offering his hand.

'It is good to see you, Julia. I hadn't expected you to be here.'

'Charles wanted me to have a few weeks in the country. Everything is so frantic – with all the talks and conferences now that the war is over. But what are you doing here?'

'I have been discharged,' Brent said. 'My father has been unwell. I am going home the day after tomorrow. I am not sure when I shall get to come back, so I decided I would drive down to see Mrs Allington today.'

'Brent is staying with us overnight,' Mama said. 'He intended to go to a hotel, but I told him he was welcome to stay here.'

'Yes, of course,' I agreed. 'I do hope your father's illness is not serious, Brent?'

'It must have been serious enough or he would not have written to me. Hopefully, he is over the worst.'

'I am very sorry that he was ill.'

'Yes, so am I,' Brent said. 'We've argued often enough, but I am fond of him.' He smiled ruefully. 'How are you, Julia? I believe congratulations are in order?'

'Yes. I am having a child. We are both very pleased.'

'Of course. I hope everything goes well for you.'

'I am sure it will,' I replied. 'I am very well. Mama says I have even more energy now than I did when I was a child.'

'Julia is always doing something,' Mama said with an indulgent look at me. 'Did you know that she is learning to drive?'

'Yes. She mentioned it in one of her letters,' Brent said and grinned. 'Would you like a little spin in my car after tea, Julia?'

'Yes, very much,' I said. 'If you are prepared to trust me?'

'Why not?' His eyes crinkled at the corners as he gave me a huge smile. 'You took a chance on me after all.'

We laughed and the conversation turned to other things.

After tea, Brent led the way outside. He helped me into the driving seat of his car, explained that the brake was a little sharper than most, and then we were off.

We drove at a sedate pace around the grounds, then ventured out on to the roads as far as the village, Brent encouraging me to go a little quicker. It was beginning to get dark by the time we returned.

'You did very well, Julia,' he said. 'Would you like me to leave the car here for you to use?'

'But – don't you need it yourself?' I looked at him in surprise.

'I can get to Liverpool by train. My ship leaves from there and I'm not sure where I should leave the car. I would rather you had it, Julia. Otherwise it will stand in some garage until I come back – which might be months or years.'

'You do intend to come back then?'

'Yes.' He gave me an odd look. 'It may not be for a while, but I'll be back – like that bad penny.'

He was helping me down. I glanced up at him. 'You're not a bad penny, Brent. Thank you for letting me borrow your car. I have my own but it is at Rondebush.'

'Well, now you have another here.'

'You are a darling,' I said and impulsively kissed his cheek.

Brent caught me, pulling me close and kissing me on the lips. For a moment I was still, and then I found myself responding, my arms up around his neck, fingers tangling in his slightly too long hair. It was a deep, intense, passionate kiss, and when it ended we were both breathless and shaken.

'We shouldn't have done that,' I said at last.

'No, we shouldn't,' Brent agreed, but there was a gleam in his eyes.

'It must never happen again.'

'No, of course not – unless you want it to happen, Julia.'

'What do you mean?'

'You know what I mean. You wanted that as much as I did.' His eyes seemed to burn into me. 'There has always been something between us, Julia. Deny it if you will, but it is there – a fine thread holding us – despite what you feel for Charles.'

'Yes, there has always been something,' I admitted. 'But it can never come to anything, Brent. I love Charles, and I am carrying his child.'

'You love him, but are you *in love* with him?' Brent looked deep into my eyes. 'I think you fell for his reputation, Julia. He was a war hero, older, sophisticated . . . you fell for the image, not the man. He doesn't give you enough . . . something is missing, isn't it? You know it in your heart even—'

'Stop!' I placed my fingers to his lips. 'I won't hear this, Brent. I won't! We must go in and change or we shall be late for dinner.'

'You asked if I was coming back,' Brent said, and there was a harsh, wild note in his voice. 'I'm coming back for you, Julia. Married or not, one day you are going to need me, and when you do I'll be here.'

'No, Brent,' I whispered, my throat closing as I choked back the stupid tears. 'I love Charles. I shall always love him.'

And then I turned and ran into the house before he could stop me.

Brent entertained us all that evening at dinner. He told amusing tales about life in the RFC, making it seem as though it had all been one huge game. His stories made light of the suffering so many of the brave young men had faced, telling us only about all the practical jokes they had played on one another and people who had taken them into their homes.

'Shorty Mallen's dog always slept on his bed with him,' Brent said. 'So one day when he had a rather friendly young lady to stay with him, Shorty shut the dog in the shed because his young lady didn't like dogs. It howled all night – and every night Shorty's girlfriend came to stay – rather giving the game away.'

'What will he do with the dog if he gets married?' I asked.

Brent frowned. 'Shorty won't be getting married,' he said. 'One of the chaps tried to adopt the poor beast when Shorty didn't make it back, but it wouldn't stop howling. In the end we had to have it taken away.'

'Oh.' I said. 'How very sad. I am so sorry.'

Brent's eyes met mine across the table. 'It was just one of those things, Julia. Life goes on in the midst of death.'

A shiver went down my spine at that moment, but I merely nodded. I knew Brent would not have told me that part of the story if I hadn't asked, but he hadn't tried to hide it from me when I did. He must have faced death so many times these past months, losing people he loved and admired.

I thought about Brent as I lay in bed that night. It was wrong of him to have kissed me like that, and very wrong of me to have kissed him back. I could not understand why I had allowed it to happen.

I *was* in love with Charles. Of course I was. Brent's words had made me uneasy, but I would put them right out of my mind. He was going back to America and I would probably never see him again. Besides, my life was with Charles – and I wanted it that way!

Twelve

B rent left early the next morning. I took him to the station in his car. We stood on the platform in silence for a moment, and then he gave me an apologetic kiss on the cheek.

'I am sorry if I pushed you too far yesterday, Julia.'

'It doesn't matter. I *am* fond of you, Brent.'

'But you love Charles.' He nodded in acquiescence. 'I know, but I meant what I said – if you need me I'll be there.' He took a printed card from his waistcoat pocket. 'This is my address back home. Write to me if you want to.'

'Perhaps . . .' I slipped the card into my purse. 'I am not sure that would be fair to you, Brent. I promised to write while you were in the RFC – this might be the time to stop, for both our sakes.'

'I shall miss your letters,' he said. 'I shan't forget you, Julia.'

I watched him board the train and I felt a sharp ache somewhere around my heart. I didn't want to say goodbye to Brent, and yet I knew it was best this way.

'Take care,' I called as he poked his head through an open window. 'I hope your father is better.'

'He's a tough old bird, like me,' Brent said and grinned wickedly. 'You take care of yourself, Julia. I'll send a postcard sometimes.'

I waved until the train left the station, then returned to the car parked outside. For some reason I didn't understand I burst into tears. I felt lonely and miserable, and I wished I were in London with Charles.

I was getting very emotional over nothing! I scolded myself, blew my nose and wiped my eyes. All this fuss! Just because Brent had kissed me and made me feel . . . I shut out my thoughts quickly. Best not to analyse what I had felt for him in those brief moments.

The truth was that I was missing Charles. I had enjoyed the intimate side of our marriage, but we had not been together that way for a while now. Charles had been too busy or suffering from one of his wretched headaches. It was because I was feeling lonely and a little neglected that I had responded so passionately to Brent's kiss.

I felt better now that I had convinced myself of the reason for my feeling so low. I would telephone Charles that evening and tell him I was coming back to town at the weekend, if not before. This separation was not good for our marriage.

I parked the car outside the house. There was a bite in the air and the wind felt chilly, making me shiver as I got out of the car. I glanced at a vase of flowers on the table in the hall. They had begun to droop and needed attention. I picked the vase up, intending to take it to the little flower room where we always did our flowers and freshened the water.

Mama came out into the hall. 'Ah, there you are, darling,' she said. 'Would you leave the flowers for a moment please? I would like to talk to you.'

Her expression was serious, and something in her manner frightened me. She looked upset, almost nervous. What could be wrong? Setting the vase down, I followed her into her parlour. Papa was already there, and his face was so grave that I began to tremble.

'Papa – what is it?' I asked in a whisper. 'Is Phil in trouble again?'

'No, Julia. It isn't your brother. I am so very sorry, my darling. The call came while you were out – it is Charles.'

'Charles? Did he ring me?' Why was my father looking at me so oddly? 'Is something wrong with Charles?'

'Sit down, dearest,' Mama said in a gentle voice that frightened me to death. 'I am afraid the news is bad—'

'Charles is ill, isn't he? Those dreadful headaches . . .' I felt the ice begin to spread through me as I saw their expressions. They were devastated, afraid of telling me something they knew would distress me. 'Please, you must tell me! What has happened to Charles?'

'Mrs Watts found him in bed this morning,' Papa said. 'He didn't suffer, Julia. She said he looked peaceful – as though he had just gone to sleep.'

'What do—? Oh, no!' I stared at him in horror. What was he saying? He couldn't mean that Charles was dead? But he did! I could see it in his eyes. I sat down as my legs went weak. 'I don't understand. How . . . how did he die?'

'I received a letter from Charles this morning,' Papa said. 'He must have planned this very carefully, Julia. He enclosed a letter for you. Apparently he has known about this . . . trouble of his for months and kept it to himself.' Papa paused as I looked at him, wanting him to go on, though I had already begun to suspect the truth. 'There was a tiny fragment of shrapnel in Charles's brain. He was warned months ago that nothing could be done. It was in too sensitive an area and an operation would have damaged him too badly. It was just a matter of time.'

'Yes. Yes, I see.' I spoke calmly, though inside I was screaming a protest. This couldn't be happening. It couldn't! Charles wasn't dead. He was in London planning another surprise for me.

'Was there never any hope?'

'Charles kept going to see different doctors. He hoped that one of them would say an operation was feasible – he had his last consultation this week. He was finally turned down and warned that the fragment might have moved, that he could lose his sight at any time. He believed it might affect his personality, that he might be prone to sudden and violent mood swings, and of course the pain was bound to get much worse. So he decided that it would be best for everyone if he chose the easy way out. He took some pills . . .' Papa stopped speaking as he saw my look of denial. 'Perhaps it was best for Charles, Julia.'

'No!' I felt a surge of anger. 'He had no right to do this! Sending me here to you like a child while he—' I choked on the words that seemed to clog my throat with bitterness.

Jumping to my feet, I began to pace the room in agitation. How could Charles have kept this from me for so long? How long had he known? Why hadn't he told me there was something seriously wrong? I was his wife. He should have told me. I would never have left him to face that last consultation alone if I had known.

'Julia . . . my darling.'

I heard my mother's distress but I avoided her. I did not want to be held and comforted like a little girl who had fallen and cut her knee. My grief was sharp and deep, cutting me to the heart, but there was also anger.

Charles had petted and indulged me, but he had not confided in me. He had not shared his worries with me. He had constantly told me he needed and loved me, but he had not thought me adult enough to face the truth.

That hurt me so much. I wanted to shout and scream in my turmoil of pain and grief. I had given Charles my love and by this act he had cast it back in my face.

'He had no right to do this,' I said and looked at Papa. 'You know he didn't. I should have been there with him. I should have been told.'

'Yes, I agree,' Papa said. 'Charles did what he thought best, Julia, but he was wrong. He should have allowed you to share this. It would have been far better for both of you.'

'He wanted to spare you pain,' Mama said. 'Try to understand how he felt, my darling. I know it hurts you, but don't be angry, don't be bitter.'

I shook my head. I wanted to scream or shout, but I didn't.

'Charles must be buried at Rondebush,' I said, my chin going up. I was amazed at how clearly I was seeing things. The pain and grief were being controlled by a strength I had not realised was there. 'His parents will want that. I am not sure if he will have written to them.'

Even as I spoke the telephone had begun to ring in the hall.

'I will answer that,' Mama said and went out at once.

'Would you like me to go up to London?' Papa asked. 'I could arrange all this for you, Julia – if you would like me to?'

He was asking, not telling, knowing that my pride as well as my heart had been hurt. I was not a child and I could make my own decisions, but Papa would help me if I needed him.

'Yes, please,' I said. 'You will know what must be done there. I shall go down to Charles's home. Mary will need help in arranging that side of things. Lord Hamilton may not be able to stand the shock. He is a very frail and dear man. I want to be with him now.'

Papa came towards me. He looked at me for a moment, then leaned forward to kiss my forehead.

'You will cry when the shock wears off,' he said. 'But I know you will cope, Julia. Would you like your mother to come down with you? I can join you both at Rondebush when everything is settled.'

'Yes, that might be best.' I smiled at him, because he understood. 'Shock isn't good for the baby. Yes, I should like Mama to be with me – just in case.'

'That was Lady Hamilton,' Mama said as she came back into the room a moment later. 'It seems Charles had written to her, too. I told her you would probably be down soon. Was that all right?'

'Yes. I should like to go tomorrow – if that is possible?'

My father explained what had been agreed between us. He would leave for London that afternoon on the train and see to all the formalities, and he suggested that our chauffeur should drive Mama and I to Rondebush the next day.

'I shall join you both in a few days, Jenny. Julia will be glad of our company until after this is all over.' His look of love seemed to embrace me. 'Why don't you take Charles's letter up to your room, my dear? Perhaps it will help you to understand things more clearly.'

'Thank you.' I took it from him, slipping it into my skirt pocket. 'I'll read it later. I must speak to someone about those cuttings from Mama's garden. I shall want to take them with us tomorrow.'

I saw Mama's expression of alarm, but Papa shook his head and she let me go. She wanted to comfort me as if I was her little girl, but Papa knew that I must be allowed to find my own way through the maze of pain and grief that now plagued my mind.

I felt curiously calm as I left the house in search of the gardener who had been helping me. Later, I would read Charles's letter, but for the moment I needed to walk. The anger was building inside me again. If I did nothing I should go mad!

Charles had had no right to hide his illness from me! I was his wife. He claimed to love and need me. He should have trusted me. By taking his own life in this way he had robbed us both of so much.

It was the action of a coward.

Anger sustained me throughout the day. I kept going over the things Charles had said to me, searching for clues. I was so stupid! I should have guessed long ago that something was seriously wrong.

I had seen for myself what could happen in a similar case. The young pilot in the hospital had died because a tiny piece of metal in his brain had moved suddenly and without warning.

Was that what Charles had feared? He had been warned that the symptoms might be severe and he had been unable to face them. But he would not have had to face them alone. Our love would have seen us through, however bad it had become.

'Oh, Charles, Charles . . . Why didn't you tell me? Why didn't you let me share your fears?'

He had not wanted me to suffer with him. He had petted me, spoiled me, and treated me like a fragile flower that might wilt in a storm. Why had he seen me as being so vulnerable? I was not a foolish child, nor yet a weak and clinging vine. Yes, it would have hurt me dreadfully to know that my husband could die at any time, but I would have been strong for him.

Anger turned eventually to deep, despairing grief as Papa had known it would. The tears came that night as I read Charles's letter before I went to bed:

> Forgive me, my darling,
>
> I know you will be angry. You do not deserve that I should do this to you, but I cannot bear the pain any longer – the pain of what I have done to you. I should not have married you, Julia. I knew that there might be a physical cause for my headaches when I returned from seeing Rosendale last Christmas. He warned me that if the tests proved positive I might have only a few months to live – though it could have been longer – and that the headaches would become gradually worse.

I should have told you then. I ought to have released you from your promise to marry me, but I snatched greedily at the chance of happiness. You were so strong and full of life, so lovely. I wanted you so much, Julia. But I should have let you choose.

What I did was utterly selfish. I have ruined your chance of finding happiness with someone else – or perhaps not? Perhaps you will find someone nearer your own age, someone who will give you the kind of life you deserve. I pray that you will be happy again one day.

I love you, Julia. My mother was right about me. I am weak and I am selfish. Yet you meant so much to me, gave me so much happiness. Please forgive me, my darling. Remember me kindly.

Your loving Charles.

'Oh, Charles,' I wept as I laid his letter aside. 'Oh, Charles. Why could you not have told me this before? Why did you only let me into your thoughts when it was too late?'

I lay sleepless for a long, long time that night. I felt so hopeless, so empty. How could Charles have thrown away what we had? Even if our time together was destined to be short, we could have spent it together.

He had sent me away, because he had decided to end it if the final consultation proved useless. He had sent me to my mother where I would be safe and then he had died alone.

It hurt. It hurt me so much, to think of him writing his letters, taking the pills and going to bed in that empty apartment.

'Charles! How could you? How could you do this?' I cried in agony, burying my face in the pillow as the storm of weeping wracked my body.

I felt betrayed, abandoned. Marriage was the joining together of two hearts and minds as well as bodies. This act of Charles's was independent, almost as if I did not exist. I was merely another possession, to be disposed of at will – a much prized, much loved possession, but no more.

I felt that my whole marriage had been a sham. Charles had

known from the beginning that we might have only a short time together.

He should have told me!

'Charles should have told you.' Mary said after she had kissed me and made us welcome in her parlour. My mother had been taken upstairs to refresh herself and we were alone. 'I do not mind that he chose not to confide in me – perhaps I have deserved that – but you had a right to know.'

'I would rather have known,' I replied. 'It would have been painful, but I believe I would still have married him. We had some happy times together, and now I can understand why he was moody for the later part of our marriage.'

'Charles was always moody.' She bit her lip. 'Forgive me, Julia, but I cannot change the habit of a lifetime. Charles was my son, and despite the arguments, I cared about him, though it might have appeared otherwise at times. He could make me so angry! When I first visited the hospital, I was furious with him for such reckless bravery that I may have said things I now regret. What I cannot pretend is that he had no faults. Of late I had thought him stronger, but the weakness was always there. Charles took the easy way out.'

I could not defend him when her words echoed my thoughts.

'I feel betrayed.'

'Charles betrayed himself, Julia. He had everything to live for. He should have fought to the bitter end, even if it was painful and hard to bear.'

'He was ill, Mary. His judgement may not have been as clear as it might. I am angry too, but I shall try to understand why he acted as he did.'

She nodded, her eyes thoughtful. 'That is what I would expect you to say, Julia. You are a very brave young woman.'

'I have only done what is right. Charles belongs here.'

'Yes, of course. Exactly.' She hesitated, then, 'What will you do when the funeral is over, Julia? I know you have not yet had sufficient time to think, but I wondered if you would prefer to live with your parents? You will not want to live in London?'

'No. I shall close the apartment. I could not bear to go back there. I shall arrange for everything to be sent on here.'

'Here, Julia?' She arched her brows. 'I know you told Henry the child would be born here, but we would both understand if you changed your mind.'

'I have no intention of changing my mind,' I replied. 'Charles knew I wanted to live here. If you are prepared to have me, I shall make this my home.'

'Nothing would please Henry more,' Mary said. 'And I shall be very happy to have you here, Julia – for as long as you wish.'

'I see no reason why I should ever want to leave,' I said. 'I shall devote myself to my child – and to my garden, of course.'

'Are you sure you want to stay on here?' Mama asked the afternoon she and Papa were due to return home.

The funeral had taken place two days earlier. I had not wept as I stood in church, or when I watched the coffin lowered into the ground. I felt empty. Calm and composed, but emotionless. Charles had gone and I felt that he had abandoned me. I could not yet find it in my heart to forgive him.

'Yes, I am sure,' I said.

'You would be welcome to come with us, darling. Why not stay with me until after the baby is born and then decide what you want to do?'

'I know I can come to you whenever I want,' I said and put my arms around my mother, laying my head against her shoulder, and inhaling her soft perfume. 'But this is my child's home. I promised Lord Hamilton that his grandchild would be born here. Besides, I want to live here with Charles's parents. They need me, Mama. Henry is so frail – and Mary is lonely. She never says it, but I know she feels it deep down inside. You have Papa and the boys and I shall visit you sometimes. You can come here, too. Next spring my garden will be beginning to take shape. You must come and stay.'

'I shall come for the birth – if you want me, Julia?'

'Of course I do!' I smiled at her. 'Don't look so worried. I can manage. I shall be fine, Mama.'

'That's what Philip says.' She smiled ruefully. 'Forgive me for fussing, my dearest. I know you are not a child, but—'

'I shall always be your little girl?' I teased her in the old way.

'I know that, Mama, and I love you for it, but I do need to do this. Can you understand how I feel? I have to learn to live without Charles. I know I can come home if I need to, but I want to try – I want to be myself.'

'Yes, Julia,' she said. 'I do understand your need to live your own life. After Gérard died I wanted to die too, but I was carrying you. I had to live for you, and then Philip found me. It was a while before I would let myself love again, but in the end I did. I pray that you will find happiness one day.'

'I shall never marry again.'

'Oh, Julia,' Mama said and looked sad. 'Don't shut yourself off from life. You are so hurt now, but the pain will heal in time. You will see things differently.'

'No, Mama. I loved Charles. I thought he needed me, but he shut me out. I don't want anyone to do that to me again.'

She touched my cheek but said no more on the subject.

'I love you, Mama.'

'I love you, Julia, and so did Charles. He was wrong but he was only trying to protect you.'

'Yes, I know.'

I knew, but it did not make the pain any easier to bear.

We parted then, and I went up to my own room. I sat down and wrote a long letter to Brent. I told him about Charles – how he had known he was dying, and that he had kept the truth from me. I also wrote that this was my last letter. 'I intend to devote my life to my child and my garden. Please do not attempt to see me again, Brent. I have nothing to give you.'

Then I sealed the envelope and took it downstairs to the hall.

Christmas Day was very much like any other. I spent the morning walking, tending the pots of herbs in my garden, and looking for signs of life in the cuttings we had transplanted from Mama's garden. Mary and I had a light lunch together, and in the afternoon I spent half an hour reading to Henry.

The war was over and our country was beginning the long slow business of healing itself. I suppose this quiet time was a healing process for us all, though I was still hurting too much to allow myself such thoughts.

194

We had exchanged gifts earlier, though there was no tree in the drawing room. Nor had we given a large party for our friends.

'I think it best to wait for a while, Julia,' Mary had said a few weeks before Christmas. Unless you would like to invite some of your particular friends?'

'We shall wait until the baby is born,' I said. 'But I would like to ask Sarah and her husband for lunch on Boxing Day. I know they have their own arrangements for Christmas lunch.'

'Of course, Julia,' she said, nodding approvingly. 'Sarah is welcome to come whenever she wishes. It was someone else I thought it wiser not to invite just yet.'

'Are you speaking of Lady Watson?'

Mary's gaze narrowed. 'I have heard that she has been behaving oddly,' she said. 'They say she drinks too much these days.'

'I was not aware of that . . .' I lifted my eyes to meet hers. 'How long has this been going on?'

'Since the middle of October, I understand.'

'Oh . . . I see.'

'Yes, I thought you might,' Mary replied. 'Now, Julia – what shall I buy for your parents as a Christmas gift? And what would you like?'

'Some more roses for my garden – or a supply of note-paper.'

She laughed. 'You do have rather a lot of letters. I noticed there was another card from America this morning. A view of San Francisco, this time. Do you suppose he actually visits all these places?'

Brent's cards had started to arrive at the end of October. He never wrote more than my name, address and a brief line on them. His message was usually 'thinking of you' or simply 'love Brent'.

I had done my best to ignore them at first, but they continued to come every few days, each one different. It was almost as if Brent were giving me a guided tour of America through postcards.

I did not send him a Christmas card, nor did I write. I had not changed my mind. There was no point. Brent would be wasting his time if he continued to hope. I had been married once, I had no wish to marry again.

'The boxes arrived this morning,' Mary said that cold January day. 'Would you like me to unpack them for you? I think these must be Charles's personal bits and pieces. Mrs Watts said she would send them last of all.'

'I think I would like to do them myself later – if they could be taken up to his room?'

'Yes, of course.' Mary never argued or tried to dictate. 'As long as you don't tire yourself, Julia.'

I was becoming extremely large and very uncomfortable. Often now my back ached and I felt tired most of the time. It was so unlike me that it was a little worrying.

'Perhaps you could help me?' I suggested. 'I would rather not leave it to the servants, and it might be easier if we did it together.'

'Yes, I should imagine it might. I can do most of the unpacking and you can tell me what you want done with everything.'

'The clothes can be given away,' I said. 'I imagine there must be a charity that would welcome them?'

'Yes, I think that is a sensible idea,' she agreed. 'It is the more durable things you might like to keep – books, pictures . . .'

'Yes. Charles painted some nice pictures.'

Mary nodded but made no comment. The boxes were carried upstairs and we began the task of unpacking them. There were brushes and combs backed with silver and tortoiseshell, articles of jewellery, silver cigarette and card cases, and a leather writing set for a desk, besides various other items of a similar nature.

'All these can stay in his room,' I said to Mary. 'Put them in the top drawer of his tallboy. If I have a son he might like to have them one day.'

'Yes, of course,' Mary agreed. 'Even a daughter might want something of her father's.'

'Will you mind if it is a girl?' I asked. 'I know you wanted the family to go on.'

'The family goes on while you and the child live,' Mary said.

'I am proud of belonging to this family, Julia, but I have come to love you, my dear.'

Tears stung my eyes. I turned away so that she should not see.

'Oh, this is rather lovely,' Mary said. 'Idealistic, of course, but that was Charles.'

I turned to look at what she had discovered. It was a little oil painting of a girl in a yellow dress holding a white rose in her hand.

'Charles said he wanted to paint me. He did some sketches, but he never showed me this.' I took it from her. The girl in the picture looked sweet and innocent. It was me and yet it was not. I had never been as angelic as that girl. 'Oh, Mary—'

Suddenly I was crying, sobbing as if my heart would break. Charles had painted me as I was to him – as he had wanted to keep me for all time.

'Julia, my dear.' Mary put her arms about me, rocking me as I sobbed out my grief and pain. 'Cry it out of you. You've been such a good brave girl, but it had to come out, my dear. It had to come out.'

'It was seeing what he had done . . . how he thought of me.'

'Actually, it is rather good,' Mary said. 'I think I shall have it framed and hung in the gallery – if you don't mind?'

I blew my nose hard on the large handkerchief she had given me, which was one of Charles's. 'I think that would amuse him,' I said. 'He used to find a lot of things funny when we first knew one another. We laughed together often.'

'You should remember that, Julia,' Mary said. 'Remember the good things. I have remembered the times when he was small and used to come to me for a cuddle – before Billy's accident.'

'Charles changed . . . became withdrawn.'

'He was ill,' Mary said. 'I did not make allowances, but I should have done. *I* should have done.'

I knew she was not speaking only of the last few months. Mary had at last forgiven Charles for not being able to save his brother from drowning in the millpond.

Thirteen

It was early in February, two weeks before the baby was due. I had grown so large that I found it difficult to walk, but I refused to lie around doing nothing and I made a point of visiting my garden every day, though I could not bend down to tend my herb pots.

I came in to find yet another card from Brent lying with other letters on the hall table. I was glancing through them and about to open one from Marina when the first pain struck. The letters fell from my fingers as I gave a startled cry. Surely the baby wasn't coming? It was too soon!

'Julia?' Mary came out into the hall. 'What is the matter? Is it the baby? You are in pain, aren't you? I'll have the nurse called.'

'It is too soon,' I said, looking at her anxiously. 'What have I done, Mary? You told me to rest more, but I couldn't.'

'Don't blame yourself,' Mary said. 'With all you've had to put up with it's a wonder you managed to get this far. There is no need to panic, Julia. Fortunately, Mr Meacham sent his nurse in plenty of time. She will look after you, and I shall send for Doctor James.'

I could not answer her because another terrifying pain was ripping through me. I gasped and Mary put her arm about my waist, helping me up the stairs.

One of the maids saw us, and at a nod from Mary went flying ahead of us to warn the nurse to be ready.

'It is just as well I was here,' Nurse Joan said as she saw us. 'Mr Meacham thought you might give birth early. There's nothing to worry about, Mrs Hamilton. Some ladies do tend to carry less than their full term. Quite often that makes it easier on them. Nature is a wonderful thing.'

198

I could only gasp as the pain struck again. It was far worse and far more urgent than I had expected.

'I should advise you to scream if you feel like it,' Mary said. 'This is one of those times when it is best not to be too brave, Julia. Scream as much as you like. No one will mind.'

I bit my lip. I was determined not to let the pain beat me.

It was less than an hour before I began to scream like a wild thing. The pain was truly unbearable. I wondered desperately how long I would have to endure such agony, and then, just as Doctor James arrived, my son was born. A few seconds later his sister joined him.

'Good, good,' the doctor said beaming at me. 'That's what I like to see, Mrs Hamilton. No fuss and no nonsense. I wish all my patients gave birth as easily as you.'

'I am so glad you are pleased,' I murmured and then closed my eyes. If that was an easy birth I pitied all the other women!

I was so dreadfully tired. They were showing me my babies, telling me how beautiful they were, but I could hardly keep my eyes open.

'Well done, Julia,' Mary said. 'I've sent someone to tell Henry the good news, and I've telephoned your parents. They will be here as soon as they can.'

'She is very tired,' Nurse Joan said. 'Please – we should all leave Mrs Hamilton to rest. You can talk to her later, when she is feeling better.'

I was so very, very tired. I was drifting away . . . drifting into a deep sleep.

There was only a shaded lamp burning when I awoke with a start. I lay back for a moment, wondering what had woken me. Then I became aware of something – a strong smell of heavy perfume. The perfume I had smelt just before someone pushed me down the stairs.

I opened my eyes and saw her. She was standing at the foot of the bed staring at me. Her eyes had a peculiar, glazed look about them, and I thought she was obviously intoxicated.

'So, you are awake,' she said, her voice slurred and indistinct. 'I wanted you to wake up before I did it – I wanted you to know why.'

'Why you tried to kill me before?' I said warily. I glanced round the room looking for some means of calling for help. The door to the dressing room was slightly ajar. 'You poisoned poor Miss Henderson, didn't you? That was rather unnecessary, wasn't it?'

'She was going to tell you. The silly bitch saw me that night. She switched the lights on again before I could disappear.'

'Yes, I thought it might have been something like that.' I stared at her. 'But why do you want to kill me now? It is too late, isn't it?'

'Charles is dead,' she said, and there was a sob in her voice. 'I was always in love with him. He threw me over for Angela – even though I told him she was Paul Langan's lover, that it was still going on even after she married him. I had to watch her queening it over me, but I got rid of her. I taunted her about that horse and then . . .' She giggled foolishly. 'When she was lying in bed helpless I took a pillow and smothered her. I was going to arrange a little accident for that bastard I married, but Charles went off to the war and then he met you.'

I was fully awake now, but I felt so weak. She was obviously drunk or mad – perhaps both. She had been obsessed with Charles for years. I remembered him telling me she was becoming a bit of a nuisance.

'But that is all over,' I reminded her. 'You cannot gain anything from my death now. Charles is dead. He can't marry you even if he wanted to, but then, he never did, did he? That's what you couldn't stand, isn't it, Anne? You murdered Angela and arranged it so that he blamed his mother, but he still didn't want you.'

'Damn you!' She picked up a large cushion. 'I hate you! I've hated you since the moment I first saw you. Charles gave you everything that should have been mine. I can't have him, but why should you have all this? You've given Mary her heir, but you won't live to enjoy it.' She moved toward me, a purposeful gleam in her eyes. 'I killed Angela and got away with it—'

'But you won't murder Julia,' a voice said. The door to the dressing room was pushed wide open and Mary came into the bedroom, Nurse Joan just behind her. 'I heard every word you

200

said, madam. I've had my suspicions since you pushed Julia down the stairs, but I was not certain enough to accuse you. Now I shall speak to your husband.'

'You can't prove anything,' Anne Watson cried. 'I was just talking. I'm drunk. Everyone knows I drink too much. You couldn't make it stand up in court. They would laugh at you.'

'Your husband will not laugh, Lady Watson. I shall insist he takes you away – somewhere you will not be a danger to my daughter-in-law. Otherwise, I shall be forced to go to the police. It will cause a scandal, which I shall dislike, but I believe Lord Watson has a political career in mind?'

'Bitch!' Anne Watson threw the cushion to the floor. 'I could have killed her while she slept, but I wanted her to know.' Her eyes blazed suddenly. 'I had an abortion when I was eighteen. The child was Charles's. I wasn't ready to get married then and afterwards . . . afterwards, he shunned me.'

She burst into tears and fled from the room.

'Dear me,' said Nurse Joan, picking up the cushion. 'What a very disturbed lady she is.'

'I understand she is unable to have children,' Mary said. 'I suppose the news of your delightful twins pushed her over the edge, Julia. How are you feeling, now? Less tired I hope?'

'Oh, Mary . . .' I gave a slightly hysterical laugh. 'Apart from almost being murdered in my bed and a slight case of shock, I am feeling much better.'

'Surely not shock?' she said with a smile. 'You guessed it was her, of course – because of the perfume. I had thought . . .' She turned to Nurse Joan. 'Would you go down and ask Alice to bring us some tea please?'

I waited until the door closed behind the nurse. 'You thought Charles might have smothered Angela because he couldn't stand to see her in pain, so you bamboozled Doctor James into signing the certificate of natural death. Charles thought you had done it.'

Mary nodded, accepting that I had guessed the cause of the bitterness between them.

'Yes. God forgive me. I did think that at first. Charles was so angry when he went off to the war. I imagined he could not bear to live with what he had done, but then I began to realise he blamed me. I saw then that it must have been someone else, but it wasn't until the night you were pushed that I realised *she* must have wanted Angela dead, too.'

'Oh, Mary. I wish Charles had known the truth.'

'I think in his heart he did at the end, Julia. His letter seems to indicate that he no longer blamed me for Angela's accident. He asked me to forgive him for what happened to Billy. I have done so, Julia, and I pray that he is at peace now.'

'Yes.' I looked at her wistfully. 'Do you think he knows about the twins?'

'We must hope that it is possible.' She sighed, then, always practical, 'I have arranged for a wet nurse, Julia – a very reliable woman I know of. Doctor James thought it unlikely that you would be able to produce enough milk to satisfy both twins, but you should at least try. Shall I bring them to you? We put them in Charles's room so that you could rest. Someone can sleep there for the time being – perhaps Alice?'

'Are you keeping a watch over me, Mary?'

'For the moment,' she said. 'I have ever since you came back to us. I think the danger is over, but we shall see.'

She went into the next room, then returned with a baby in each arm, smiling as she gave them to me.

'There, that is where they belong,' she said. 'What do you intend to call them, Julia?'

'Henry, Philip, Charles – and Adele, Mary, Jennifer.'

'Poor little mites,' Mary said. 'To be burdened with so many names.'

'Harry and Della for short,' I replied and laughed. 'I've been very clever, haven't I, Mary? You wanted a boy and I wanted a girl – it is no wonder I was so fat and uncomfortable!'

'I wondered if you might be carrying twins, but your doctor did not mention the possibility.'

'He probably thought it would scare me,' I teased.

'Then he does not know you, Julia,' Mary said. She nodded approvingly as Harry began to suckle. 'I am not sure that anything frightens you.'

'Yes, it does,' I said. 'I was frightened of Anne Watson until

I caught the scent of lavender water. Then I knew you were near and I wasn't frightened anymore.'

She looked amused – an almost tender, indulgent look, very similar to one I had seen in Charles's eyes when we were courting.

'That's enough for Harry,' she said. 'Greedy little thing. Leave some for Della. Give him to me, Julia. I'll put him back in his cot, while you see to his sister – then perhaps we can have our tea in peace.'

'Twins!' Mama was so excited. 'We could hardly believe it, Julia, and you look wonderful, darling. Was it very terrible?'

'Doctor James wishes all his ladies gave birth so easily. I wish he could change places with one of them just once.'

'Julia!' Mama laughed delightedly. 'You sound like your old self at last. It is nice to hear you being naughty again. Are you feeling a little better, my darling?'

I reached for her hand, taking it to my cheek. 'Yes, I do feel less empty now – now that is a silly thing to say!' I glanced at my flat stomach as I reclined against a pile of pillows on top of the bed. 'But you know what I mean. I have Harry and Della to love, and that doesn't leave much room for feeling self-pity. I just wish Charles were here to see them.'

'Perhaps he can,' Mama said. 'After I lost Gérard I felt him close to me for a long time. He came to me in dreams, Julia, but after I married Philip he went away.'

'I have never felt Charles near me,' I said sadly. 'After his death I felt angry, cheated – and then empty. It wasn't until Mary found his portrait of me that the emptiness began to go away, and now I have the children.'

'I felt much as you do,' Mama said. 'But I found love again – and I believe you may one day.'

'No, I do not think so,' I said. 'I do not wish to marry again.'

Mama smiled a little secret smile but said nothing.

My parents stayed at Rondebush for a week, by which time I was up and about again, despite Doctor James's pleas that I should stay in bed for at least three weeks.

Mr Meacham had come down from London to see me. He made a brief examination and said that I had coped well with the birth of the twins.

'I would normally caution a woman in your situation not to have another child for at least two years,' he said. 'But in the circumstances . . . I am sorry, Mrs Hamilton. I thought you should be aware of the situation. Otherwise, you are perfectly healthy.'

'So there is no need for me to stay in bed for three weeks?'

He looked horrified. 'None. I sincerely hope you will not do so.'

'I do not intend to,' I replied. 'Though some people will think me very foolish.'

'Ah, I see.' He smiled. 'You may refer any doubters to me, Mrs Hamilton.'

I got up as soon as he had gone, but for the next few days I contented myself with sitting in my private rooms wearing a dressing gown. By the end of the week I was downstairs and showing Mama the snowdrops in my garden.

'It isn't completely white like yours,' I told her. 'But this bed is white – the far side is planted with creamy yellow flowers, the opposite bed is bright yellow and this wall is planted with climbing roses that are a combination of pink and yellow, and apricot. And I shall have a mulberry tree in the middle. There was one here once, you know – a huge glorious thing, so Mary says. But they had to cut it down some years back.'

'You will always have something different to look at,' Mama said. 'And a garden goes on for ever. You will find it changes as it grows. Wild things appear as if by magic, and you must decide whether to let them grow or pluck them out.'

'Yes, I suppose one has to be ruthless if order is to be preserved.'

'But wild things are pretty,' Mama said, a little smile on her lips. 'Sometimes they give a lot of pleasure. You may not want to pluck them out.'

She was teasing me. I was not sure, but I suspected there was a hidden meaning to her words. What did she know that I did not?

My parents left the next morning. Before they went, I had a few moments alone with Papa.

'How are you, Julia?'

'Much better, thank you.'

'I have been wondering . . . if I had not sent Charles to your mother you would never have met. Have you ever regretted your marriage?'

'No, Papa. I do not regret my marriage – only that Charles chose to end it the way he did.'

'It was not well done of him,' Papa said. 'But he was ill, Julia. He could not be expected to make a clear judgement. You should try to forgive him if you can.'

'I have forgiven him, Papa. After all, he gave me the twins.'

'I meant *truly* forgive,' my father said. 'Charles hurt you by what he did, but he did it because he loved you too much. It was not that he thought you would not be able to bear it – he could not bear to make you suffer. It was his weakness, not yours. He knew that he might have to suffer a slow descent into what might have become a piti-ful state.'

'Yes, I know,' I said and kissed him. 'I know Charles meant to save me pain, and though I thought it cowardly at the time I now realise that it was for him a very brave thing to do, but I would rather have known.'

'You were strong enough to share his pain, Julia – are you strong enough to accept that he was too weak to let you? Forgive him for being so much less than you expected him to be. Forgive him and love him for what he was.'

'I love you, Papa,' I said. 'Mama was lucky to find you.'

'Oh no,' he said and smiled. 'I was the lucky one.'

Over the next few months, the twins were a source of delight to us all. Henry eagerly anticipated the times I took them to visit him.

'Harry is just like Billy was as a baby,' he told me one morning as he touched the soft down on my son's head. 'Della is more like you, Julia. She will be a beauty when she grows up.'

'And a handful,' I said. 'She screams twice as loudly as Harry. I think she has a temper.'

'She must get that from Mary.'

'Henry!' He grinned at me. I laughed and replied, cheekily, 'You know Mary never loses her temper.'

He grimaced. 'Not so much these days, I'll grant you, but she did when she was younger – before Billy was drowned. She was very different then. I had almost forgotten what those times were like, but she has become more like her old self of late.'

We talked for a little longer, then I rang for Nanny to take the twins back to the nursery. After they had gone, I read to Henry for a few minutes.

'You are such a comfort to me, Julia,' he said. 'The estate is not entailed, you know. I have left the house to you. Mary is to have life tenancy of course, but you won't mind sharing it with her?'

'Of course not,' I said. 'But the estate should surely go to Harry?'

'When I'm gone there will be taxes to pay, Julia. There are trust funds for the twins, but I don't want this house and its history to be a millstone round their necks. You must be free to sell it when Mary is dead.'

'I shall never sell Rondebush. I love it. I want to stay here for the rest of my life.'

'You may marry again, Julia. You are very young to live alone for the rest of your life. Charles would not have wanted that. He loved you. He would have wanted you to be happy.'

'I am happy. I have everything I need,' I said, yet even as I spoke I knew that was not quite true.

Henry died that night, very peacefully in his sleep. Mary and I shed tears for him together.

I grieved for my father-in-law, but there was no bitterness. He had loved and trusted me. I had nothing to reproach him for, no parting regrets. We had known each other a short time, but it had enriched us both.

It was after the funeral that Sarah told us the news about Anne Watson.

'She was heard to have a terrible row with her husband,' Sarah said. 'And then she went off abroad with someone – they say he was a Russian count or something of the sort. She met him at a party in London, and apparently he is mad about her. Lord Watson is going to divorce her.'

'That is interesting,' I said carefully and glanced at Mary. 'I don't suppose we shall see her again.'

'I doubt it very much,' Sarah said. 'She told me that she was bored with her life and wanted to visit all the exciting places she had never been to with her husband. I don't think she ever loved him.'

'No,' I replied. 'I think you must be right, Sarah.'

'So that is that,' Mary said when we were alone. 'I believe Anne will never dare to show her face here again – after all, I could carry out my threat and report her to the police. She murdered two people, Julia. Perhaps she deserved to be arrested and punished for her crimes.'

'Yes, perhaps, but that would not have brought them back, would it? And it would have been an unpleasant scandal.'

'Careful, Julia,' Mary warned with a wry laugh. 'You are in danger of sounding just like me.'

It was high summer when I came in from my garden to discover that I had an unexpected visitor. I had been on my knees, planting and weeding in my rose beds. It was a job that Mary felt I should leave to the gardeners, but something I enjoyed doing myself. I wore gloves so as not to get dirt beneath my fingernails, which would have been unforgivable, but I refused to leave everything to the gardeners. It was something I loved doing, and it made me feel at peace with myself.

So, I was feeling relaxed and happy when I walked into the drawing room, where I had been told Mary was entertaining a guest.

'I am not fit to be seen,' I announced, brushing some debris from my skirt. 'But I am dying for a cup of tea – Brent! What on earth are you doing here?'

'Julia!' Mary reprimanded. 'That is no way to treat our guest, and especially one who has travelled such a long way to see you.'

'Of course it is very nice to see you,' I said, and sat down so that he could resume his own chair. 'Why didn't you let us know you were coming?'

'Hello, Julia,' Brent said and smiled. 'You look wonderful. I think you have caught the sun.'

'She is getting a dreadful tan,' Mary said disapprovingly. 'She will garden, Brent – get down on her knees and dig in the earth. I've tried to tell her it isn't fitting, but she never listens to me.'

'Mary! That isn't true,' I protested. 'I am forever asking your advice.'

'But do you take it?' Mary laughed. 'Sometimes – when it suits you – is the answer. But I do not mind, Julia. It makes life interesting. As your cards do, Brent. I quite look forward to seeing where the next one is coming from. Tell me, do you go everywhere yourself?'

'I fly myself around the country in my own plane,' Brent said, 'but some of the cards are a cheat. I get someone else to post them for me.'

'Ah,' Mary said and nodded. 'We did enjoy them – didn't we, Julia?'

'It was nice of you to send them,' I said. 'How is your father now?'

'Better but his heart attack was a shock for him. He has decided to retire and spend more time enjoying his life – actually, he came over with me on the ship, Julia. He wants to do a tour of England and Scotland. Some of his ancestors from way back may have come from there. Now that he has the time he wants to discover his roots. And as I was coming over he decided to accompany me.'

'I am glad you are getting on with him now.'

'Oh, we still argue all the time,' Brent said cheerfully. 'But we understand each other so it doesn't matter.'

I accepted a cup of tea from Mary. 'So – are you going to stay here or go back to America?'

'It depends on whether I can find somewhere I want to settle,' he said. 'I rather like your house, Julia. I was asking Mary if she knew of anywhere like this in the area. I would like a house like this one. Somewhere that will be a home for

208

a family, not just a house, but there also has to be good pasture land for the horses, of course.'

'I told him he won't find another Rondebush anywhere,' Mary said. 'But Kent is the garden of England so the land is good. I dare say if it is good pasture you are looking for you could find it easily enough near here. And, as I have already told you, you are more than welcome to stay here while you have a look for something to suit you, Brent.'

I looked at her, feeling slightly bewildered by the way she seemed to have taken to him. I knew Brent's free and easy ways usually appealed to most people, but this was Lady Hamilton!

'You are very kind,' he said. 'I should be grateful – if Julia doesn't mind?'

'Mind – why should I mind?' I asked, pretending to an indifference I did not feel. 'We were thinking of having a party soon. We might as well give it while you are here. I'll write and ask Marina if she would like to stay, and Mama and Papa.'

'I think that is an excellent idea,' Mary said. 'And now there is something I really must do. Forgive me, Brent, but I shall see you again later. Perhaps Julia will point you in the right direction for my stables. She doesn't care for horses, of course, but I know you are considered something of an expert and I should value your opinion of my latest acquisition. She's a pretty mare, but I'm not sure she has strong enough hindquarters to make a good breeder. With the breeding programme you were telling me about I should value your advice.

'Yes, of course,' Brent said and stood up as she did. 'If I find suitable premises near by I shall be glad to help out any time.'

Mary nodded approvingly, gave me an odd look and went out.

I finished my tea and got up to put my cup on the tray. 'Well, I think I ought to go and change, Brent. Anyone will show you the stables, if you ask.'

He caught my arm as I turned away, preventing me from leaving.

'Is that all you have to say?'

'What else did you expect? I told you in my letter. I warned you not to go on hoping for something that will never happen.'

'And I told you a long time ago that I never give up on what I want – and I want you, Julia. I'm willing to wait for you to get over your grief. I'm not a fool, and I know you aren't going to fall into my arms just like that, but—'

'Let me go, Brent,' I said. 'I told you I didn't want to marry again. I have decided that I want to spend my life here – caring for my children and this house.'

'That's OK,' he said easily. 'I can live here. I'm not a caveman. I don't need to drag you off by your hair. I can buy land in the area and build my stables.'

'I don't want you to live here,' I replied. 'Let me go, Brent – please?'

'I'll let you go for now,' he said. 'But you were always meant for me, Julia – and in your heart you know it. What you had with Charles was good, but it wasn't your destiny. You belong to me, and this time I don't intend to let you go.'

I wrenched away from him and ran out into the hall, then up the stairs to my own room. There, I closed the door and leaned against it, trembling from head to foot.

Oh, why had Brent come? I had begun to live again, to feel content with my life, and now he made me start to feel again – to feel the forbidden things that I must not feel for him.

I had been in Brent's arms the night that Charles was preparing to die for my sake, thrilling to his kiss and for that I must be punished. I had blamed Charles for his betrayal, but I had also betrayed him. To marry Brent would be a betrayal of the love I had felt for Charles.

Fourteen

I was very polite to Brent that evening, but my politeness was a two-edged sword, keeping us apart. Brent knew what was going on but chose to ignore it. He turned the full force of his charm on Mary, and she melted beneath it. I watched her blush like a young girl as he talked to her in a way no one had bothered to for years, and I tried to be angry with him for making up to her. Since he was clearly interested in what she had to say about horses, however, and she was equally absorbed in his comments on a whole range of topics, I was unable to accuse him of merely flattering her for his own gain.

I was forced to admit that he was a charming, even fascinating companion, and had I not been determined to resist I, too, would have been eating out of his hand by the end of the evening.

'I like your friend very much,' Mary told me as I said goodnight to her later. 'Underneath all that charm and wit is a very warm, caring person. I am not surprised that you did not wish to give up your friendship even after you married.'

'Brent is fun,' I replied. 'And I know he can be caring, too. He wrote Marina a wonderful letter when Johnny was killed.'

'Yes, I should imagine that young man runs deeper than you might imagine, Julia. You would be wise not to underestimate him.'

I asked her what she meant, but she merely shook her head and smiled.

I found it difficult to sleep that night, tossing and turning in a bed that suddenly seemed far too large. My thoughts churned incessantly. I felt so confused, so uncertain. Until Brent's arrival I had been almost serene, wrapped up in my own little world. Now my body seemed to tingle and I knew that I had been thrust back to reality. I was being forced to think about something more than babies and gardens.

Mary and I had breakfast alone. Apparently, Brent had had his at the crack of dawn.

'There is a house he rather wants to see,' Mary told me. 'And some good pasture land. He wanted to visit the agents as soon as they opened. Brent moves fast when he wants something.'

'Yes, I expect so. He can be very determined, and he takes too much for granted.'

I spoke harshly, unreasonably irritated by Mary's support for Brent.

She gave me an odd look but said no more. We separated, Mary going off to her beloved stables while I went out to my garden.

Nanny brought the twins out in their prams, settling them in a shady corner near where I was working. I was no longer breastfeeding either of them. It had proved too much for me and they had long been weaned on to a bottle. Harry was taking quite a lot of soft foods, though Della was more difficult. They were both contented babies most of the time; they seemed wrapped up in each other, always aware that there should be two of them and never satisfied unless they were together.

At lunchtime, Nanny took the twins in for their feed, and I went to wash and tidy myself. When I entered the dining room Mary and Brent were drinking sherry and investigating the contents of the cold buffet on the sideboard.

'Ah, there you are,' Mary said. 'Brent has thought of something rather exciting for us, Julia. He thinks we should consider opening the gardens and perhaps a part of the house to the public for a few days in the summer.'

I stared at her in shock. 'Open the house – for people to walk round? Of course we shan't do any such thing, Mary. I'm surprised you should even consider it.'

'It might pay a few bills,' she said calmly. 'Brent only suggested it because I asked his advice about investments.'

I was silent. Mary and I had never discussed money. I knew

212

Charles had left everything he had to me, and the lawyers were sorting out both his and Henry's affairs. I had imagined they paid the bills, at least until it was all settled.

After lunch, I spoke to Mary alone.

'Naturally, I shall pay for the upkeep of the house. As soon as the lawyers tell me what is left I shall set up an account at the bank. Charles always paid the bills. I had only what he gave me for small expenses, but he said there was plenty of money.'

'Yes, of course there is,' Mary replied. 'We had to pay tax on the estate when Henry died, but there should be sufficient income, although I have no idea how to manage Henry's investments. Both he and Charles were good at things like that, buying and selling stocks and shares. I doubt if the income in itself is as much as they were able to make through dealing. This house is expensive to maintain, Julia. That is why Henry made it possible for you to sell if need be.'

'But – it is a treasure cave. All the pictures, paintings and silver . . . to say nothing of the porcelain and my jewels.'

'Would you really want to sell anything? If for instance we needed a new roof?'

'No, of course not.' I stared at her. 'Mary! I've been so selfish. I never gave it a thought. I've never had to think about money.'

'Nor have I, my dear – that is the problem for us.' She smiled. 'We are certainly not in difficulties yet, but over the years we may see our investments dwindle unless we manage them successfully. Brent says his father will advise us. I have asked him to invite Mr Gregory to stay, and I shall take Brent's advice about my stables. I could make them pay in various ways rather than simply indulging myself. It will be quite a challenge. I am very excited about it.'

'But – open the house and gardens? Could you bear that, Mary? To have people you don't know in your house?'

'You know, I think I should rather enjoy giving them a guided tour of certain rooms. We should keep the family rooms private, of course. But it is up to you to decide, Julia. It is your house.'

'I must think about it,' I said and frowned. 'Did Brent look at the house he was interested in?'

'He bought it and the land,' Mary said and smiled. 'We shall have a new neighbour soon, Julia.'

'What do you mean?'

'Oh, didn't I tell you?' Mary gave me an innocent look. 'Henry sold the Dower House years ago. It is such an old-fashioned notion, don't you think? Charles said there was no point in keeping it, as he couldn't see me ever wanting to live there. Well, it was rather damp and unappealing then. Apparently, the last owners modernized it. Brent is going to install central heating! Such an American thing, but they have been doing it successfully since the second half of the last century. He says the house will be cosy then – what a wonderful word!'

'Did you tell Brent the house was for sale, Mary?'

'It was just what he was looking for, at least for the moment, and it will be pleasant to have him so near. I am going to help him set up his stables and he will help me with my new ideas.'

'How very *cosy*.' I looked at her in disgust. 'I wish you hadn't told Brent. He might never have found the Dower House then.'

'Oh, I doubt that,' Mary replied serenely. 'I believe he would have left no stone unturned in his search. When Brent wants something, Julia, he gets it.'

I glared at her. 'Not always, Mary. There are some things that even Brent can't manage.'

I walked away from her feeling aggrieved. Mary was on Brent's side. Well, if she imagined I was about to cave in and let him win, she was wrong!

Mama came down for our dinner party, but Papa was too busy.

'He sends his love, darling,' she said. 'He had to go somewhere with Phil. Your brother is determined on a military career so Philip is trying to get him enrolled as an officer at the Royal Military Academy Sandhurst.'

'Well at least the war is over, Mama.'

'Yes, the Great War as they call it – though goodness knows why it should be called that after all the slaughter! However, there is always trouble somewhere. I would much rather your

214

brother came home to help run the estate, but Philip says we must let him have his way.'

'Papa is right,' I said and kissed her. 'You cannot keep Phil wrapped in cotton wool for ever.'

'No,' she agreed with a wry smile. 'We all have to let go. How nice for you that Brent is to be your neighbour, Julia. He will be a big help to you and Mary, and Mr Gregory is such a nice man. I think Philip would like him. I have invited him to stay when he returns from his trip to Scotland next month. After all, there is a slight family connection – and who knows what the future will bring?'

'I'm glad you like Brent and his father,' I replied with dignity. 'But there is no point in you and Mary putting your heads together. I am not going to marry him.'

'Of course not, Julia. Has anyone said you should?'

'Not yet,' I admitted. 'But it is only a matter of time.'

'Brent is very attractive, don't you think so?' Marina asked. She was carrying her first child and at five months looked blooming with health and much smaller than I had been at the same stage. 'He has a new maturity after his time in the RFC. It suits him. If I weren't so happily married I would set my cap at him.'

'I don't want to marry again.'

'Why not? Did you hate the intimate side of things?'

I blushed at the direct question. 'No, of course not. It's just that . . . just that I don't want to be married. I prefer my freedom.'

Doesn't it get a bit lonely at night?' Marina asked. 'I'm not saying you should rush things, but don't leave it too long, Julia. If you don't want Brent, someone else will.'

'I do like your friend,' Sarah said to me as I showed her a new rose I had just acquired. 'Howard is keen to do business with him. He says Brent will be a great asset to the neighbourhood. We are very lucky that he has decided to settle here.'

'Mary says the same. I suppose it will be useful for her having him near. They get on so well. They are both mad about horses, of course.'

'Oh, but there is so much more to like and admire about Brent,' Sarah said. 'He is quite clever enough to have followed his father into banking if he had wanted to – it is simply that he loves the country life. Any woman would be fortunate to marry a man like that.'

'Sarah! Are you matchmaking?' I saw her wicked smile and laughed.

'Why not? You should marry him, Julia. He is obviously in love with you. What are you waiting for? Surely you don't imagine Charles would want you to mourn him for the rest of your life? Charles loved you almost too much, my dear. What he did was wrong, but he did it for the best of motives. He wanted to set you free . . . to give you the chance of finding happiness again.'

Tears welled up in my eyes. 'I am not sure I can ever trust again, Sarah. I'm afraid – afraid of being hurt.'

'I cannot tell you that you will never be hurt again,' Sarah said. 'You could – God forbid! – lose one of your children.'

'Sarah! Please don't.'

'Life isn't all sunshine and roses, Julia – and even roses have thorns.'

'Yes, I know.' I brushed away the stupid tears. 'But wouldn't it be wrong of me to be happy when Charles is dead?'

'I think that is exactly what he would want you to be, Julia.'

'Yes.' I looked at her thoughtfully. 'I suppose you are right.'

I stood in the gallery gazing at the picture Charles had painted of me, and the tears slipped down my cheeks.

'I am so sorry, Charles,' I whispered. 'Forgive me.'

I love you, Julia. Be happy.

For a moment I felt Charles close to me. It was as if somehow he had touched my cheek, and then he was gone. I turned with my face wet with tears to see Brent watching me.

'Mary told me you might be here,' he said and his voice was harsh, almost angry. 'I'm sorry. I shouldn't have intruded.'

'You haven't,' I said. 'I was just about to join everyone for tea.'

216

'You were crying over that picture,' Brent said, his eyes glinting. 'It isn't you, Julia. You were never that vulnerable. You had spirit when I met you. Don't let what happened ruin your life. You've made Charles into some kind of a god. He wasn't. He was just an average, fairly selfish man.'

'Please don't say that!'

'I'm telling you for your own good. He had no right to marry you with all that hanging over him, Julia.'

'Brent, don't . . . please? Charles is dead.'

'But you can't let him go, can you?' He glared at me, coming closer to gaze down into my face. 'You know I love you. You feel something for me – or you would if you let yourself. I know you will never love me as you did him, but—'

'No, Brent,' I said quietly. 'I don't love you as I did Charles.'

His face went white. 'I suppose I deserved that, Julia. You did warn me, but I thought if I came here – if I forced you to see me every day . . . but it's useless, isn't it? I'll go to Scotland with my father. The lawyers can put the Dower House up for sale.'

He was turning away and I knew that if I let him go it would be for good. I laid my hand on his arm.

'Please don't go,' I said and my voice was husky with emotion. 'I don't love you as I did Charles – I love you far more. In a way that I hadn't even begun to imagine was possible when I married. I did love Charles very much, Brent. He was like Papa in some ways and I enjoyed being spoiled at first, but then I began to resent being treated like a little girl or a fragile flower. I am a woman now, Brent, and it is as a woman that I offer you my love.'

He stared at me in wonder, and then that irrepressible grin broke through.

'If we get a special licence, we can be married before my father leaves for Scotland,' he said. 'You don't want a big wedding, do you, Julia?'

'I would like to have the wedding here at Rondebush,' I said. 'You did mean it when you said you could live here, didn't you?'

217

'I love the house. We can repair the old wing and have that for ourselves.'

'I thought we were going to open the house?'

'The gardens maybe. You won't have to bother about money in future, Julia. My family has rather too much of it.'

'But I do want to open the garden,' I said. 'And I thought I might develop a nursery to sell cuttings and plants grown from seed.'

'Want to be independent?' Brent laughed. 'I can see I've lit a fire in both you and Mary. You can sell ice to Eskimos for all I care, Julia. Just as long as you let me share the fun with you.'

I gazed up into his eyes as he reached for me.

'Oh yes, Brent,' I murmured softly. 'I think I can promise there will be plenty of good things to enjoy together in the future.'